THE COST OF ELECTRICITY

THE COST OF ELECTRICITY

Kathryn Holzman

Mills College, 1921

The bright young Mills College students stroll into the library in short-fringed dresses and floppy hats, calling each other "baby." All white ankles and high heels; strings of long beads rattle as they shimmy by the librarian's desk.

Shiny new things, Lulu thinks, remembering that frisson of electricity. Her desk abuts the 900s. She depends on the Dewey Decimal system these days to keep things in order. As she pastes card pockets into a new shipment of books, a cocky young history student, her black hair cropped in the popular bob, asks for a book about the early settlers. Without referring to the card catalog, Lulu directs her to Carey's *History of Oregon*. "978," she says. "Just around the corner."

A fledging scientist slams a geode on her desk, leaving a sprinkle of golden dust on the oak veneer. "I found this when I hiked the switchbacks up to Crater Lake," she says. "Where would I find a book to identify it?"

"Try Scott's *Oregon Geology*." Lulu doesn't mention she knew the author.

The students hurry off for dinner, and the library settles into a comforting quiet. Lulu loads the books the patrons left behind onto a wooden cart.

Despite her affinity for the 978s, her own short stories appear in magazines on the display shelf next to the reference desk.

1

Categorization can be tricky. Her father's diaries, for example, are preserved in a wooden file cabinet next to the window. History, perhaps. Possibly politics or land use. "I was the first white boy in Indian country," he used to brag, a starting point against which to contrast his self-evident success as a Republican land surveyor and railroad commissioner.

But the cocky young student who couldn't care less has hit a nerve. When the girl walked away, leaving "My father was a pioneer" hanging in the air, Lulu father's voice lingered on the tip of her tongue, along with a dozen more. The tales queue up, eager to be heard. A writer's disability, Lulu supposes, and not an unpleasant one. She completes her routine, putting the library to bed.

The students take pride in attending the first women's college west of the Rockies, and rightly so. But Lulu longs to tell them she too was in the vanguard. She graduated from the coeducational University of Oregon, class of 1904, when women students were a novelty. Intellectually, she easily competed with the young men in her freshman class, but her aspirations didn't end there. Like Mary Shelley, she wanted to write, but she also longed to live and love freely. Hence the Dutch cap in her dresser drawer in the room she rented before the university provided housing for women. Let the flappers shimmy. She had stories of her own.

Lulu pushes her cart through the narrow aisles, eyeing the books like old friends, several capable of making her heart flutter. She saves the fiction section for last, cherishing the sunlit room with its plush armchairs. Large windows encourage a reader to dawdle. As the motley crew of memories compete for her attention, she decides to take a break and give them an audience from the comfort of an overstuffed chair.

The overhead fan whispers. The blades stir the air. In their whoosh, she hears the familiar voices of everyone she has ever loved, as well as everyone who got in the way. The fan revolves. The pages of the magazines flutter. Lulu temples her fingers. When she closes her eyes, she sees each of them as clear as day. Young and hell-bent on distinguishing themselves. But just as she gets them into focus, the audience applauds and heads for the door.

Lulu hoists herself up, cursing her sore feet and the hint of a headache niggling at the sides of her vision. She's grateful no students hear her decidedly middle-aged groan. She clicks off the overhead lights, locks the library door, and descends the library's stone steps.

We were so young. How surprised the bobbed-hair girl would be if she knew the turmoil she had triggered in this staid librarian's head! But really, was any of this a surprise? With a bit of effort, any diligent researcher can uncover a snake bed of broken hearts and betrayal left behind by even the most unremarkable of lives. Biographies 920. Who could possibly believe the circuitous routes we choose to arrive at our destinations? In reality, who cares? Not her students. Certainly not the aspiring flapper.

Like that of her father, the pioneer, Lulu's journey started with a dream, and then she had a life. From time to time, the two even ran in parallel.

Before heading up the walkway to the cozy cottage she now calls home, Lulu watches a bright star appear in the clear California sky, the center of a universe. *I was there,* she thinks, *when they turned on the electricity. I did my best to pursue a life beautiful. But baby,* she wishes she had warned the disinterested student, *the journey from there to here wasn't at all what I expected.*

Part I: Eugene

Chapter 1 Portland

At the end of an endless day, the trolley deposited Lulu and her stack of luggage outside the familiar stairs to her parents' home. How glorious to stand on solid ground after so many days of travel! She'd spent the last week riding the rails: first the 20th Century Limited from New York City to Chicago, then across the Rockies on the Southern Pacific's Overland Limited. Now she struggled to pick up her aching feet, as weary as if she had crossed the country like her grandparents, walking beside a stagecoach.

Her parents' house, on the outskirts of Portland, lorded over the newer residences. Grand two-story pillars bellowed the home's importance. Despite her new, more worldly perspective, she gazed at her bedchamber window, eager to stretch out on her cozy bed. She couldn't wait to fall into that veritable nest of comforters and feather pillows.

Before she lifted the brass knocker, her sister Lizzie threw open the heavy front door. "Lulu, you're home!" Lizzie barreled into her, nearly knocking her off her feet. "I thought you would never get here! Tell me everything." She repeated the word for emphasis. "Everything."

"Where's your father?" Behind Lizzie, their mother, Kitty, craned her neck to examine the street below. At the sight of the streetcar pulling away, she pursed her lips.

"Father had to stay on the East Coast. He had business to attend to," Lulu answered, careful to keep her tone light.

Lizzie rolled her eyes.

"He sends his love." Lulu took her mother's arm. "Oh Mother, I had such a lovely trip. The Atlantic crossing was everything I dreamed it might be." She opened her bag and extracted gifts: a copy of *Le Journal* for her sister and a silk scarf from Harrods for her mother.

Lizzie scanned *Le Journal* with only a modicum of interest. "There's something I want to show you."

"Your sister has a new fixation," Kitty sighed, her wrinkled forehead expressing more skepticism than her words.

Lulu would have preferred a quick nap, but Lizzie insisted they visit the stable "pronto." Leaving their mother to finish the preparations for supper, the two girls headed outside, arms entwined.

Every dwelling on their block had a curbside iron-cast horse ring, but, since streetcars had replaced horses and carriages, the Cleaver's home was the only one with its own stable. In a not unusual act of rebellion, Lulu and Lizzie had refused to part with their horse, Diamond, whom they considered a member of the family.

The shed was redolent of hay and feed. Diamond snorted when the girls opened the wooden door. Lulu kissed the gelding's nose as Lizzie reached for a large brush from the shelf above his stall and began brushing him. Lulu took the opportunity to settle on a hay bale and rest. Her sister's enthusiasm only heightened her exhaustion.

"Spill it." Lizzie plopped down next to Lulu, setting the brush down on the prickly hay.

"First, tell me what has Mother all in a twitter."

Lizzie pointed to a shiny new cross saddle hanging from the wall on a wooden peg. Lulu examined it, fingering the well-oiled leather. She had never considered riding face-forward on a horse. "I always assumed the purpose of a sidesaddle was to accommodate long skirts."

"Balderdash. Do you know they invented the sidesaddle to protect the virginity of Princess Anne of Bohemia when she traveled across Europe to wed King Richard II?"

8

Lulu looked sideways at her sister. "Riding sidesaddle all these years didn't prevent me from succumbing to a dashing Frenchman's proposition."

"Oh Lulu, I knew it!"

"I did. And it was marvelous."

"Did you meet this Frenchman on the ocean liner?"

"A scholar and a gentleman," Lulu replied, a coy smile tickling the corners of her mouth.

"Just like in a novel," Lizzie sighed. She kicked up her feet and spread her petticoats. This was going to take a while.

"Behave yourself, and I might even show you my prized souvenir."

"Are you in love?" Lizzie's eyes brightened.

"No, of course not."

"Okay, sis, no more stalling." Lizzie lit the oil lamp that sat on a wooden stool, leaving it to flicker on its lowest setting, filling the stable with shadows.

Lulu settled next to her sister, removing her boots with a sigh of pleasure. Diamond's ears twitched. "I already told you the ship was enormous. It dwarfed any downtown Portland hotel." Lulu rested her head on the rough barn board, not the pillow she had looked forward to.

"Tell me about the boy," Lizzie insisted. "Not the ship."

"Hardly a boy," Lulu corrected her. "A man. Just between the two of us?"

"Of course."

"I spotted him that very first day as I followed Father up the gangway, a very handsome, slender young man with wavy blond hair. As I walked by him, he said, 'Bonjour, mademoiselle,'" Lulu imitated his deep voice.

"Bonjour," Lizzie tried the words on for size. "I wish my French was as good as yours."

"I was wearing my plaid traveling suit."

"Of course, you were. I can hear Mother now as she packed your trunk: 'There is no situation in which a lady is more exposed than when she travels.'" Their mother, who had never stepped outside of

9

the state of Oregon, had spent months preparing Lulu's wardrobe for the trip.

Lulu chuckled. "Like my suit, it was all very elegant. A grand piano at the bar. Bench cushions covered in red velvet. Chandeliers on the ceiling and waiters pouring steaming Darjeeling tea into delicate china cups."

"Enough scenery. We don't have all day."

"I'm getting there. In front of an enormous stone fireplace, I saw him again, turning the pages of a thick red book. I twisted my neck to see the title. Would you believe it? Baudelaire!"

"Perfect! Who spoke first, you or he?"

"Father excused himself to light a cigar on the deck. I realized that was my chance to approach him. I asked, in my best French, what he was reading." Lulu blushed, remembering how her heart had pounded as she worked up the nerve to talk to the dashing fellow. "He grasped my hand and kissed my fingers. Then he offered to read Baudelaire's poetry aloud. Not wanting to appear too eager, I agreed to look for him the following morning in front of the fire."

"Of course, you did."

"Louis was twenty, a Frenchman courteous enough to please even Mother. I told Father I had befriended a fellow voyager who offered to help me practice my French."

"How clever," Lizzie said.

"We read the Parisian newspaper together. He corrected my mispronunciations by placing a finger to my lips." Lulu demonstrated, touching her sister's lips. "We discussed the impact of La Belle Époque on the role of women."

"And..."

"French women, he told me, are increasingly concerned about the manly issues of war, peace, and colonialism. 'Moi aussi,' I said."

Lizzie stood up and resumed brushing Diamond. Clearly, sophisticated banter was not what she had been hoping for.

"Have you ever heard of a Dutch cap?" Lulu asked.

"A what cap?"

"I didn't know either." Lulu had her sister's attention now. "But I didn't let on. Louis explained. 'For the woman, comprends-tu? To make love but not babies?'"

"Lulu!" Her sister was all eyes. "And I thought abandoning my sidesaddle was daring!"

"He read Baudelaire, for God's sake. We were sailing to Europe. Where else was I going to learn about romance? Certainly not from the boys at the university. Sure, some of them are fine fellows and a few are serious scholars, but they are hardly the men of my dreams. No man besides Father had ever kissed me. Mother was a world away, and Father was nowhere to be seen. What should I have said?" Lulu's words poured out as she described the scene to her sister, the only person who might understand. "The Dutch cap, he assured me, guaranteed my freedom. In France, he said again, women were as free as men."

Lizzie settled on the hay once again.

"I had no intention of letting the chance to experience such freedom pass me by." Lulu paused. For once, Lizzie was quiet. "He invited me to his cabin."

"Stop. I think I am going to swoon." Lizzie loved this word from her romance novels.

"That's how I felt, at first. But as he stroked my thigh, the ship encountered turbulence. It lurched and rolled from right to left. I felt as if we were riding the top of an enormous wave."

"And he stopped?" Lizzie asked, with a trace of disappointment.

"No, I told him not to," Lulu said. "Oh, you can't imagine the confusion of limbs, elbows, and disheveled clothes that followed."

"How did it feel?"

"It wasn't at all like I had imagined."

Lizzie had no reply to that. Had Lulu said too much, her tongue loose from lack of sleep and the disorientation of returning home? Had she overstepped even her sister's insatiable tolerance for scandal? Lulu scooted over and kissed her sister on the cheek. "The Dutch cap is in my bag. Do you want to see it?"

At the dinner table, Kitty complained, "Lulu, I hoped you would talk some sense into your sister."

"Anyone who needs to get work done on a horse knows riding sidesaddle is impractical," Lizzie replied.

"But you are not a working woman, dear. Neither is your sister. A young lady must always be conscious of appearances."

"Whatever do you mean, Mother?" Lizzie asked, setting her mother up.

"Annie Oakley rides sidesaddle, why can't you?"

"Oakley uses a hook to anchor her leg to the horse." Their mother's belief in decorum amused her sister no end. Lizzie jumped on every chance she gave them to elicit her platitudes.

"Chaucer portrayed Joan of Arc riding astride her horse," Lulu added.

Kitty, defeated, looked down at her plate. She was no match for her spirited daughters.

"If only your father were here."

Chapter 2 - Sophomores

Eugene, Oregon, Fall 1901

Lulu's friend Vesta volunteered the sophomore girls to be hostesses for the Class of 1905's convocation. So, as the incoming freshmen spread out between the enormous firs and strolled the meandering stone paths that connected Deady and Villard Halls, Lulu was stuck in the basement. Dressed in a white lace blouse, white apron, and long black skirt, she manned the teapot and piled cookies on a china platter.

Through the ground-level windows, she watched her male classmates escape the lecture hall, shoving their way down the steps through members of the football team dressed in turtleneck jerseys embossed with a wide-eyed O.

At her side, Annabelle, by far the most attractive girl in the class of 1904, held court. Imitating the freshman class president, she flipped her perfectly waved blond hair and spoke as if she were sucking a plum. "Wondrously proud to favor the university with our presence."

Vesta, Annabelle's devoted sidekick, giggled. At the same time, she attempted to tuck her dark curls back into her updo, a pointless task since each curl seemed determined to escape captivity.

"I suppose every entering class thinks their ideas are loftier than those of the class before." Since her dalliance with the Frenchman,

Lulu had adopted a casual insouciance that she hoped distinguished her from her classmates. "The dean of women made the only worthwhile speech of the day."

"I beg to differ," Annabelle said, nibbling on a sugar cookie. "Her speech was a snooze compared to Roy's."

"Oh please don't tell me you were taken in by that dapper vest and phony red bow tie." But Lulu might as well have been talking to the wall.

Roy Bacon had dominated the stage; he had all the girls' attention. The editor of the school literary magazine, the *Webfoot*, charmed the audience with such highfalutin lines as "We lift our heads to the lofty atmosphere where angles, circles, arcs, sines, logarithms, and complements fan but never disturb our cool brows."

"Roy tries too hard," Lulu said. "He may look dashing, but he lacks the elegant sophistication of European men."

She laid out the napkins, mulling over the day's program. If only her friends shared the dean's lofty vision of a life beautiful. Instead, they giggled like schoolgirls over a pompous boy.

As she moved a pile of student newspapers to the windowsill, the hair on the back of her neck alerted her to someone watching.

"Did you read my editorial?" Roy Bacon loomed over her, holding a copy of the paper in his hand. She swore his mustache twitched in amusement.

He opened a copy of the paper and pointed out his article. "It's about time the university provides housing for female students, don't you think?"

"Every woman I know complains about the difficulty in finding rooms for boarding." Lulu scanned the article, her mouth turned down with disdain. "The need for a women's dormitory hardly requires your advocacy." She wasn't about to give the self-important boy credit for an idea that was far from original.

She was well-versed in the housing issue. In fact, she lived it. During the school year, Lulu rented a room over J.W. Kay's Furniture Store on Willamette Street. When she invited girlfriends over for tea, she told them to look for the sign that read:

"When Cupid's dart
Pierces your heart
Then come to us
We'll give you a start."

Vesta rented rooms from the owner of Geyser's Gun Store, which, despite its name, was the university supplier of gymnasium suits, tennis and football goods, and cutlery.

"I see no reason," she said, "women shouldn't receive the same accommodation as men. The university houses seventy male students for $3.50 a week. Rooms off campus are not only an inconvenience, but they are much more expensive."

"Of course, housing women is a radical experiment." Roy immediately pivoted to the opposing side of the argument. Could he be more annoying? "The current plan is a small-scale demonstration to evaluate the advisability of bringing women students onto campus."

"Why, pray tell, would housing for women not be advisable?"

Roy held up his hands as if in surrender. "All I am suggesting is that women should appreciate this gesture by the university."

Lulu picked up the stack of newspapers. "Gesture? It is about time the university started treating all students equally, men and women, not out of benevolence, but because it's the right thing to do." She pushed past him and headed to the kitchen.

She could feel his eyes following her. *What did this fellow want?*

She stomped into the tiny room where the other women were drying dishes. Annabelle and Vesta, who had spied on the encounter from behind the swinging door, rushed to her side. "What did he say?"

"Not a damn thing worth repeating," Lulu replied.

She headed out of the hall, fuming. How could Roy Bacon presume to know what a woman wanted? Absorbed in composing arguments the skilled debater couldn't refute, she stumbled on the bottom step and fell onto the concrete walkway, ripping her skirt and scraping her right knee.

"Blazes," she said, looking around to see if anybody had noticed. *Drat!* Three sweaty football players ran to her side. They regarded her with eager, flushed faces.

"Take my arm, milady." A lanky fellow extended his hand, and she pulled herself to her feet. She had ruined her skirt, exposing lacy petticoats beneath the heavy wool.

"Thank you," she said. She draped the ripped skirt over her petticoat so the boy couldn't spot her bloody knee.

"You should watch where you're going."

"You're absolutely right."

"Do you need a doctor?"

Boys, she thought. *Why is this campus populated with boys, not men?*

"Not necessary," she said, steadier now. "I'll be on my way." She thanked them and hurried along the path, despite the throbbing pain in her knee. She crossed the campus, glancing neither left nor right, her eyes fixed on the Cascade Mountains in the distance. Passing the dormitory, she became indignant once again at Roy's words. If women could live on campus, she would be home now, changing her clothes without further exposure. Instead, she had another half mile to walk.

She saw several male classmates congregating on the concrete steps of the dormitory. Al, Judge Bartlett's son, read a newspaper. The studious boy, whom she had known since preparatory school, waved to her. She recognized the familiar banner of the *Sumpter Miner*, a newspaper her father often read.

"Lulu?" Al glanced up from his newspaper. Behind wire-rimmed glasses, his blue eyes blinked as if unaccustomed to sunshine. Noticing her torn skirt, he raised his eyebrows.

"Clumsy me, I tumbled down the stairs."

Al blushed but stood up without hesitation. "Can I escort you back to your residence?" He set down his newspaper and took her arm, his light touch gentler than the athlete's grasp. "I was just reading news about your father, the esteemed Dr. Cleaver." Arm in arm, they walked down the stone path.

So, Al knew who her father was. They seldom spoke outside the classroom.

"The newspaper reports that the Union County Court granted your father the right-of-way to build an electric road from La Grande to Cove."

"Yes," she said. "They are laying track through the agricultural districts of the Ronda Valley."

"Twenty-two miles through the finest timber in the west. To the land commissioner go the spoils?"

As they walked across the Memorial Quad, Lulu parsed his words. *Was Al implying her father was greedy? Was he judging her?* She doubted it. As Judge Bartlett's son, he also came from a family used to the benefits enjoyed by the most successful of the state's pioneers.

"Not the path you might expect a dentist's life to take," she said.

"Ah, but nation-building brings out a man's true nature," Al said. "There are many examples among our parents and the faculty." Lulu wondered if this was a veiled reference to his own father, a university regent whose stern lectures were a staple of any university event.

"My father hasn't practiced dentistry since the Republicans named him land commissioner in 1883. Now that he's railroad commissioner, he prefers raising money on the East Coast and traveling abroad. When he's in Oregon, he crosses the state identifying routes for the railroad." She supposed Al already knew most of this, but she'd rather discuss their parents than her fall down the stairs.

They headed into the streets of downtown Eugene.

"I refuse to let my family history define me," she declared. "Our parents' lives are so public, especially here at the university. How many times have I heard that your father was a member of the first graduating class?"

Al hesitated at the corner, shielding her from the splashing mud of passing carriages. "We fought to keep the university open." Al imitated his father, parroting the opening line of the story that Judge Bartlett recounted at every assembly.

Lulu laughed, surprised at the boy's audacity. "I understand. They're proud of their progress. But what does that have to do with us?"

"It's refreshing to talk with a woman who is not afraid to voice her opinions."

"Contrary to what my parents think, I intend to use my education to prepare for a career, not simply to latch onto a husband. I'm going to write for a real magazine one day. Women have careers as well as men, you know."

Instead of arguing, Al nodded in agreement. "I imagine you will find a way."

Soon she spotted the sign above the door to her rooming house. She wondered what Al would make of the rhyme touting Cupid's dart.

"Careful climbing those steps." For a moment, he seemed to be searching for something more to say, but instead turned away and headed back to campus with a friendly wave. Lulu watched him disappear. *Had that been a wink*, she asked herself, *masked by his thick lenses?*

When he had disappeared around the corner, she trudged up the rickety stairs to her room, thinking of Al, Roy, and the school year to come. And of the dean of women, a proud and handsome woman, who had encouraged the female students to live "the life beautiful."

She stepped out of her ruined skirt and let her petticoats fall, then examined her scraped knee. Why was it so hard for a woman to stand up for herself without stumbling? Now that she studied with men, would she also have an opportunity to follow her male classmates into the workplace? And why were her friends attracted to a showoff like Roy rather than a sensible, courteous scholar like Al?

For the same reason, she supposed, that the Frenchman on the ocean liner attracted her, reading Baudelaire in front of the raging fire. That mysterious flutter of the heart. Even the most analytical of scholars would have to admit, the heart and the mind did not always agree.

She cleaned her wound with soap and water, smarting at the sting.

Should an ambitious woman marry for romance? Or should she settle for companionship? Maybe she would not marry at all.

But for now, she decided, she would explore her friendship with Al. Hadn't he said he respected her intelligence? That was a start. They shared ambition and family histories. Perhaps, in Al, she had identified a man who could satisfy her high standards. And with time, she hoped, her heart might catch up with her intellect. Her Dutch cap, wrapped in a lacy handkerchief in her bureau, was there to remind her. There was no reason on earth she couldn't pursue both a career and romance, just like her favorite author, Mary Shelley.

* * *

Dean Clarissa Carson presided behind a large wooden desk piled high with textbooks and student papers. Although her ink-stained fingers lacked a wedding ring, she wore ample jewelry: large stones in chunky settings and heavy silver bracelets. A black velvet bow topped her dark hair. There was nothing delicate about this imposing woman, a professor of rhetoric and English literature, who shepherded the female students at the university. Morning sunshine poured through the window behind her, silhouetting her face like the cameo Lulu's mother wore for special occasions. On a fall afternoon, Lulu perched on a leather chair, grasping a notebook and chewing the eraser of her pencil as she tapped her foot.

The assignment had been: "Interview an early pioneer. Discuss their role in the state's establishment. Identify threats to their survival, the choices it required them to make, and the impact of their experiences in shaping the state we know today."

"Was I unwise to write about my father?" Lulu asked. "Perhaps I'm too close to the subject?"

"On the contrary, your generation has unique access to the personal stories of the Oregon pioneers."

"But my father is far from a hero."

"Few are." The dean smiled. "I look forward to hearing your thoughts on his experiences."

Lulu opened her notebook and scanned the diary her father kept during his journey west: "The Oregon country is covered with peaks of naked rock, many of them capped with snow. The Sweet Water River valley provides a good road and fine grass with wood for fuel. When we lack wood, we appeal to wild sage and buffalo chips. Meats such as buffalo, antelope, and elk are abundant."

"Your father discusses survival in poetic terms. I can see where you inherited your talent as a writer."

"In 1848, the Alton, Illinois *Telegraph* published a letter written by my father from the Oregon Trail." Lulu read over the sentences she had copied from the letter silently, as if reluctant to share her father's words. "There are issues here..."

"Such as?"

"You asked us to identify the threats to the pioneers' survival. But hostility toward the Indians keeps intruding on my father's lyrical prose. For example, he wrote: 'There is a rumor that after a company of Oregon immigrants crossed the Missouri River into Indian Territory, Indians stole their horses. The immigrants pursued the Injuns and killed three.' He added that there were no grounds for the rumor. My father, you know, served for many years as the registrar of the La Grande County land office." Lulu hesitated. "It served his interests to understate the Indians' claim to the land. In the letter, he acknowledges that these false stories deterred other companies from fighting to secure the range and gave him time to claim this land for himself."

"And what, my dear, is the premise for your paper?"

"We are the inheritors of a stolen legacy."

Lulu's father had always encouraged her to be strong, to stand up for her beliefs. She wondered how he would react to her thesis.

She continued reading: "'A treaty between the citizens of Oregon and their Indian neighbors has taken place and peace followed.' Good enough. But then he says: 'The whites gave the Indians several handsome drubbings before peace was concluded.'"

"What was the price paid for that peace?" Lulu asked her mentor now, her voice trembling.

Dean Carson smiled. "I don't believe you need my guidance, dear. Your paper seems well underway. Changing the established order requires introspection and patience."

The dean spoke from experience. In 1899, when Lulu was still in preparatory school, Carson had urged the state legislature to allow women the right to vote. Along with her prep school classmates, Lulu traveled to the Oregon State Capitol to watch Carson deliver a fiery appeal. The speech, printed on the front page of the *Portland Record,* had been persuasive. Unfortunately, although the legislature passed the bill, voters defeated it in 1900. Dean Carson was the reason Lulu had come to the university.

"And how is your dear father?" the dean asked now.

"Out of town, as always. He spends much of his time on the East Coast, raising money for the Central Railway."

"And your mother?"

"Home with my sister, Lizzie."

"Women can be fine on their own," the dean replied. "A husband need not define a woman." A sly smile spread across Carson's face. "And you, my dear, all is well? I've heard rumors among the faculty you may have a beau."

With fewer than fifty students in a class, one's love life was common knowledge.

"I expect to see Al tonight, at the joint meeting of the literary societies."

"Yes, I hear the men have asked the women to join them. I bet poor Al hasn't a clue what is in store for him." The dean chuckled. "How clever of you to invite him to become the business manager for the *Webfoot.*"

"Well, I couldn't ask him to write poetry."

"Be kind, dear. The boy runs deep."

"It's his father, the judge, who intimidates me."

Dean Carson's chuckle was hearty, low, and musical. "You can hold your own in his esteemed company. All you have to do is listen and nod with appreciation at the judge's sagacity and political acumen. I've mastered the art myself over many a long Sunday afternoon."

Carson walked Lulu to the door, a protective arm around her shoulders. "You'll be fine." Lulu, as always, felt empowered by the older woman's confidence. "It's a delight to meet with you, my dear."

The dean kissed her on the cheek before turning her attention to the anarchy of her cluttered desk.

***

Roy, the guest speaker at the joint meeting of the university literary societies, sashayed into the university auditorium. On one arm, Annabelle, her golden hair held aloft by a green velvet ribbon, listened attentively to his steady patter. On the other, Vesta checked out the students entering the room. She interrupted Roy to point out Al, sitting alone in a seat in the last row.

"Hey, old man," Roy said. "I didn't expect to see you here." They shook hands. "Annabelle, let's show my dear friend to a proper seat." Roy spotted Lulu in the second row and pointed to the seat next to her. "Here's just the place." He whispered to Vesta, "Who needs Cupid? Roy Bacon is in the house."

"You know Lulu Cleaver?" Roy asked Al, pretending he had not heard the rumors about Al and Lulu. "A handsome woman and brilliant too. A class act in every sense of the word."

Lulu swatted Roy away like a pesky mosquito but shifted in her seat to let Al pass. Annabelle and Vesta watched with amusement. Al sat down next to Lulu, squirming under Roy's attention. When Lulu greeted Al with a welcoming smile, ignoring Roy's dramatic entrance, Roy winked at Annabelle, pleased by the success of his matchmaking.

"You, my dear," Roy squeezed Annabelle's shoulder, "must keep my seat warm for me. Vesta, my love," he kissed her hand, "I trust you will keep my companions in line." With the seating arranged to his satisfaction, he joined the other officers at the front of the room.

Ansel Francis, chairman of the Philologian Society, banged a wooden gavel on the dais. "I call this meeting to order."

The string band burst into the popular German march, "The Jolly Coppersmith." The last of the students had settled in their seats by the time J.C. Whiteaker rose to deliver his salutatory, a brief history of the university's literary societies.

To the delighted applause of the women's visiting society, he complimented the zeal that characterized the women's work, lauding the university's ongoing commitment to the experiment with coeducation. He reminded them that, of the eastern universities, only Oberlin admitted women. "But our inspiration will always arise," his voice gained strength as the women cheered him on, "from the congenial soil of the valleys of Oregon."

When the audience's enthusiastic response quieted, Ansel introduced Roy. After a dramatic pause, Roy recited his poem, "Night on Shasta," careful to enunciate each word as if it were a gift to his audience.

"How very close to heaven it seems up here
When noiseless night her velvet curtain drops!
I dare not raise my head above the copse
Lest I should bump some star, they are so near"

At the last word, the audience cheered. Taking an exaggerated bow, Roy strode off the stage, his eyes darting from side to side, alert for signs of appreciation from the crowd.

"Close to heaven..." Vesta shut her eyes, transported. A quartet of junior girls arranged wooden chairs in a small arc on the stage and prepared to play "Only a Dream of Home."

"Roy is certainly gifted," Al said to Lulu.

"He does a decent job of editing the university's literary magazine," Lulu replied, "but he's full of himself."

Here among friends, there was no question Roy was in his element. Two gorgeous girls at his side and even Lulu acknowledging his editing talents. But instead of further extolling his virtues, the conversation between Al and Lulu took another turn.

"Even if I convince my father electrical engineering is a worthy path of study, I'll never light up a room like Roy does," Al said. Roy waited for Lulu's response.

"Nor need you," she said. "Modesty is sometimes a virtue."

The hardest nuts to crack were sometimes those that tasted the best. Roy found it hard to take his eyes off Lulu, who seemed unaware of his presence. Only Annabelle's insistent tap on his arm refocused his attention on the two girls at his side.

By the time intermission arrived, Roy had stretched his long legs, blocking the row. But as soon as the lights came on, he offered a crooked elbow to Annabelle and followed Vesta down the aisle to the punchbowl to accept more accolades.

Lulu was no silly romantic. Roy meant it when he told Al that Lulu was a class act. If she weren't out of his league, he might have made overtures to her himself. Instead, he invited her to work with him on the literary magazine. She had agreed to do so only if he offered Al the position of business manager. Out of the corner of his eye, he saw Lulu turn and brush Al's cheek with the back of her hand.

Roy called out to Ted, his roommate and loyal sidekick. "Get a look at that." He pointed to the couple. "Bingo."

"Bully for him," Ted said.

"Lucky guy," Roy said, keeping his tone light and playful.

Ansel's gavel summoned the students back for the second half of the evening's festivities. Al and Lulu sidled back into their seats. Roy caught Al's eye, giving him an enthusiastic thumbs up. "Quite a successful evening, wouldn't you say?" Al wrinkled his forehead.

An innocent, thought Roy. He does not know what he has there. Annabelle, her eyes on the stage, rested a delicate hand on Roy's arm. Vesta chattered on. Lulu looked straight ahead, refusing to acknowledge his admiring gaze.

Chapter 3 Courtship

Lulu strolled along the Willamette River, musing about men, her father's absence, and her mother's rigid adherence to etiquette. She thought of Al, his calm demeanor and respectful attention. When she touched his cheek, the skin had been as smooth as a child's against her knuckles, the downy fuzz that of an adolescent boy. Would this be enough for her? Like Virginia Woolf, she had a room of her own and intended to put it to good use. But for the life of her, she couldn't imagine how she would get Al into bed. He was always so proper. He seldom walked on campus without a jacket and tie.

She would need more than Cupid's dart the next time they stood in front of her boardinghouse door.

Lost in her daydream, at first, she didn't notice Vesta tapping her on the back. But her friend persisted, dancing around Lulu until she blocked her path. "Annabelle and I are performing with the women's choral group, the Treble Clef, at the First Christian Church on Friday," Vesta said. "I do hope you'll come?"

Sighing as she looked for a way to escape, Lulu couldn't dodge her friend's overture. But then, she realized, this might be the perfect opportunity. She would ask Al to walk her home after the choral group's performance. A stroll along the river at twilight could be so romantic.

"With pleasure. I'll ask Al to come along," she said.

"Roy will be there too," Vesta said. "Reverend Rose asked him to do the evening's reading."

Lulu struggled to keep a straight face. "Roy, religious? That's hard to imagine."

"Roy told us at lunch he's going to deliver a lesson from the Bible. I'm thinking of wearing my red dress. Do you think red is too bright for the occasion?"

Lulu, lost in her own plans for the evening, didn't answer. Sneaking Al up the stairway to her room would not be difficult, but strait-laced Al was likely to protest. The walk home would have to prove persuasive.

"Lulu? Are you listening?"

"The evening should be lovely," Lulu said, "although I would prefer a gathering at the Bohemian Club. The conversation there is much more stimulating."

"I doubt it," Vesta said. She considered the rebellious members of the all-girl Bohemian Club a blemish on the university. Lulu loved to tease her and frequently threatened to join the club for its unconventional views.

"The church expects hundreds of young men and women for the concert," Vesta said.

"I'm sure the evening will be magnificent," Lulu said, although it was not the gathering at the church she had in mind.

* * *

Roy paced in front of the altar, his fists clenched, his stomach a knot of nerves. He never ate before an oration, preferring to arrive ahead of his audience to familiarize himself with the hall. He checked for squeaky boards under his feet and tested the room's lighting, determining the best place to stand. A random sunbeam striking his face at just the right moment could prove an effective oratory device.

The *Morning Register* predicted that the evening's social would "throng with fair maids and brave young men." When Reverend Rose invited him to speak, he asked Roy to carry His message into the world by urging the students to embody Christian values through Bible study.

Roy read and reread the evening's biblical passage, waiting for that magical moment when the words would come to him. Until they did, panic gnawed at his empty stomach. The knot, as familiar as the nugget of gold in his pocket, propelled him as he paced in front of the altar, his muscles tense and his jaw stiff.

He didn't belong here. Roy had heard his college friends say he had appeared out of "nowhere." Only he knew that "nowhere" was Kennett, California, in the heart of California gold country.

Kennett was the site of one of the largest gold-producing mines in Northern California, but it was the Crystal Saloon's whiskey, distilled and bottled in the back of the bar, that had attracted his father to the town. A large and bombastic man, he moved his family west in search of gold, but whiskey and barmaids were his stock in trade.

When the family first arrived, his father declared he had struck the mother lode. He planned to mine not gold but "investments." Night after night, his father stumbled home to their drafty cabin long after midnight, ebullient with liquor, selling his wife Alice on the opportunities he had discovered listening to drunken miners' fantasies. Why toil in the mines when the lure of gold had value in its own right? In the meantime, to buy groceries, his mother accepted a position teaching at the one-room schoolhouse.

Roy was twelve when his father came home lugging a printing press, a bulky piece of machinery as tall as Roy and his sister Jessie. Powered by a wheel as large as those on a carriage, its two long cylinders gleamed. Soon the press was humming. Roy's father printed two newspapers each week. One, with his wife's input, was the typical small-town weekly rag. Most of its articles bore a vague semblance to reality. The second, which his father distributed far and wide, contained nothing but lies. Persuasive tales of gold strikes; elaborate construction schemes that promised a tenfold return on investment. Opportunities in every form, each fail-proof scheme promising more than the last. A typical ad read: "Buy Consolidated Standard! Dividends are as sure to follow as day succeeds night. $500,000 worth of rich ore waiting to be processed."

When investors responded, Roy's father took them to his office, the Crystal Saloon. There he plied them with whiskey, putting on a dazzling show. The local barmaids, willing co-conspirators, poured and flirted as long as the tips were generous. If a night was profitable,

Roy's father arrived home with hard candy for the children and jewelry redeemed from the pawn shop for his hard-working wife. For a while, the money poured in.

At his father's knee, Roy learned the value of charm. Unfortunately, other shysters worked the suckers too. When word got out that the Kennett gold miners were crooked, an East Coast client walked out on his father before closing the deal.

"The governor of Pennsylvania is threatening to outlaw the sale of mining stock in the state," his father raved. His mother shushed him, reminding him that the children were sleeping. "For God Almighty," she said, "keep your voice down."

Roy was sixteen when his father left town. Alice's salary barely kept the family fed. Roy confided in a sympathetic minister, who fed him cookies and encouraged him to seek consolation in the Bible. Soon, he found a place at the minister's side at Sunday services. Roy blossomed, discovering in sermons a talent that would help him provide for his family.

The minister was not the only person who came to his aid. One night, a friendly barmaid at the Crystal Saloon reached under the 150-foot-long redwood bar and handed him the gold nugget, saying it was a gift from his father. Roy knew the well-meaning gesture came from pity. His father had nothing to do with it.

In Kennett, Roy discovered the compassion of barmaids and ministers. If it weren't for this discovery, he would never have received a scholarship to the university. He understood early the value of letting an audience see you struggle.

As the students filed into the First Christian Church, Reverend Rose watched as Roy paced. With each step, Roy repeated a Bible passage beneath his breath, as if mulling over its deeper meaning. With each alleluia, he filled his lungs. The reverend relaxed. The holy words fueled Roy's sense of certainty, restoring his flagging faith with the power of God, and imbuing his language with the persuasive wonder of the natural world. A confident strut replaced his nervous pacing. He thanked the reverend for his encouragement, received his blessing, and acknowledged his ability to restore confidence in the warmth of the Holy Spirit. He was ready.

28

Students filled the pews. The low buzz of animated voices echoed throughout the church as Annabelle approached the podium. With a flip of her blond curls, she sang the opening notes of the hymn "How Blest and Happy Is the Man." When the final soaring note floated to the ceiling, Roy inhaled and, following the hushed pause of anticipation, strode to the front of the room.

"Surrender to your Lord and Savior," he bellowed. With thunderous conviction, he advocated Bible study as the path to a righteous life. "An unprejudiced investigation and practical application of its truth will guide you, my dear friends, granting you a power derived from devotion."

Reverend Rose beamed.

In the front row, Vesta and Ted followed his every word as if hypnotized. As he spoke, the candles on the altar flickered. The fading rays of sunshine cast a benediction. Vesta's hands clasped in ecstasy. Roy caught Annabelle's eye when he said the devotion.

At the height of his rhetoric, Roy squeezed the gold nugget in his pocket. He rode the wave of the audience's rapt attention, drinking it in like a man lost high on Mount Shasta gulping from a frosty stream. When he finished, the church shook with applause.

The sweet harmonies of the Treble Clef that followed only elevated his mood, the angelic notes ascending as if into heaven. He returned to his chair next to his friends to soak in their praise.

Reverend Rose, ebullient, invited the guests to join him for a reception in the church basement. There, Annabelle refilled his glass of tea whenever he asked. Vesta fed him macaroons, and the high school girls giggled, their envy apparent. Lulu kissed Annabelle on the cheek. In the optimistic afterglow of his success, Roy longed to feel the brush of Lulu's lips on his face, but she shook his hand, a businesslike acknowledgment of his impressive performance. For now, that would have to do.

In a corner of the room, a reporter from the Eugene paper interviewed Reverend Rose about the annual event. The next morning, Roy would clip the article from the paper and tuck it into the mirror over his bureau. "One of the pleasing features of school life in Oregon's educational center is this annual reception where hundreds of young men and women assemble to become better acquainted and enjoy our congregation's hospitality."

The evening, Reverend Rose reported, could not have been more successful.

* * *

After the reception, Al followed Lulu down the stairs of the church. Since taking the job at the *Webfoot*, he too sported a jaunty bow tie. Unlike Roy's red calling card, his was a conservative blue. As they strolled down Main Street, he spoke with animation about the new hall of engineering, an impressive brick building trimmed in buff-colored cement with a wraparound porch of Spanish tile.

"Two horizontal steel-shell tubular boilers, eighty-five horsepower each, generate the steam for the heating system," he said. "The draft is produced by a brick chimney seventy feet high."

For the evening, Lulu had dressed in white lace with a pink sash. So far, Al hadn't seemed to notice.

"Every room and hallway in the building has radiators of a proper size and number to maintain a comfortable temperature in any weather. They drain into a large steel receiving tank in the boiler's pit."

Lulu had inserted her Dutch cap before leaving for the party, wanting to avoid the embarrassment she had felt when her Frenchman had performed the task. As Al described the heating system of the new building, she considered the possibility that Al might be a virgin. She gave his arm a reassuring squeeze. He smiled back at her fondly. "Am I boring you?"

"Not at all. I love your curiosity about how things work."

"If you ask me, engineering is the new frontier. That's why I want to transfer to the new school. Of course, even considering the move appalls Father. He always assumed I would follow in his footsteps and study law."

"Well, I think your decision is dandy. Isn't that why we're here? To follow our passions and not waste an opportunity? I say hurrah to you. I'd much rather listen to your description of a building's heating system than most of the petty discourse of our peers."

"Thank you, my dear."

"I'm so bored by Vesta and Annabelle's gossip. Vesta puts all her energy into trying to sweep your friend Roy off his feet."

"Vesta and every other woman in our class."

"When I first met Vesta, I asked her what she planned to study at the university. She replied she was here to earn her M.R.S. Can you imagine?"

"I think you are the most level-headed woman I know." Al blushed, but his compliment was sincere.

"Level-headed because I choose you?"

"Level-headed because you have more important things on your mind than snagging a man. How did your seminar with Professor Carson go?"

"Well. She continues to encourage me to tackle the ethics of the Indian question."

"I know you are up to the task." Al did not conceal his admiration. Lulu hoped he was right.

They paused at the river to watch a family of ducks. Lulu tucked her arm in Al's, moving closer as the ducks paddled by. "Al, do you want to kiss me?"

Startled, Al turned to her, his blue eyes wide behind the thick lenses of his eyeglasses. She tipped her head. Should she close her eyes?

"You wouldn't mind?" he asked.

"Not at all."

After two tentative pecks, he pulled her closer. The ducks were long gone by the time he pulled back, breathless and flustered.

Al wrapped his arm around her as they walked toward her rented room. Their bodies brushed against each other, a pleasant sensation that Lulu found encouraging. Soon they stood under Cupid's sign.

"Unlike Vesta, I don't believe in marriage," Lulu said. "But I do believe in love."

"Do tell me more," Al said, holding her hand.

"Like Mary Wollstonecraft, I believe a man and woman who love each other should be free to sleep together outside the bonds of marriage. Mary had extramarital affairs with two married men, Henry Fuseli and Gilbert Imlay, before marrying William Godwin."

"But..." Al sputtered. "You know I'm not married?"

Lulu laughed. "I know, but I wanted you to know I will never be a slave to any man." She thought of her mother. "My career and independence are important to me. But that doesn't mean I want to be alone."

Al inhaled, mulled this over, and then exhaled. "Lulu, my dear, you take my breath away."

She took that as acquiescence. "Will you come up to my room then?"

He reached for her hand, and they headed for the rooming house.

It had taken no persuasion at all. She had underestimated the man.

They tiptoed up the stairs, careful not to make any noise that might alert the other tenants. Once she shut the door behind them, Al embraced her with a confidence that surprised her. She untied his bow tie. He took over from there, taking off his shoes and stretching out on the bed. She sat down, her heart fluttering madly. Gently, he stroked her arm and then held her face in his hands. In no hurry, he explored her body. "I'm an engineer," he whispered in her ear. "I need to know how things work."

He studied for the rest of the evening, mastering the task at hand. Lulu let him take the lead, pleased by her body's eager response as he explored. This time, Lulu was not disappointed. Free love was everything she had dreamed it would be. She didn't require a Frenchman. In Al, she had found a sublime partner, methodical and considerate. Just the companion a suffragette like Lulu required on her journey toward fulfillment.

* * *

Al's father was livid. "We must do everything we can to protect states' rights." He sat at the head of the dining room table, his invited guests a captive audience. "The Act of February 1903 contradicts all precedent by awarding concurrent jurisdiction to the federal courts," the judge bellowed.

"An outrage," his colleague Dr. Dunham agreed, pounding a beefy fist on the Bartletts' elegantly set table, causing the china to tremble.

Al rolled his eyes, taking care that only Lulu could see.

"What does Section 60 cover?" Dean Carson interrupted the men's conversation.

With a snort of condescension, Dr. Bartlett explained: "Suits that cover preferences or fraudulent conveyances."

In 1902, the judge had delivered the state court's most important constitutional decision, establishing how initiatives and referendums could support a republican form of government. Since then, he considered himself the preeminent authority on the state's inherent rights in federal jurisdictions.

"It is blatant overreach like this that makes us wish you were back on the state's supreme court," Dr. Dunham said. "Under your leadership, Oregon held its own against an intrusive federal judiciary."

Since his term ended four years ago, Al's father, on top of his teaching responsibilities at the university, had spent most of his time preparing to defend his ruling to the Supreme Court of the United States. For months now, he had immersed himself in the Constitution, seeking guidance on the coordination between federal and state legislation.

Beneath the heavy table, Lulu's foot sought Al's. In response to her gentle nudge, he poked her ankle with the toe of his boot. After the previous night's intimacy, this touch was electric, traveling up his leg like an electric current. Lulu's uncharacteristic silence said everything he needed to know about her reaction to the judge's monologue. Through her, Al watched the all-too-familiar scenario with new eyes.

"Young Mr. Bartlett?" Dr. Dunham turned his attention to the judge's eldest son. "I do hope you'll follow in your father's footsteps. Oregon needs fine minds like yours speaking up if the state is to maintain the progress of the last forty years."

A year ago, Al would have smiled at the inquiry and passed the roast beef. But today, Lulu's expectant gaze demanded more of him. At the end of the table, his maternal grandfather, Thomas Scott, paused with the gravy spoon in his hand. His mother, seated at the old man's side, slipped a china saucer under it to protect the lace of the crocheted tablecloth.

"While I have nothing but respect for my father's accomplishments," Al said, his voice quavering, "my interests lie in another direction." He avoided his father's eyes, seeking the kinder attention of his grandfather at his mother's side.

"Young Al," Grandfather Scott, a geologist and one of the first professors at the university, said. "This is a surprising development." Scott's bushy eyebrows accentuated the delighted twinkle of his eyes. He ladled a second spoonful of gravy onto his pile of mashed potatoes and, circumventing his bushy mustache and long beard, shoved a heap into his open mouth. Al's mother watched with alarm. Whether her concern was about the possibility of a stain on the linen or the result of Al's unexpected announcement was not clear.

"I'm thinking of enrolling in the new School of Engineering," Al said. Lulu stroked his thigh under cover of her napkin. His voice steadied. He had rehearsed this speech the previous night to Lulu's approbation. "My choice is the obvious one. I was born the day they wired the first fifty-nine customers in Manhattan with electric current." Encouraged by his grandfather's nod of approval, he turned to his father. "By the time you, Father, were appointed to the Oregon Supreme Court, long-distance power lines crisscrossed Portland and an electric railroad spanned our county. I entered the university a year after the discovery of alternate current." Lulu squeezed his leg. "Electricity will run our new nation, and I want to take advantage of the opportunities it offers."

From the end of the table, Judge Bartlett glowered. He banged his fist like a gavel on the table. The china rattled. "How"—the judge let the word hang in the air. The guests held their breath, waiting for him to complete his sentence. "How can you begin a course of study in electronics at this late date?" He pronounced "electronics" as if the word itself offended him.

"I'll finish the coursework for a Bachelor of Science. To receive a degree in Electrical Engineering, I'll stay for a postgraduate year."

"Harrumph." The judge rendered his verdict. Al tried to ignore the tears gathering in his mother's eyes.

"I believe Al's talent for scientific investigation has great value to the state," Lulu said.

"The School of Engineering offers excellent opportunities and equipment for young men inclined toward a scientific or industrial career." Dr. Scott, having much experience in defending the university's scientific advances, spoke up.

"Industrial?" the judge sneered.

"Especially fitting," Scott continued, smiling at his grandson, "in the Pacific Northwest, where enormous resources await our development."

Dean Carson winked at Lulu. Lulu directed her most flirtatious smile at the geologist. "Dr. Scott, it is such a pleasure to meet you. I so admire your work." Ignoring the room's stony silence, she continued. "I think the university has benefited from your unique ability to give scientific truth a moral energy."

Al's grandfather put down his fork. "That is the job of any scientist," he said. "The earth is God's holy book. The earth's strata—its seas, lakes, rivers, mountains, valleys, trees, and flowers—are his word." Lulu listened without once letting go of Al's thigh.

The judge shifted in his chair at the head of the table. Cleared his throat.

"And yes, young Al, I do believe electricity is part of God's design." Al received his grandfather's benediction with gratitude, a wan smile, and a beating heart.

"Is this your doing, young lady?" the judge thundered, turning his fierce, dark eyes on the young woman who had arrived on Al's arm. Lulu did not flinch.

"I am confident Al can make his own decisions," she replied.

The judge snorted again, pushing his dinner plate aside and folding his unblemished napkin on the table. "Darling, can you please clear the table?" He stood up. "Gentlemen, join me in the parlor for a cigar?"

Al remained at Lulu's side. Facing his father had taken every ounce of courage he had.

Did his father know him so little? Perhaps one of Al's brothers would follow his father into the study of law, but he would not. Could not. Had never even considered it.

Lulu knew this. Lulu understood him. Turning to her, he felt a wave of love sweep over him. This gorgeous, brilliant woman had invited him into her bed. She had given him the confidence to become his own man.

Dr. Scott also remained at the table. When the other women jumped up to assist Cornelia in clearing the dishes, Lulu addressed Al's grandfather. "Tell me, sir, how did you choose your course of study?"

"When I first discovered geometry, it seemed a pure, beautiful logic, the perfect chain of reasoning."

"Did I not tell you that Dr. Scott is an inspiration?" Back from the kitchen, Dean Carson sat down next to the geologist who spoke with a charming Irish lilt.

"Soon after I arrived in Oregon, I joined up with a party of cavalry carrying supplies to the Harney Valley. There, I uncovered my first fossils on the John Day River." The old man lit up as he recounted his discovery. Soon, the other women gathered around the revered professor, ignoring the men's booming voices competing in the parlor.

None of the professors had challenged his father's dismissal of his announcement. Al's mother had not spoken up in his defense.

"Excuse me, Mother," he said when he could no longer bear it, "but it's time for us to leave."

Lulu stood up. "Must we go now? Your grandfather is truly amazing," she said. "I'm loath to go."

Al's mother smiled wanly at Lulu's praise of her father, wiping her eyes and warily watching her son enfold Lulu's hand in his.

Cornelia did not kiss Al goodbye. His father's wrath awaited her and for this, and only this, he was sorry.

Lulu and Al headed back toward campus. Sunshine dappled the tree-lined road. Lulu spoke with animation, rehashing the conversations that had taken place during the evening. "Dr. Scott is truly a marvel."

As they stood outside Lulu's room under Cupid's verse, Lulu imitated the "great man," as she called the judge. In a deep, self-important baritone, she proclaimed: "We have brought the rule of law to these savage lands." Al did not come to his father's defense.

Instead, Al silenced her with a prolonged kiss, his hands embracing her narrow waist. He pulled her toward him, drawn to the warmth of her lithe body. This time, she did not ask. They took off their shoes and tiptoed up the rickety stairs in stockinged feet. In Lulu's room, the judge wielded no power. In Lulu's arms, Al prepared to pursue his path wherever it might lead.

* * *

Crater Lake, 1902

Lulu and Al followed Roy as he paraded up the Fort Klamath Military Road like a lieutenant leading soldiers into battle. Behind them, Annabelle lugged a large basket filled with the day's picnic. The dirt road forked a half mile west of the Cascade Divide.

"Sheer upward ride the great Cascades," Roy recited, disappearing around a bend. The familiar lilt of his resonant voice echoed in the canyons that opened up on either side of the road.

> *"The sunbeams flash from peak to peak*
> *And touch with fire the ancient streak*
> *I hear a pebble loose itself and break*
> *The deep blue mirror of the lake."*

In the silent interlude after his recitation, they heard a pebble fall into the water with a satisfying plop.

"With Roy, it's always a show," Al said, shifting the weight of the basket to his other hand.

Annabelle, Lulu, and Al rounded the curve. The lake appeared. Roy's timing was impeccable. A wide expanse as smooth as glass painted the bluest blue reflected delicate puffs of fair-weather clouds.

"Worth the trip?" Roy asked. With an expansive sweep of his arm, Roy gifted his followers with the view of the lake, mountains, and sky that surrounded them.

No doubt about it, the mountains were impressive.

Only Lulu dared to challenge Roy's magnanimous gesture. "Thank God President Roosevelt made Crater Lake a national park. The mining industry gave him quite a fight."

Roy waved aside her commentary. "Who needs a park? I've hiked these mountains my entire life." He pointed at the tall pines. "For me, this is a sacred spot. I would never wish it defiled by politicians or miners."

The jaunt had been Roy's idea, a fitting conclusion to their sophomore year. Lulu and Al jumped at the chance to spend a few more days together before they separated for the summer.

"I could live without the dramatic commentary," Al confided to her now. "The scenery doesn't require interpretation."

"But you have to admit," Lulu said, "it's a beautiful poem." Louder, she added, "And a spectacular view."

"Worth every moment of the harrowing trip up," Annabelle said. She was still recovering from the ride on the Southern Pacific railway, which Roy called "the Old, Slow, and Easy." "It's a miracle we didn't die when the steam locomotive crossed those rickety covered bridges."

"You may be beautiful, my dear," Roy snorted, "but up here in the mountains, beauty only gets you so far."

"Annabelle is a trooper," Lulu said. "You ought to give her credit for making the arduous journey to spend the day with us."

At yet another breathtaking overlook, they spread out a red plaid blanket on the delicate spring grass. Inhaling the mountain air, Al said, "This is the tonic I need before settling into a summer of study." Gazing up at the sky and the towering trees, he exhaled reverently. "Invigorating."

Lulu helped Annabelle dole out sandwiches. Annabelle presented the food with a flourish, singing out each of their names as she handed them the sandwiches. Since Roy had invited her to join the outing, she had held her head higher, a diva preparing to walk onstage.

"Your voice lessons are paying off, I see," Lulu said.

"I'm hoping this summer at the conservatory will polish my skills for the fall musical. My father pulled a lot of strings to get me in."

Lulu knew Annabelle's father, an influential businessman, had plenty of strings to pull.

"I'm certain you will return to campus a star," Lulu said, winking at Al. Roy, of course, encouraged the girl. Perhaps she would get to know her friend better during the summer, when they would both be in Portland: Annabelle at the conservatory and Lulu at home. "I wish we could stay here forever. The moment I arrive home, I become a child again."

"At least you don't have to perform manual labor," Roy commiserated. Al's cousin Will had recommended Roy and Ted for summer positions with the Condor Water and Power Company. By June, the two boys would be hard at work building a power ditch in the Rogue River Valley.

But this afternoon, all their summer plans faded in the glorious sunshine.

"Joaquin Miller camped for several days on the rim last summer," Roy said. As they lay on their backs, sated by the hike and the hearty lunch, he recited from the *Sea of Silence*: "The lake took hold of my heart. Unlike other parks, I love it almost like one of my family."

"Beautiful," Lulu said. "Who better captures the spirit of Oregon than the state's poet laureate?"

"I hereby nominate Roy to be our personal poet laureate," Al said.

"Hear, hear." Annabelle gazed at Roy with undisguised adoration. She lit a cigarette and watched the wisps of smoke dissipate into the clear sky.

"If Roy is our poet laureate, I want to be something just as significant," Lulu insisted.

"You can be our muse," Al said, taking her hand and kissing the knuckles one by one.

"Not sufficient." Lulu pulled her hand back.

"Our literary star?"

"Better." She turned back to him. "I will write the story of this day, this fleeting moment of our lives, and it will take your breath away."

"And I," Annabelle broke in, "will star in the play made from your story and receive thunderous applause from audiences far and wide."

"You both will be remarkable," Al said, reaching for Lulu's hand again. This time she allowed him to hold on to it. "While you three dream of new worlds, "he said, "I will build them. "

Lulu stretched out next to Al on the grass and closed her eyes. The noonday sun warmed her face, filtering brilliant and blazing red by her eyelids. The warm breeze lulled her to sleep. Roy tickled Al's nose with a feathery blade of grass, causing him to sneeze and ending her reverie. Moments later, Al chased Roy across the field as Lulu and Annabelle cheered them on, laughing. The two boys wrestled in the grass, each determined to establish a supremacy that neither was likely to achieve.

When he'd had enough, Al conceded. "I'm no match for you."

Roy lifted Annabelle up by her narrow waist and spun her around, her blond hair waving in the wind, her skirts and petticoats a cloud of lace.

"Never forget you said that," Roy said to Al. And then setting Annabelle down, he asked her, "Did I sweep you off your feet?"

"The day I met you," she said, breathless.

"The Lord smiles on us all then," he said.

"Do you think," Al asked Lulu later as they followed their friends down the dusty mountain road, "Roy believes any of his malarkey?"

"What do you mean?"

"His sermonizing about God and faith. His religion and poems evoking heaven. I, for one, have never seen him read the Bible despite his golden words about Bible study."

"Roy is a poet who needs words to survive."

"I think Roy enjoys an audience."

Lulu kicked a pebble, mulling this over. "When Roy and I work on the *Webfoot*, I see another side of him. A serious side. His childhood was tough. It lacked many of the comforts you and I take for granted. The church became his sanctuary."

"Maybe." Al walked on, silent now, a thoughtful frown on his face.

"You're not jealous, are you?" she teased.

"I just can't help but wonder what convictions lie beneath his melodrama." He chose his words with care. "Even his attention to Annabelle seems an act. It's impossible to tell whether or not he likes the girl."

"Roy loves these mountains," Lulu responded. "Didn't your Grandfather Scott say that a love of nature does not differ from a love of God? I, for one, am touched that he brought us here to share his glorious mountainside. To open up to us. Can't you leave your scientific skepticism behind for one day and enjoy the scenery? Be thankful Roy brought us together."

Al snapped. "Roy had nothing to do with that." He stopped and picked a daisy from the roadside.

"You love me, you love me not," he said, plucking the petals one by one.

"I love you, silly," Lulu said, pulling him close, crushing what remained of the flower as she kissed him. Annabelle and Roy disappeared ahead. "And I love making love to you," she said, poking him in the stomach.

They ran, hand in hand, to catch up with the others.

Chapter 4 The Explosion

Medford, Oregon, 1902

"The moon makes a good light for our town after old Sol has retired for the night," one of Medford's citizens had been heard to say. *"Yes,"* said the other, *"but the moon is unreliable—she goes out sometimes. We are going to have an electric light system and then the moon won't be in it."*
"The Town Talker," Medford Mail

Two weeks after successfully completing their sophomore year at the university, Roy and Ted traveled by carriage to the town of Woodville, a hamlet on the Rogue River forty miles south of Medford, to report for their summer jobs. The Condor Water and Power Company had recently been granted a franchise to construct a power ditch abutting the river, and they were to provide the muscle to get the job done.

Their boss, C.H. Leadbetter, was a large man, a cigar-chomping, red-faced corporate officer of the power company. He eyed his new employees before providing a brief history of the project. He took most of the credit for having sold the undertaking to a skeptical public. "I explained to those yokels that the power ditch would supply drinking water to the town as well as electric power. When that didn't do the trick, I promised to supply water to the community at no charge during the term of the franchise."

C.H. cast a dubious gaze on the students he had hired for the summer. Roy rewarded him with a complicit smile. C.H. named him team supervisor on the spot, to the disappointment of Ted and Al's cousin Will, who had gotten them the job. Will figured the position was rightfully his.

The tasks assigned to the summer employees were tedious. Building a power ditch involved excavation by hand. As their first task, C.H. said, the crew would shovel a ditch three feet deep and eight feet wide. Once they completed the digging, they would place dynamite in holes along the center line of the ditch, spaced so the detonation of one stick exploded the next. A blasting cap and fuse would prime the starting charge.

C.H. pointed the students in the right direction and returned to his office, not to return until the end of the day, when he would assess their progress and berate them for their white-bellied, aristocratic negligence. "We've got a deadline to meet," he reminded them, chomping on his cigar and kicking the slag dismissively. "I'm not paying you to lollygag."

Before long, the students fell into a mind-numbing routine and experienced the job's unforeseen benefits. Roy's pasty white arms tanned nicely. During their infrequent breaks, Roy and Ted compared the impressive contours of their new muscles. In contrast to the sedentary life they led as university students, the summer work left them feeling strong, almost powerful.

Roy walked along the right side of the ditch, testing the depth of the holes, the width of the exposed earth. Two feet behind him, Will, bored with digging holes, took a break from cleaning up slag. He stretched out his stiff legs on a boulder they had uprooted during the previous day's detonation. To make more room for himself, he pushed aside an open box of dynamite caps labeled *DANGER, property of Prospect, Jackson County, Oregon.* Ted strolled by, jabbing a metal bar into the earth, making one last hole at a thirty-degree angle just below the waterline, eight inches deep. He twirled the bar like a baton before inserting a one-and-one-quarter by eight-inch cartridge packed with fifty percent nitroglycerine dynamite into the hole. "That's the last of 'em," he said. His task done, he joined Will's perch on the boulder. "'Spose it's not a good idea for us to smoke," he joshed.

Roy, intent on capping the waterproof fuse for the blast, manipulated the cap in his hand. His movements were slow and cautious, just as C.H. had taught him. The middle hole had to be charged right before the blast so that the blasting cap in his hand and the fuse would not remain underwater longer than a few minutes. He tuned out his coworkers' shenanigans. At his command, the detonation of the charge would set off the adjacent cartridges in either direction, almost instantaneously.

The drama of each detonation thrilled Roy; the glory and the danger of the explosion made the dreary job bearable. And the wages weren't bad. Unlike his more affluent classmates, Roy needed the money to pay for his junior year.

Later, he could not recall what went wrong. All he knew was that before he had time to finish his task and shepherd the others a safe distance away, a spark came out of nowhere, kissing the fuse that danced alive in his palm and triggering an explosion so loud it was heard in the next town. One second Roy was studying a small red cap in his palm, and the next he held the sun in his hand.

But the boys who set it in motion heard nothing at all. They were instantly deaf. Silver darts of dancing metal shot into the air and splattered the side walls of the power ditch with a spray as powerful as a fireman's hose. The burning orb shot fire bolts toward the earth and the sky. At Roy's side, Ted watched stunned, numb.

Pyrotechnics lit the excavation site brighter than the fourth of July. Gray rock glistening like silver. Ted screamed "what the hell?" and then "damn." A shard of metal cauterized his outstretched leg. Will threw his cigarette to the ground one moment before he too was lying in the rubble, blood spurting through a gash in his work pants. Roy, mesmerized by the fire in his hand, at first didn't feel the stab of lightning that exploded in his abdomen. Pain burst as bright as the light right before the metal shards peppered his face and pierced his left eye. Until the day he died, he would swear he saw Lulu's face in the explosion's flash. Her eyes golden. Her dark hair like sunbeams framing her elegant face. He clung to the vision like an amulet as he descended into darkness.

Roy swam his way back to consciousness. He felt nauseous, despite the sensation that he was floating on a cloud.

Lulu held his hand. Her fingers felt warm, reassuring. "Poor thing."

"The doctors say that's the ether," Al said.

Roy touched his head. His eyes were swathed in bandages. Even the sockets ached.

"Where am I?"

"Medford," Al said. "Dr. Kendall's hospital. They brought you here by buckboard during the night."

Horse hooves clopping, the jarring of a wooden vehicle on potholed roads. The memories floated by as if they had happened to someone else. A violent flash followed by unremitting pain, alarmed voices. The last thing he recalled was holding the fuse as his buddies laid dynamite, preparing to blast power ditches for the lucrative summer job he had used the best of his blarney to talk his way into.

"Ted and Will are okay. The doctors removed fragments from their legs, but you got the worst of it," Al said.

"There's a stained-glass window right over your bed." Lulu changed the subject. "I know you can't see it, but the light passing through it makes it seem like you're lying in a rainbow."

Al said, "You were in surgery all night."

White sheets, blinding lights like knives. Nurses and doctors in starched aprons silhouetted by a large window filled with moonlight. A mustached man wearing gloves looking down at him, dead serious. A nurse perched next to a large gurgling machine, holding a hose. Bowls lined up on a metal table at his side. Surgical instruments in a stew pot of boiling water. He recalled a doctor holding a soft cloth redolent of chemicals over his nose. Dusk descending on him, darkness, a relief from the pain as the blinding lights faded into dancing colors, into nothingness from which he could not escape.

What if he would never see her again?

"My eyes?"

"They are hoping there will be no permanent damage." Al, a straight shooter, delivered an honest assessment of his condition. "At worst, you may lose sight in one eye."

"Dr. Kendall's hospital is the best in Oregon." Lulu described the elegant Victorian mansion, the oversized windows, and the towering ceilings. "The stables for the horses are the cleanest I have ever seen. Dr. Kendall is the most qualified surgeon in the state."

Roy listened for horses in the backyard, their impatient snuffling.

A nurse entered the room, her starched skirt rustling like wind rattling autumn leaves. She probed his aching limbs, checked the bandages covering the wound in his abdomen. He felt her fingers on his feverish flesh. *Did Lulu flinch at the sight of his wound? Al*, he supposed, *draped a comforting arm around her.*

"No sign of infection," the nurse said, her voice low and businesslike. She did not touch the bandages that covered his eyes. "He needs to rest," she told his friends. "That's the best medicine for him now."

Despite the nurse's instructions, Al and Lulu remained at his side for the rest of the afternoon. Al rambled on about his summer catching up with his classmates in the School of Engineering. "Dr. McAllister lets us tinker with the engines and dynamos and other electrical apparatuses. I feel like a child on Christmas morning, unable to decide which toy I want to play with first."

Behind bandages and through the foggy residue of anesthesia, Roy listened, catching a word here, a word there. He suspected his friend was uncomfortable in the hospital and his incessant talking masked his fear. Mostly, he listened for Lulu, seeking comfort in the swish of her petticoats as she smoothed his blanket, poured him a glass of water.

"We left Portland as soon we heard about your accident," she told him. "Will's mother told mine. A friend of the judge gave us a ride to Medford in his Rambler automobile. Annabelle would have joined us, but the conservatory asked her to sing in this weekend's oratorio."

Al said that only three of the newfangled automobiles had been purchased in Eugene that summer, each of them a prized possession of a wealthy citizen, an item of wonder to all who watched their progress on the muddy street. The image of Lulu and Al riding out of town on the tufted black seats of an automobile pierced the darkness of Roy's blindness, stressing the seriousness of his accident. "We promised your mother we would stay by your side until she and Jessie arrive in Medford."

As the anesthesia cleared, Roy realized he was in dire straits. There was no way his mother could pay the exorbitant cost of a hospital bed. He had counted on his summer wages to pay for next year's expenses. His physical pain paled next to the mental anguish that overcame him.

"I imagine Ted will be quite the dandy on his crutches," Lulu said.

Al asked the nurse where he might arrange overnight accommodations.

"The Nash Hotel has rooms to rent," she said. "Our patients' families often stay there."

"In that case, I'll be back in a jiffy," he said.

Roy knew Al had left the room when he heard footsteps fading in the corridor. He sank into the sullen gloom. His entire face throbbed.

"You're going to be all right," Lulu whispered, stroking his hand.

C.H. Leadbetter arrived at the hospital moments before the nurses insisted all visitors clear the ward. His heavy footsteps thundered through the quiet corridors. Even here, Roy imagined, an unlit cigar hung from the blossom of his boss's mouth. Although blind, he could imagine the man's corduroy vest stretching across his protruding belly.

"I'll leave you be then," Lulu said. "We'll be back in the morning." He wished he could grasp her hand tighter, hold her nearer.

"My boy," C.H. boomed from the doorway. "This is a most distressing development."

A second voice, reedy and businesslike, interrupted him. "Now C.H., there is no need to alarm the boy. We need to reassure him. He is in excellent hands."

Mr. Webb, C.H. told him, was an attorney representing Condor Water and Power, here to make things right.

"We"—and by "we," Webb meant the company—"insist that each of you young men receives the highest level of care. We have already spoken with the esteemed clinic doctors and informed them that no expense is too dear when it comes to your rapid recovery."

That got Roy's attention.

"Nurse Lydia here has my card. Whatever you need, we will arrange for you to have it."

"You will pay my bills?"

"We will, my son. Not only will Condor Water and Power pay your medical expenses, but we have arranged to pay the balance of your summer's wages and have increased your pay rate by five percent. All we ask of you is a speedy recovery." The man's enthusiasm reminded Roy of his father selling snake oil in a bar.

He would, when he was up to it, get more out of this man. In the meantime, Roy thanked him, playing up the frailty in his voice, touching the bandages on his head. Groaning as Lydia ushered the businessmen out of the room.

Lydia, who had received instructions from the doctor that her patient should feel no pain, doubled the doctor's prescription for laudanum, squeezing the bitter liquid onto his tongue with an eyedropper. Soon Roy drifted off into a spongy world of stars exploding over snowy mountain peaks, of hucksters dressed as physicians cradling his bleeding brain and miners prospecting for gold while Roy, wearing the short pants of a young boy, shouted from a mountaintop, poetry echoing in the valleys below, where newfangled cars ferried admirers to sit at his feet.

With his mattress like cotton and the curtains blowing in the nighttime breezes, he thought for a moment that this might be heaven.

When he woke in the night, his mother was at his side. In his mind's eye—the only one that worked—he sensed her lined face braced for yet another disaster. His sister Jessie sniffled. He assured them this might be a blessing in disguise.

"God works in wondrous ways," Reverend Rose had taught him to say.

Dr. Kendall kept telling him, "There is every reason to hope that the sight in your remaining eye is not impaired." But Roy listened to the tone of the doctor's voice, not his words. As an experienced orator, he understood subliminal messages, the art of twisting the meaning of words. Now, he too reassured his mother and sister he was going to be all right.

* * *

Lulu and Al rented rooms in Medford's Nash Hotel, conveniently located across the street from the railroad depot. Outside, the small city bustled with activity. Excavators scraped the dirt road all day long, preparing Main Street for paving. Cars and carriages bounced along the street, sounded impatient horns, and left clouds of dust in their wake.

Al paced his small room like an animal in a cage. "My summer work has been a revelation," he told Lulu as he hung his suit jacket up in the closet. "So many opportunities to explore and not enough time. As soon as Roy's mother gets here, let's catch the next train back to Eugene."

"How can you say that when our friend languishes in the hospital?" Al's lack of sympathy took Lulu aback. She could not shake the sight of her classmate lying on the starched white sheets; the cocky man's helplessness as he lay pale, blind, and bandaged, in obvious pain.

Al kissed the top of her head.

Lulu said nothing. The sight of Roy in the hospital had unsettled her. Al's composure seemed out of place. Insensitive.

"It's an unfortunate situation, but I'm sure he'll be all right."

Lulu excused herself, telling Al she needed to freshen up. Instead, she studied her face in the hallway bathroom mirror. What must it feel like to be blind? Her reflection stared back, wide-eyed, unblemished. Unchanged by the day's events. The overhead lamp illuminated her hands, rose pink and soft. She pictured Roy's, swathed in bandages. *Handling dynamite*, she thought. *What the hell was he thinking?*

Al did not appear to share her sympathies. When she returned to his room, he said, "Trust Roy to milk the situation for all it's worth." He removed his glasses and cleaned the lenses with a fresh white handkerchief from his pocket.

The summer night wasn't cold, but she trembled as if she too had suffered an injury.

Men, she was learning, often misread what women wanted. Her father, for example, assured her mother had become accustomed to his absences. In a recent letter, he wrote: "Your mother has no desire to accompany me on my travels. A woman needs a man to provide for her, and I would never let your mother down, nor fail to provide for you or your sister." He added that Lulu, having the benefit of a university education, should choose a young man who could do the same for her. "As always, my dear daughter, you have excelled in the task. It thrills both your mother and me that you are keeping company with Al Bartlett."

Small comfort, she thought. Lizzie suspected their father had a lover on the East Coast. Al, obsessed with his studies, was unfazed by the explosion that had injured their friend.

"Al," she said, "do you sometimes think progress comes with a price? That the sacrifices it requires can do irreparable harm?"

"Dear one," Al turned to her, cupping her face in his hands, "there have always been accidents, progress or not. Roy is lucky to live where medical care is available. The power company has accepted responsibility for his bills."

"It's not just the money... Roy could have died." He massaged her shoulders, methodically releasing the knots in the tense muscles, sending shivers down her spine.

"But he didn't. Roy's tough. He'll get through this."

She closed her eyes, giving in to the comfort of his touch.

"I've missed you this summer," he said.

"Balderdash. You've been busy, fiddling with your gadgets in the lab."

"On the contrary, I hear your voice every day, standing up to my father. Urging me to pursue my passions. I think about you every night..."

Lulu relaxed. She closed her eyes.

"Poor Roy," she said again, this time with less emotion, grateful that Al was at her side.

"He'll be okay," Al said.

The sun faded outside the window. Al escorted her to her room. Always the gentleman, she thought. Steadfast. That's how her father described Al. Thank God that wasn't his only charm.

They didn't make love that night in that tawdry hotel room, but she wouldn't have minded if they had.

Instead, they slept separately in single beds in closet-sized rooms. In the morning, after verifying that Roy's mother and sister had arrived late in the night and had taken up the vigil at their friend's side, they said goodbye and boarded the train back to Portland.

* * *

Before removing Roy's bandages, Dr. Kendall asked Nurse Lydia to close the curtains. The surgeon turned off the room's overhead lights. In the artificial twilight of the hospital room, Roy imagined his mother watching from the armchair where she had spent most of the preceding month, her hands worrying, her eyes bright with fear.

"As you know, your left eye was damaged in the explosion. Despite our best efforts, we had to remove it. For the time being, you can wear an eye patch. When your recovery is complete, we will refer you to an oculist to prepare a prosthetic. The Germans have developed a superior glass formula for the making of artificial eyes. A hollow cryolite glass prosthesis is nearly indistinguishable from a natural eye."

"Only the best for our patient," Mr. Webb said, logging the expected expense in his ledger. His daily visit had become an elaborate accounting of Condor Water and Power's beneficence.

"Avast ye," Roy chuckled. "All hands ahoy." For days now, he had been using his idea of pirate lingo. Unlike his mother, Roy was feeling no pain.

Doctor Kendall administered anesthesia prior to the unveiling. To prepare for the removal of the bandages, he upped the daily dose of laudanum from two drops on the tongue to four. Before uncovering the damaged eye, he waited for the drug to take effect. "A few drops of cocaine solution on the patient's cornea renders the eye temporarily immobile and insensitive to pain," Kendall said, playing to his audience.

With methodical care, he removed the bandages.

Riding the wave of laudanum and numbed by the cocaine, Roy waited. For weeks now, he had lived in muffled darkness. Now ghosts emerged from the cloud he called home. The first thing he saw was the doctor's face, his beady eyes magnified by the lenses of his wire spectacles, his bushy gray eyebrows gathered in concentration. Bony pink fingers with large knuckles held a scope two inches above Roy's face, its light so bright the sharp beam felt like a knife.

"Can he see?" Alice's faint voice trembled.

"Give him a moment." Kendall handed the scope to Lydia.

The pain the scope's light triggered eased. Fuzzy shapes emerged in the darkened room. Roy noted that the nurse was fleshier than he had imagined, a loaf of bread kind of girl, soft. Mousy brown hair and one of those ridiculous white caps. He had imagined her as more statuesque, of the same body type as Lulu, perhaps with Annabelle's blond hair.

"How many fingers?" the doctor asked, raising two.

"Shiver me timbers." Roy amused himself, thinking the phrase apt since the tableau unfolding in front of him jarred every corner of his battered body. "Two," he said, tired of looking at the doctor's serious visage. The man had no sense of humor.

The examination that followed was excruciating despite the doctor's liberal application of an anesthetic. Kendall took his time admiring the elegance of his surgical craftsmanship. After twenty minutes of undivided attention to Roy's bloodshot but functioning eye, he proclaimed the surgery a success.

"We'll have you out of here in no time," Dr. Kendall said. Mr. Webb made a note. Alice scurried to her son's side.

The weariness etched into his mother's face sobered him, despite the medication humming in his veins. She seemed to have aged years since he last saw her. He had become used to his mother's disembodied presence, her vigilance during his illness, but, like everything else he had experienced since the accident, her presence lacked a physical dimension. He had felt her concern, but without seeing her, she had seemed ethereal. A mythical mother, part and parcel with the caring nurse and the domineering doctor.

But here she was, perched nervously on his bleached white sheets. He looked down and took in the angry stitched gash across his abdomen. In the doctor's mirror, he saw the horror of the gaping hole where his left eye belonged. He groaned.

"Are you in pain?" Nurse Lydia asked, her hand rosy on his pasty white arm.

"Always," he said, drinking her in, a helping hand holding a small vial of the brown liquid he depended on. "Always."

His sister Jessie watched as the nurse administered another two drops of the laudanum and then gently covered the offending socket with a black eyepatch held on by a narrow strap that tied behind his head. "Are you better now, matey?" Jessie asked, admiring his eye patch. The twelve-year-old had prepared a list of pirate terms to use when speaking with her brother.

"Aargh," he said now, feeling the warmth of opium rocking him. *This is heaven*, he thought, *the crepuscular light of the room, his mother and sister by his side, the plump nurse at his beck and call.*

As he practiced pirate terms with his sister—poop deck, power monkey, scallywag—Dr. Kendall shook his mother's hand, accepting her effusive gratitude as if it were his due. Mr. Webb slapped shut his ledger, informing the family he would return the next day to coordinate discharge plans.

Floating several inches above the bed, Roy saw the brilliant white sheets. The ceiling was smooth ivory, plaster embellished by elegant crown molding. Where the sun circumvented the white linen curtains, its glow bathed the room in multicolored prisms. Like rainbows, Lulu had said, the day after the accident, the day she sat by his side. "Shark bait. Son of a biscuit eater. Walk the plank." Jessie giggled, and with his good eye, Roy watched her red curls dance with the rhythm of her laughter.

He was going home. Soon he would return to the university.

* * *

Roy, dandily decked out in a suit, linen vest, and black bow tie the exact shade of his eye patch, read the president's Thanksgiving proclamation with gusto, standing at the head of the table. He employed every tool in his oratorical repertoire. "We are thankful for all that has been done for us in the past, and we pray that in the future we may be strengthened in the unending struggle to do our duty fearlessly and honestly, with charity and goodwill." Jessie, dressed in her finest calico party dress, beamed at her brother's words over centerpieces she had constructed herself: elaborate sculptures of pinecones and berries, gourds, and bright red fall leaves. Ted, Al, and Lulu, each the recipient of one of Jessie's homemade invitations, nodded in appreciation. At the end of the table, Alice wiped tears from her eyes.

Theodore Roosevelt had written the speech, but you'd never know that listening to Roy. He delivered the president's words with aplomb. Loaded silences between phrases, a faint quaver in his voice signaling his sincerity, a heartfelt sigh at the finish. Before sitting down, he looked each guest in the eye and thanked them, his voice restored to its previous tenor.

The minute Roy sat down, Ted leaped from his seat to claim his favorite cut of meat. Al stood at the sideboard, admiring the enormous, aromatic turkey, a holiday gift from Condor Water and Power. "I have dibs on the drumstick," Ted said, pushing Al aside. Before helping himself to the traditional sides of stuffing, cranberry sauce, and mashed potatoes, Ted took an enormous bite of the oversized piece of turkey. "I love this holiday," he said, waving greasy fingers through the air for emphasis.

"I see years of education have not civilized you, my friend," Al said.

"Not a bit," Ted grinned. As the other guests heaped their plates with the holiday meal, Roy continued to sit at the head of the table, basking in his return to the limelight. Before serving herself, Jessie prepared a plate for her brother and her silent mother, who watched the young people with relish.

"Do tell," Roy asked Al, "how have you amused yourself in my absence?"

"It's been a struggle, but I'm doing my best." Al launched into an elaborate description of his projects at the School of Engineering. "I've become quite convinced that electricity, not gold, is the key to Oregon's prosperity. Your benefactor, C.H., has positioned himself right smack dab in the middle of things."

Lulu sat on Roy's right side, the side with his good eye. She watched, fascinated, as Roy evaluated his options. At first, Roy turned his head ninety degrees to the left and focused his good right eye on Al, but soon he was rubbing his neck, tired from the effort. Then Lulu watched as Roy pretended to look Ted in the eye, even when it was obvious he could not see him. The act of listening was a skill that Roy had yet to master since his accident. A pity, since an effective debater was by necessity a skilled listener. For now, Roy's attempts to follow Al's conversation were clumsy. Al cut his response short when Roy put his head into his hands, complaining of a throbbing pain in his right eye.

"Al, sweetheart, perhaps Roy would rather not talk about the power company today."

"Sorry, old boy," Al said.

Old boy. How many times had Roy addressed Al by that phrase?

Their usual roles had been reversed. Al, secure in his standing, would have to learn to be more solicitous to his friend who, it was clear, was still not right.

"Your mother tells me you will return to school in the fall?" Lulu came to Al's rescue. Since she sat on Roy's right side, he could look at her without undue effort.

"My ocular prosthesis will be ready in the spring. I have every intention of returning to Eugene soon after."

"If the doctor clears you," his mother cautioned, her first words of the evening. "You are just getting your strength back."

Roy ignored his mother. "And how, my dear," he said to Lulu, "are the literati at the school newspaper coping with the loss of their beloved leader?"

"The *Webfoot* is but a shadow of its former glory, I assure you," Lulu laughed. "Winston tries his best, but..." This wasn't exactly true. Things at the magazine chugged along nicely without Roy at the helm, but she knew this was not the report he wanted to hear.

"The blind leading the blind?" At Roy's words, his sister looked shocked, but the rest of the diners relaxed at his lack of self-consciousness. "We'll put an end to that soon." He pushed aside his uneaten dinner.

When flashes of panic crossed Roy's face like a curtain muffling his studied animation, Lulu didn't look away, encouraging him to continue his dissimulation with a flirtatious smile that, as it always had, elicited an immediate response.

Roy was still Roy. Milking a dramatic situation for all it was worth. Only now, Lulu didn't mind when he winked at her. When Al scowled in response, she squeezed his hand. *You'd think, with things going so well between them, Al would follow her lead.* "Give the poor guy a break," she said, covering her mouth with her napkin. "Can't you see how hard this is for him?"

Roy's sister fawned over their guests, delighted to have the company.

Long into the evening, the college friends lounged in front of the living room fireplace, sipping brandy. Al stretched his legs out on the worn carpet. Ted plumbed the conversation for puns. Roy, having fortified his drink with a drop of laudanum, relaxed and, to Lulu's relief, stopped trying so hard to prove he was okay. His expression softened and his usually busy hands lay idle in his lap. Lulu collapsed into an armchair near the fire. Jessie, careful not to wrinkle her party dress, scooted over and settled at her feet. Her gaze of admiration mirrored those of the inebriated men.

"Your mother's sweet," Lulu said to Jessie.

Al patted a spot on the floor beside him. After a moment's hesitation, Lulu moved to sit next to him. Curling her legs beneath her long skirt, she leaned against him.

And then, perhaps in response to having been asked to assist with the evening's domestic chores while the men lolled, Lulu said, "I have been so inspired by my work with Dean Carson this semester.

Because of her persistent efforts, NAWSA will hold its convention in Portland next summer."

"What's NAWSA?" Jessie asked.

"The North American Woman Suffrage Association. A group of women campaigning for our right to vote."

"Whose right?"

"Our right. Yours and mine. Women deserve the same rights as men. I do hope you know that."

Jessie looked over at her brother for an explanation.

"If anyone can achieve such a lofty goal, it's Lulu," Roy said.

Reassured by his approval, Jessie asked Lulu, "Are you going to attend the convention?"

"Try to stop me."

"We wouldn't dare," Ted chuckled, his enunciation sloppy, his words slurred. "Right, Al? Your girl's a lion."

"I believe you gentlemen are ready for bed," Lulu said. Roy's gaze, directed her way, lacked focus. At her words, Al took a last sip of his brandy before lifting himself up off the floor.

"A lovely evening, Roy," he said. "Such a refreshing change. You rescued me from yet another tedious holiday with the judge. My brothers were beside themselves with envy when I informed my parents that I could not join the family Thanksgiving."

"We are so relieved to see you up and about," Lulu added, extending an arm so that Al could pull her to her feet. "Come back to us soon. We need you to restore the *Webfoot* to its rightful glory."

"You're sweet," Al said to her as they adjourned to opposite sides of the guest room where Ted was already snoring.

"It's not that hard to say whatever helps the chap to mend."

When Al asked her if she noticed a new slowness in Roy's speech, Lulu waved off the question. "Roy did a lovely job of reciting Roosevelt's Thanksgiving Day speech," she said. "Watching him, I realized how much we have to be thankful for."

"As long as you stick with me," Al muttered, "I will always be thankful."

Lulu gave him a gentle shove. "Go to bed, old boy," she said, mocking the friends' favorite affectation. "You've had too much to drink."

Chapter 5 Seniors

Portland, Oregon, December 1904

Lulu couldn't avoid the splashing mud. The trolleys and horse carts showered her with filth. Three blocks from the trolley stop to her mother's house, and her petticoats clung to her legs, wet and soiled.

Her mother's note was mysterious. Could she please return home at once? There were "important considerations" they needed to discuss.

Lulu hadn't finished her contribution to the *Webfoot,* a promising short story. She would have preferred to stay in her room over the department store to prepare for her last semester at the university. Dean Carson had selected her to be her teaching assistant in the spring, a great honor, and she had lesson plans to review. Al, for once, had agreed to set his studies aside for the Christmas holidays. They had planned to take advantage of the rare opportunity to spend time together unobserved on the deserted campus. But here she was, climbing the brick steps to her parents' house, a trail of mud behind her.

Her mother opened the door before Lulu raised her hand to the copper knocker. "Darling, you look a fright."

Lulu shed her wet clothes and put on the robe her mother handed her. "Maybe, just maybe, I can salvage your dress." Kitty took on the project with a fierce intensity. Five minutes inside, and Lulu had been returned to helpless adolescence.

Kitty dabbed at the mud stains. "How is your handsome young man?" She didn't wait for a reply. "Your father is so pleased. Such a handsome, polite man. And, dare I say it, a suitable father for a future family?"

Lulu had heard this all before. After every visit home, she resisted the temptation to dump poor Al just to make a point. Instead, she changed the subject. "How is Father?"

"Off to Boston again. Chasing money for the railroad." Her mother's smile faded, and she scrubbed harder. "Your father travels on the whim of the politicians who named him to his prestigious office. The Republicans have been calling the shots in Portland since the turn of the century."

"He must be livid, now that Uren pushed through the initiative and referendum system," Lulu said. Oregon voters had just approved William Uren's reforms designed to break the power of Oregon's political bosses. "Uren's ticket for change has so much momentum that now he is advocating for the direct election of U.S. senators, direct presidential primaries, tougher conflict-of-interest laws, and the right to recall public officials."

Kitty looked up blankly at her daughter. She rinsed Lulu's skirt in cold water and held the fabric up to the light to be sure she had not missed a spot. Satisfied, she hung the wet garment to dry.

"There is something I want to show you," she said.

Already apprehensive, Lulu followed her mother up the stairs to her parents' bedroom, a large room lavishly decorated with gifts her father sent home from his frequent travels—overstuffed quilts from the finest New York department stores, a red and gold Oriental rug that had crossed the nation on one of the earliest steam trains, fine pottery, and a redwood jewelry box filled to the brim with bead necklaces, cameos, and her mother's precious string of pearls.

A garment bag lay on her large poster bed like a dummy stretched out for a mid-day nap.

"With all the holiday mania, we haven't discussed your intentions," her mother said, positioned between the door and her bed like an assistant in a magic show trying to distract the audience from the reveal.

"My intentions?"

"Sweetheart, you and Al are entering your last semester at the university. It's time."

"Mom, you know Al changed his major midstream. He has to stay at the university for a postgraduate year to complete his degree."

"And you, I assume, plan to keep him company?" Again, the coy twist of phrase. The inexplicable brightness in her mother's eye.

"Actually, I've applied for an instructor's position in the Department of English," Lulu said. She had been wondering how to tell her mother her plans.

This news caught her mother unprepared. Kitty had never held a job. For as long as Lulu could remember, her mother had filled the role of loyal caretaker, gracious hostess, and uncomplaining wife.

"But sweetheart, is that necessary?"

"Necessary, no. Desirable, yes. Mother, I have always wanted a profession." Buoyed by Dean Carson's encouragement, Lulu had applied for the position when it became available. "Eventually, I want to write professionally, but teaching is a good start." Lulu pulled her mother's flowered robe around her, tying the sash to hide her corset.

"Most teachers are spinsters," her mother said. "What does Al say about your plans?" Here it was, the reason her mother had summoned her home. "Darling, I don't think you've heard me. It's time."

"Time?"

With a frustrated harrumph, Kitty turned her back on her daughter and unzipped the garment bag on her bed.

Lulu watched in astonishment as her mother held up an elegant ivory wedding suit.

The dress had the popular Edwardian collar, an exaggerated cinched waistline, and a long, flared skirt with just the hint of a train. The lower sleeves were full, narrowing at the wrist, but, despite the faddish details, the suit's tailoring was impeccable. An Edwardian wedding suit trimmed in contrast braid just a whisper darker than the dress itself. Flawless and undoubtedly expensive.

"Collar details are all the rage," her mother said. "But I think the sophistication of this dress is perfect for you. You would not believe the excess on display in the lace Bertha collar styles."

Lulu was speechless.

Her mother continued to fuss with the dress, smoothing the fabric, humming, waiting for Lulu to respond. When her daughter remained quiet, she tried again. "Would you like to try it on?"

Lulu glared. "Why on earth would I?"

The dress, a presence in its own right, seemed poised for a response. Unable to come up with a retort that would accurately express her disgust, Lulu pivoted and left the room. She would have walked right out the front door, but her mother's plotting could not have been better planned. In her corset and her mother's flowered bathrobe, Lulu had no choice but to wait for her dress to dry.

Her mother followed her downstairs, her stockinged feet noiseless in the wake of Lulu's infuriated retreat. "I just want you to be happy." Her mother's voice was plaintive.

"I want a career, Mother." Lulu fought to keep her voice level, to throttle back the anger that threatened to choke her.

"I thought the boy loved you."

Lulu twirled around, a tornado of seething anger. What did her mother know? Had she any notion of the delight on Al's face when they were together? The respect with which he treated her? "My God, Mother. How dare you?" The scent of her mother's robe nauseated her, the musk of her perfume vying with the cloying sweetness of dying flowers. "Love is not a matter of pragmatism. Al loves me. And I love him. But what we feel will never come between us and our careers. If either of us has any interest in getting married, the time is certainly not now. This will be our decision to make. Not yours."

Lulu took a breath. "And should that time come, I am perfectly capable of buying my suit for the occasion." Lulu untied her sash and threw the irritating robe on the floor. Relishing her mother's open-mouthed shock, she marched out of the room half naked. "There must be a dress somewhere in this house that will suffice for my trip home." With spite-filled pleasure, she emphasized the word "home."

From the closet she had once shared with Lizzie, she pulled out a dress she had worn in preparatory school, a navy-blue shift with a sailor's collar and sassy red tie. The perfect antidote to the elegant gown on display in her mother's room. The virginal schoolgirl's outfit was dated, but she figured Al would find it amusing.

She adjusted her skirt, straightened the tie, and then walked downstairs, stone-faced.

"Tell Father I'm sorry I missed him," she said. Her mother sat at the kitchen table, head in hands.

"Tell him yourself," Kitty said, her voice small, defeated. Looking up, she surveyed her daughter's outfit. "I always loved that dress."

Lulu hesitated. *Her mother was clueless. She came from another time. What did she know? Her gesture had been well-meaning, if thoughtless.* Lulu had not meant to hurt her mother. She meant only to stand up for herself.

"Mother," she sat down next to Kitty, who cradled the folded robe in her lap. "Things are changing. Soon, women will have the vote. I'm only trying to take advantage of the education you and Father have generously provided me."

Kitty shook her head, a slow, despairing "no." "Some things never change," she said. Lulu watched as her mother pushed back her chair and walked over to the counter. "Do you want tea?" She filled the teakettle and lit the gas flame. Methodically, she measured tea leaves and took two china teacups from the cabinet.

Her voice calm now, weary, Kitty said, "Your father rented an apartment in Boston. He says it's for convenience. So much of his business is on the East Coast." Turning to Lulu, she added, "If we weren't married, I fear I would already have lost him. Marriage is a contract. It protects women against the unpredictability of a husband's impulses."

Balancing the two cups, she returned to the table and set each down with care. Not a drop spilled. Lulu watched her mother perform the domestic task flawlessly, as she had her whole, sad, lonely life.

"Well, if Uren has his way, the Republicans may soon find their influence much diminished. Father may be home before you know it," Lulu said.

"And if I have mine, one day you will wear that dress," Kitty answered.

They drank their tea in silence. Having scored her point, Lulu was at a loss for what to say next. Fortunately, Lizzie broke the stillness, slamming the front door. She was home from school, a whirlwind of braids and books. Spotting Lulu's unlikely attire, Lizzie collapsed into hysterical laughter.

"There's a story here somewhere, right?" she asked. "I'm on the prowl for plots," she said, palming two cookies. "I'll be in the stable whenever you're ready." Lizzie kissed her mother dramatically and headed out the door. "Pronto," she hissed, draining the room of any remaining tension.

* * *

Eugene, 1904

The sign in the State Street shop window said: "*Let's become acquainted.*" For months, Al had passed the new jewelry shop every time he went downtown. The greeting lodged in his memory. Soon their friends would graduate, but he and Lulu would remain in Eugene as a couple. Lulu had accepted the position of instructor in the English department, and he would complete his Engineering Certificate. It seemed right—no, more than that. He wanted to commemorate their change in status with a meaningful gift. But every time he resolved to purchase a token of his affection, the aggressive sales pitch of the jeweler on Main Street intimidated him. The slick salesman must have recognized him as the judge's son. In a small town like Eugene, rumors flew like birds over the river.

The handwritten sign went on: "*Come in and get acquainted. We will serve you to the best of our ability.*" Below the announcement, a spidery signature: Chas. H. Hinges.

Braced by the promise of anonymity, Al entered the small shop, where two men stood behind a glass display case containing small boxes lined with purple velvet. Shuffling his feet and glancing nervously over his shoulder, he studied the silver lockets, charm bracelets, and gold bands. He couldn't make head or tail of the trinkets. The older gentleman, sporting a dapper thick mustache that curled over his upper lip, extended a beefy hand. "Something for your wife?" he asked. His eyes followed Al's gaze to the display case.

The wife part threw Al off. Behind the counter, the gentleman's assistant smirked at his discomfort. The lad wore a starched white collar and elegant tie. He'd stuck a pen behind his ear and held a receipt pad in his hand.

"Your girlfriend?" he asked.

Al fled. But the desire to buy Lulu a gift remained. What item of jewelry would Lulu prefer? While he respected Lulu's strong opinions, it didn't make choosing a gift any easier.

"Can I ask you a favor?" he asked Annabelle one day after English class. The girl's tasteful jewelry had given him an idea. He needed a companion to help him shop.

The following afternoon, Chas H. Hingis and his assistant stood at their stations behind the counter. When Al and Annabelle entered the jewelry store, Chas extended a welcoming hand. This time, Al accepted. The assistant smirked once again. But when Annabelle directed her charming smile at him, a solicitous grin replaced the smirk.

"How can I help you, my dear?"

"My friend is looking for something tasteful."

"A gift for you?" The jeweler practically drooled.

"For his girlfriend. An elegant lady. A scholar."

Al stood up taller, as if to prove her point.

The assistant opened the glass case with a key. Furrowing his brow, he searched through the contents and then laid out an assortment of necklaces, each displaying a precious stone. Topaz, opal, amethyst. "What is the lady's birthstone?"

"No, those won't do," Al said. He knew nothing about jewelry, but he knew jewels weren't right for Lulu. "I'm looking for something solid, understated. Not cheap, but..."

"Gold?" Hingis asked. He studied the young man with an expert's eye.

"What would Dean Carson wear?" Al asked Annabelle, ignoring the man's calculating stare.

"Chunky," she said. "Definitely chunky, but classy."

The assistant renewed his search, looking for something chunky but classy. Bracelets might fit the bill, he suggested. He showed them several with unobtrusive stones. The one Al chose was unadorned, a braid of three colors of gold.

"Her wrist is slender," Annabelle added. A practiced shopper, she was enjoying herself now, making the salesman work for his money.

"If the lady requires, I can easily adjust the bracelet's width," the assistant replied. His eyes never left Annabelle. She instructed him to wrap the gift in a simple box with a silver bow and supervised as he followed her instructions.

Meanwhile, Al counted out bills from his wallet. When the assistant turned his back to place the sum in his lockbox, Al thanked Annabelle for her help. She, in turn, thanked the jewelers. "Lulu is a lucky lady," she said.

"Do you think she'll like it?" Al asked.

"Dear Al, it will thrill her. What girl doesn't like jewelry?"

Lulu might be exactly that girl, but Al dismissed the thought as he pictured the tasteful bracelet on Lulu's delicate wrist.

"What fun," Annabelle said as they headed back to campus. "Since returning to school, Roy refuses to 'socialize with the silly underclassmen.' Not that I blame him," she added, stopping to admire her reflection in the window of a dress shop. "It has to be tough, not graduating with your friends."

"Roy's quieter now. Humbled, I think, by his experience."

"I know, I know," Annabelle said. "Patience is in order. Brilliance is often brooding. Think of Chekhov. Roy is at least as talented."

Annabelle was back on the chase, Al thought.

"He's writing poetry again, you know." Annabelle chattered as they turned toward the river. Two men rode by on bicycles, dark stockings pulled over their tweed pants, hands clutching the handlebars as they whooshed by.

"Do you want to hear his latest poem?"

"Of course." Not an honest answer, but she had done him a favor.

Annabelle cleared her throat, imitating Roy's dulcet delivery:

"The shadows, doubting lead their release,
Creep from their lairs beneath the walls
And on the earth there comes a peace
That like a benediction falls."

"Lovely," Al said when she had finished. *What did he know about poetry? This was Lulu's field.* Still, he noticed that "peace" was the word Annabelle emphasized. Roy's other striking image, dark shadows creeping from their lairs beneath the walls, went right over her head.

"Roy kissed me last night."

This is what the girl had wanted to tell him all along. Roy had finally made his move. Of course, Annabelle was over the moon. She had been chasing him since they were sophomores. Vesta, who had also set her sights on him, would be heartbroken. *Still,* Al thought, *a courtship might do Roy some good. Brighten the injured lad's spirits. And if Annabelle and Roy got together, Lulu need no longer worry about their injured classmate.*

He began to whistle, only to discover that Annabelle hadn't finished.

"I have to admit the kiss ended much too soon. As soon as we got going, he pulled back."

Al whistled louder. *Didn't this girl keep anything to herself?*

"But the kiss was lovely," she said. "I do wish he had kissed me some more."

To Al's relief, Annabelle soon changed the subject. Roy had promised to help her run lines for the college social that upcoming weekend. Encouraged, she had asked Roy to accompany her home afterward, but she had trouble reading his reaction. His glass eye revealed nothing. "It always seems focused on the horizon. He said, 'Break a leg, sweetheart,' whatever that means."

By the time they arrived at his dormitory, Al was happy to see the girl off. One afternoon with Annabelle and he appreciated Lulu more. Lulu was one in a thousand, and now he had a gift to show her how much he cared.

* * *

Given the choice, Lulu would have skipped the college social, but Annabelle and Roy insisted she attend. They had been preparing for the event for weeks now. Reverend Rose had asked Roy to deliver the sermon, and Annabelle would sing. Annabelle, the lead soprano in the church's Chorale Study Club, had decided to pursue a career in the theater. Or so she said.

"She's not about to let that man out of her sight," Al said. He kissed Lulu and fell in beside her on the street side of the busy boulevard.

"Annabelle is serious about her aspirations," Lulu replied.

As they headed for the annual get-together at the First Christian Church, Lulu reflected on how much her life had changed. Two years before, she had attended the event as an ambitious and idealistic sophomore. Now she arrived as a respected senior and teaching assistant, accompanied by her longtime boyfriend. Younger students nodded in recognition as they passed, and she smiled graciously, used to the attention of students awed by their knowledge and accomplishments. Their own, not those of their parents, nor the legacy of earlier pioneers.

How young the gathering students appeared! With the joyous volume of youth, clusters of giggling girls played to the self-conscious men. The same students who sat in her classroom doodling in their notebooks as they watched the clock now flirted shamelessly and jockeyed for position. Lulu pointed out their antics to Al, her new bracelet gleaming in the sunlight.

Reverend Rose greeted them as they climbed up the church stairs.

"Thank you for all you have done for Roy," Lulu said.

He took her hand. "It is my greatest ambition that my parish remain a sanctuary. I'm pleased Roy finds comfort in my guidance."

Vesta and Ted had already taken their seats. Vesta whispered to Lulu, "Did you hear the news? Ted and I got engaged over the Christmas break." The girl glowed. "But never fear, I firmly believe that even wives should take time away from their domestic tasks to enjoy an occasional outing with their friends. After Ted and I marry, you can count on me to be there when our friends need cheering on."

Lulu bit her tongue. To each their own. She did not begrudge her friend her happiness. Ted loved every minute of his fiancée's attention, that was clear. His big loopy grin beamed wider than ever; his eyes twinkled with their usual mischief. Al and Lulu slid in beside their friends in the front pew as the organ powered up Bach's "O Wunder" and waited for the crowd to quiet.

When the pews stopped creaking, the students settled, and Annabelle burst into song. Each note rose like a bird taking flight. Her friend's talent no longer surprised Lulu. She vowed to cherish these moments when art transformed the quotidian.

Roy's oration came next. Despite his renewed vigor, he appeared painfully slender in his loose slacks, and his crooked red bow tie highlighted his pale skin. Behind wire-rimmed frames, both eyes— good and glass—flashed black and severe. The crowd quieted, fascinated by his ghostly demeanor. In almost a whisper, he quoted John: "Except a corn of wheat fall into the ground and die, it abideth alone: but if it dies, it bringeth forth much fruit." Then with thunder: "We are not alone."

Lulu watched her friend pace in front of the crowd. Watched how he rallied the audience. The young girls couldn't take their eyes off him. The boys admired his magnetism.

And yet, her friend had changed. The clenched hand he held up like a hammer trembled. His words lingered a moment too long on his tongue. Only his passion continued unabated. His intense expression, no longer the leer of a cocky boy, made him even more attractive. As his oration built to a dramatic close, he looked out on the crowd with a fierceness that demanded respect.

"John taught us: He that loveth his life shall lose it, and he that hateth his life in this world shall keep it unto life eternal." Lulu doubted the assembled young people heard a word he said. Instead, his uncompromising belief and the conviction of his delivery swept up the students. In his shadow, the frivolity of the occasion ebbed. He transfixed the audience. Annabelle, who had joined her friends in the front row, couldn't take her eyes off the man she adored.

The reception that followed the formal program was lively. Al and Lulu remained on the sidelines, greeting students confident enough to approach them while waiting to congratulate Roy on his powerful performance. Vesta circulated around the room, displaying her glittering diamond ring and reiterating yet again a blow-by-blow account of Ted's proposal. Ted happily filled in any details she omitted. Annabelle, surrounded by the choir, milked her diva moment for all it was worth.

Neither Roy nor Reverend Rose joined the raucous crowd.

Al excused himself to join a circle of his engineering colleagues. Over the summer, the future engineers had formed flourishing friendships based on the exchange of upcoming opportunities. Al's confidence grew by the day. The first class enrolled in engineering expected to be highly in demand, he told her.

Lulu scanned the crowd for Roy. She walked toward the now empty apse, mulling over the words Roy had used to dazzle the receptive crowd. "He that hateth his life." Why had he selected such a dark and depressing passage?

All semester, Lulu had watched Roy, who had enrolled in her American Authors course, with concern. The Roy Bacon she knew would have led any classroom discussion, insisted on having the last word, left a *bon mot* hanging in the air after his departure. But this year, he had taken a seat in the back row. Maybe he hadn't wanted to call attention to his relationship with the teaching assistant, but, as the weeks went on, she wondered if he was hiding behind his eager classmates. Too often during the term, Roy let inferior analysis pass uncritiqued. His weary eye lost focus. His mouth softened into a befuddled frown.

When she questioned him, he dismissed her concern. To bolster his self-confidence, she assured him his classmates admired his resiliency and would benefit from his insight and astute perceptions. His accident and recovery only heightened his reputation among his classmates. Like her, his friends admired the strength it had required to return to school.

In the vestry, she spotted Roy on his knees beside Reverend Rose.

Roy wept, head in hands, his dark hair hanging limply over his ashen face. Between sobs, he begged the Lord for light and beseeched the reverend for forgiveness.

Roy's classroom demeanor paled in light of the man crouched in front of her now. Gone was the scripted drama. This was a young boy howling his pain. Reverend Rose looked up and shook his head as if warning her off. Instead of backing away, she approached the two men.

"Roy, my friend, what's wrong?"

"It's his medication," Reverend Rose whispered. "It got the best of him."

"Medication?" Lulu asked.

"The pain medication. He hasn't been able to shake it. He's made a valiant effort, but tonight he overindulged, emptying the vial he carries in his front pocket. Right after his speech, he collapsed on the vestry floor. Thank the Lord, I was removing my robes and saw him collapse."

"I'm such a fool," Roy moaned. Stripped of his cockiness, every word ached with vulnerability.

"Thank God you were there to revive him," Lulu said. She meant to attribute the rescue not to God but to the reverend. Her heart went out to the poor boy.

Reverend Rose nodded in agreement. "I've done what I can, but I'm neglecting my parishioners," he said. "Would you mind keeping Roy company until I can return?"

"Of course not." Lulu put an arm around Roy's trembling shoulders. His fragility alarmed her, the protruding bones, the clammy feel of his skin.

In the small room where holy vestments and sacred vessels hung on hooks on the wall, the two sat quietly while Roy struggled to regain his composure. When at last his sobs subsided, he sniffled, wiping his nose with his sleeve.

"I'm such an ass," he said.

"You are an ass," Lulu said. "Why didn't you ask your friends for help?"

"I'm sick to death of sympathy," he turned to her, his one good eye fixed on her two sympathetic blue ones. "Everywhere I go, I feel people staring at me. Feeling sorry for me and my ruined face. I can't abide any more pity."

"Roy, you're wrong. Your fortitude is an inspiration to everyone who knows you."

Roy reached for her hand. "Lulu, watching you in front of the classroom, I realized how much I've fallen behind. I thought I would be the literary star of the class of 1904. Instead, I sit behind a wooden desk, a year behind, like an idling child."

"Oh, Roy. Don't be so hard on yourself."

"I can't bear it. God tested me, and I failed to rise to the challenge. I've let my friends and family down."

"Rubbish, Roy."

"I'm faking it. Just like my shyster father, I'm pretending to be someone I'm not."

"You are twice the man your father was, and you know it."

"Lulu, what would I do without you?" He drew her close, wrapping trembling arms around her. When his body quaked, she willed him to be still. She inhaled deeply in the hope he would do the same.

When she exhaled, she felt his body relax. He rested his head on her shoulder like a devoted child.

"It's okay, Roy," she said, rubbing his back.

They sat together. He was calmer now. She could feel his breath, warm and wet, next to her ear.

"At last, you came," he said. He looked up at her.

"What is that, my dear?"

"Lulu, I knew you would come." His black eyes met hers, deep pools of misery. He pulled her closer. She closed her eyes. When his parched lips brushed hers, she didn't realize at first what was happening. Before her brain could signal danger, her lips responded to sensation.

His next words caught her by surprise. "Al will never be enough for you."

He doesn't know what he is saying, she thought at first. The dark ocean of his need carried her away. And then, when the initial surge of passion abated, she pulled back, confused.

"No, Roy." An attempt to protest that even she knew lacked conviction.

Roy silenced her with another kiss. The salty taste of his saliva stung. His tongue explored her mouth as if trying to wiggle inside of her, a strange but surprising sensation. His hands, steady now, explored her body hungrily.

She knew she had to stop him but was paralyzed by the passion he aroused. With a determined sigh, she forced herself to open her eyes. Emerging from the fog of desire, she regarded the man before her. Not the vulnerable friend she had sought to comfort, but a predator claiming his prey.

What the hell was he thinking? By the time she pushed him away and stood up, it was too late.

"Roy, stop. You mustn't," she sputtered. Her voice shook, her customary aplomb blown all to hell.

"Why not?" He gazed up at her through long lashes, a drunk mid-flirt, a toddler longing to nurse, a serpent. She backed away.

"Stop it," she said again, this time more sternly. A wave of regret overcame her. She turned to the door, ready to flee.

But when she turned, she saw Annabelle standing there, resplendent in her performance attire, a bouquet of red roses clutched in her arms.

Annabelle hovered for a moment, transfixed, and then pirouetted away. Every ounce of dramatic talent tapped to portray the role of a woman betrayed. Betrayed by Roy. And by Lulu. She stomped out the door and down the main aisle of the church, the echo of her footsteps lingering in the rafters.

Roy slumped into the wooden chair, his eyes no longer bright. His shoulders crumpled. When Lulu turned back to face him, he shrunk even smaller, as if trying to disappear.

"Shit," he said. "What have we done?" He turned to Lulu. She jerked away.

"What have WE done? What on earth were you thinking?"

Roy held up his hands, begging her to understand, but she had no sympathy left to give him.

"What have YOU done?" She turned away from him and followed Annabelle out the door.

* * *

Al had a headache. Too many nights in the lab exacerbated by the high notes of Annabelle's hymn and Roy's thunderous sermon. Would this evening never end?

"Knob and tube wiring is to blame," Al's colleague Geoffrey complained. Geoffrey wore a cardigan sweater and waved an unlit pipe. A strong whiff of tobacco accompanied every heartfelt gesture.

The cluster of engineering students had sought a corner of the parish hall, where they stood, ignoring the boisterous crowd exiting the evening's performance. There, they engaged in an animated discussion on the best way to wire new construction sites for electricity.

"Builders need to consider electrical requirements," Al said, "right from the start."

"It's the architects' fault," Geoffrey replied. "They don't add electrical wiring to their drawings until after they finish the building. Then they must make the connections outside the walls."

Geoffrey and Al had spent every night that week in the lab working on their thesis, a plea for metallic conduits. They hoped to submit it to their advisor by the end of the semester.

"It is our contention," Al said, "that the best method for installing low potential wires for light, heat, and power is with an iron conduit system." He paused, prepared to entertain any inquiries from his fellow engineers. When none came, he took off his glasses and wiped them clean with his handkerchief.

Where the hell was Lulu?

"Hey Al," Geoffrey poked Al in the ribs to get his attention. His colleagues waited, eager to hear how the plan would work.

"After the builder finishes, he draws the wires through outlets in the walls. This makes the system accessible year-round."

"Brilliant, my boy," Willard said, squinting as if to imagine an electrical outlet on the inside of a wall.

"With Al's design, electricity will become the backbone of every residence!" Geoffrey beamed.

"If you will excuse me." Al's throbbing headache had become unbearable. He headed toward the front door, desperate for a breath of fresh air.

At the foot of the stairs, he encountered Annabelle. "Have you seen Lulu?" he asked.

The girl looked at him as if he were speaking a foreign language. She held a bouquet of ragged roses. Her striking green eyes, accentuated for her performance, simmered with emotion.

There must be some trouble with Roy, Al figured. *There was always trouble when Roy was around.* Tonight, the last thing he wanted was to hear details of their tempestuous relationship. What he needed was silence and a dark room followed by a quiet weekend to complete his project.

He blamed Lulu. She had abandoned him in the crowd. Before he could escape, Annabelle burst into tears.

"Oh, Al. I'm so upset." He should have remained with the engineers, but Annabelle considered him a friend. He hoped he wouldn't have to listen to a discussion about her love life.

With Roy, Annabelle had her hands full. He could see that. Tonight's sermon had seemed overwrought, the thunder of doom and gloom excessive. Annabelle's melodic hymn, although somewhat ear-splitting, had been more to his liking. No matter how talented Roy was, his friend would be better off sticking to his studies. He'd told Lulu as much. He didn't trust the man, even when Lulu attributed Roy's religious fervor to a deep loyalty to Reverend Rose.

"I'm furious with Roy," Annabelle said, reopening the one subject he wanted to avoid. "That fickle bastard." He was in for it now. As the crowd exiting the church thinned. Annabelle spat her expletive out with an actress's scorn. Fury lit her flashing eyes.

"Don't let him ruin your evening," he said to Annabelle, hoping to steer around any thorny issues. "After such a delightful performance."

"But he has ruined my evening, and you should know why. I discovered them in each other's arms. He was kissing her."

Where was Lulu when he needed her? Annabelle waited for Al to ask for more details, the obvious question being: Who was Roy kissing? Al did not want to know. Annabelle could not trust Roy. He had said that all along. He didn't need details.

"I thought he loved me," Annabelle said, turning to Al as if he were somehow to blame.

"The man is not well," he said. His head pounded out a warning.

"I trusted him, and I trusted Lulu." Standing there like a defeated beauty queen, Annabelle clutched her dying roses. She faced him down, demanding something. What, he did not know. "She is my closest friend. How could she?"

How had the subject somehow turned to Lulu? What had Roy done that caused Annabelle to question Lulu's friendship?

And then, through the fog of his headache, he pictured them.

Lulu. Lulu and Roy in an embrace. Lulu kissing Roy.

"You're not saying..."

If only the streetlights would go dark. If only the beautiful woman blocking his egress would leave him alone.

Lulu. His beacon. The woman with whom he was constructing a life, his inspiration.

"You must be mistaken," he said.

"I saw them," Annabelle repeated. "The Reverend said Roy was not well, so I went to find him in the apse, but she got there first."

It was true then. Lulu had kissed Roy. How many times had he held his tongue, telling himself that her compassion was one of her many charms? Now, it had come to this.

"I didn't mean to upset you." Annabelle apologized, but it was too late, and he refused to listen.

"I have a headache," he said. He left her on the steps and walked off toward campus. Pain flooded the conduits of his brain, electricity gone mad.

* * *

Lulu dodged a football as she crossed the wide lawn of the Sigma Nu fraternity. The large, rambling house, the first residential fraternity on campus, was a hive of activity. A half-built kayak rested on its side between the columns of the expansive porch. Al's roommates, Geoffrey and Willard, circled the project, positing next steps for rendering it seaworthy. Geoffrey, Willard, and Al had been inseparable since abandoning the dormitory for the companionship of like-minded brothers. Knowing how quickly gossip spread among the tight-knit community, Lulu held her head up high and avoided their gaze. She hoped they wouldn't see her. Heart pounding, she approached the house's front door.

But nothing escaped the eagle-eyed engineers. Geoffrey and Willard greeted her with bright smiles. "Al, your instructor's here," they called out, waving her in. "Hey fellows," she said, before entering the cluttered lobby. The room was littered with dirty dishes, stacks of books, piles of newspapers, balls, and bats. As she stood among the chaos, she tried to imagine Al in his bedroom, engrossed in an undecipherable analysis of the future of electrical waves. Resisting the urge to pick up a rain slicker that had fallen to the floor, she wondered if Al's bedroom was equally unkempt. If she could see his room, perhaps she would have a clearer idea of what to expect.

Al pulled on his jacket as he emerged from his room. Face solemn, he said, "Let's take a walk."

They ambled toward the Willamette River as they had so many times before. Out of habit and long practice, he walked on her left, shielding her from the splashing mud from horses and carriages and the shiny new automobiles that had recently appeared around town. He strolled with his hands in his pockets, his jaw clenched, his gray-blue eyes fixed on the horizon. When they arrived at the bench where they had lingered so often, he continued to stand, covering his mouth with his hand and staring out at the water.

Lulu waited for him to speak.

"Annabelle tells me..." His fretting hand muffled his words.

Lulu sat down first. *Here it comes*, she thought. She folded her hands in her lap. Her fingers were cold, her palms clammy.

"Annabelle tells me they've admitted Roy to the university clinic."

He sat down, leaving a large space between them.

"When?" The word, laced with concern, escaped her lips before she could edit the emotion.

"After the reception. He was suffering from exhaustion, I'm told. But I guess you already know that."

She chose her next words carefully. "He was in awful shape after his performance."

"So, I hear."

Lulu wondered how long they could sit like this. In silence, or worse, continuing their stilted conversation. Al might be capable of such restraint; she couldn't bear it, the not knowing. She took a deep breath, held it a moment, and turned to face him. Better she addressed the matter head on, whatever the consequences.

"Al, what did Annabelle say?"

"No, Lulu. You tell me. What did Annabelle see?"

"Oh Al, it was awful." A wave of relief flooded through her. She needed him to understand. "Reverend Rose found Roy passed out on the floor. I was distraught."

"Because?"

"Because I care about him. We care about him. Roy is your closest friend. Wouldn't you rescue him if you found him in distress?" She looked up at him, her eyes wide, pleading.

"I would not have kissed him." Al's tone was bitter. He avoided her gaze.

Lulu worried the fabric of her skirt, as if testing its quality. If only there was a way to make Al see the incident through her eyes.

"What was I to do? Roy was a mess, clearly disoriented. When he tried to kiss me, he didn't know what he was doing. I was taken aback. Al, you know you are the only one..." A vision of Hester Prynne silenced her, the moral rectitude of her students' essays. "How can I prove to you that there is no need to question my devotion?"

Al, never one to raise his voice, lowered it instead. "I'm afraid you would find the proof that would be meaningful to me unacceptable."

"Whatever do you mean?"

"Lulu, I have never asked you to marry me because I admire your determination to be self-reliant. But how can you ask me to trust you when you offer comfort to any man you please?"

"Al, that's not fair. I comforted one friend. Our friend. Once. Nothing more. But I do love you. I've demonstrated this from the day we met."

"You made love to me, Lulu. Is that love? Sex and love, they're an incomprehensible pairing. I don't know if I am prepared to live in these modern times, Lulu. I can't bear to lose you, but I'm afraid of what will happen to me if I stay with you."

"No more afraid than I." Lulu looked down at her feet.

"So, what do we do now?" His voice broke.

Lulu watched two ducks float side by side down the river. Their lives seemed so easy, their orange feet fluttering below the surface as the current carried them onward without conflict. Despite her reservations, she knew this moment demanded a decisive action. A declaration of love. She wanted Al to trust her; she wanted to be worthy. He was the rare man who would support her career and allow her to live her life on her own terms. If there was only one way to prove her loyalty, then that was what she would do.

"If we were to get married," Lulu said, leaving no room for argument, "there could be no fuss, no bother, no frilly dress. If a piece of paper is what it takes to earn your trust, I want you to know I have no reservations."

Al met her gaze at last. His pale eyes probed hers. "But Lulu, how many times have you said you don't believe in marriage? That your career will always come first."

"True. But if Mary Shelley could write *Frankenstein* while not only married but pregnant, I can show my devotion to you without giving up my dreams. We can do this our way, two equals with careers and aspirations of our own." As she spoke, she convinced herself that this was possible.

Al stared into the river for five minutes without saying a word. Lulu waited. For once, he would determine the course of their relationship, not her. When she could no longer bear the silence, she asked him again. "Al, will you marry me?" On impulse, she fell down on her knees and offered her hand. He did not take it.

His face reflected his calculations. But even behind his thick glasses, she could see he was struggling not to laugh.

"Lulu, you are the most bewildering woman I have ever known. Get up. Get up now, before you make a spectacle of yourself."

A wave of relief swept over her. She did as he asked, but still offered her hand.

After what seemed like hours, he took it. "I suppose we could arrange for a civil ceremony over the February break." He sat up taller, waiting to see what she would do now.

He was considering her offer. She could see it in his eyes. Theirs was a delicate game of chess, each move crucial to the outcome.

Lulu responded to his gambit. "No one will question our absence over the long weekend."

Only then did they turn toward each other. Al wiped the tears from her cheeks. She took his hand in hers.

"But," Lulu said, "no one must know. Otherwise, they will never offer me the salaried instructor position after I graduate."

Lulu asked Kitty to arrange the small ceremony. "No fuss, Mother," she insisted. "No church, no reception."

"But darling, your wedding should be the happiest day of your life."

"No flowers, no music." Lulu stared her mother down.

Kitty held her tongue, although Lulu remained on guard for chinks in her armor. She laid out their plan. Her grandmother's home in Baker City was far enough away from campus to escape attention. No need for Father to make the long trip back from Boston.

"If you insist." Kitty sighed. "I suppose I should be happy that you have come to your senses and have agreed to marry the man. I believe the poor lad is a saint."

"We'll send a cable to Father after the deed is done."

"But Lulu..."

"Mother, if you prefer, we can elope."

"But certainly, you intend to invite the judge and his wife to the ceremony?"

"Absolutely not. Don't you understand? If anybody at the university gets wind of this, my academic career is over."

Kitty nodded her head in bewilderment.

A week after an engagement that went unannounced, Al and Lulu rode the stage to Baker City, where Lulu's mother, sister, and grandmother waited for them in the modest living room. In a wrinkled brown judicial robe, the local justice of the peace read vows from a well-thumbed book and pronounced them man and wife before joining the family for a cup of tea. A fire crackled in the hearth, but, as Lulu had requested, no flowers graced the mantel, not even from her grandmother's well-tended garden.

Lizzie held her tongue. When Lulu had arrived in her usual white blouse and long black skirt, Lizzie had asked if the elegant wedding suit that hung in their mother's closet would now be passed on to her.

"It's all yours," Lulu had answered, chucking her sister under the chin.

During the brief ceremony, Al had extracted a simple 18-karat gold ring from his pocket and slipped it onto his bride's finger.

"Al, you know I can't wear this on campus." She'd kissed him, swept away by the trust and generosity of his gesture.

The justice of the peace, accustomed to such irregularities, did not comment. Before the newlyweds headed back to campus, Lulu entrusted the ring to her mother for safekeeping, saying she would retrieve it after Al had graduated and they had made their plans.

"I'm happy you have married at last," her mother said. "Al is a catch. Now I know your education has been worth our investment. Your father will be so proud."

* * *

The evening before commencement exercises for the nineteen students of the class of 1904, Ted, Annabelle, Vesta, Lulu, Al, and Roy gathered for a picnic on the common. As they settled in, Lulu steered Al to the opposite side of the blanket from Roy, separated by Ted and Vesta. She didn't want to make a scene, but no good would come of seating the men together. She smoothed the blanket and Al sat down at her side. "Dear," she said, "look, the California poppies are in bloom."

All the trees on the common had flowered at the same time. Cherry blossoms, like pink cotton candy, competed with white-flowering dogwoods. She pointed the flowers out to Al, keeping her back to Roy.

Vesta flashed her engagement ring as if it were a gold medal she had won in the Olympics.

"The graduation frocks this year are so dainty," Vesta said. "Mine has a three-layered skirt of white organdy and an embroidered yoke. There are the most delightful patches of shirring between the shoulder epaulets. They cover the elbow sleeves and the stole drop."

"Is the girl speaking English?" Ted asked.

"I think it's French," Al replied.

In frustration, Vesta turned to Lulu, hoping to find a more receptive audience.

"Don't drag me into this," Lulu said, holding up her hand in warning. Her bracelet reflected the bright rays of sunshine. "My recent experience with fashion has been less than stellar."

"I'm hoping I can survive the governor's speech," Ted said. "'Official Delinquency: Its Cause and Cure.' Kill me now."

Lulu groaned. Her father was due to arrive from the East Coast that evening for the festivities. The stress at home had tarnished any anticipation she felt. She had pleaded with her mother not to tell her father about her marriage. "Not yet." Her mother's tight-lipped forbearance overshadowed what she felt was her more significant news—her appointment as an assistant instructor in English Literature and her nomination for the prestigious Beekman Award. The last thing she needed now was for the governor to put her father on the spot. The politician had been on a tear, attributing modern-day corruption to prominent Republican businessmen with unjust advantages.

"At least my father won't be on the podium," Al said.

"Just think," Vesta said, "four years ago, we joined this class together, fresh from our 'little red schoolhouse on a hill.'" She then bit her tongue, remembering that Roy had not attended Portland Preparatory School with the others. Vesta glanced over at him, stretched out on the lawn languidly, his pant legs wet from the damp grass. She'd put her foot in her mouth again. Fortunately, he seemed not to have noticed, his good eye half-closed behind his wire-rimmed glasses, long locks flopping in front of his face like a curtain closing him off from his classmates. The only thing about him that hadn't changed was his bright red bow tie.

"And here we are, four years later, all grown up and graduating." Annabelle finished her friend's thought as she emptied the contents of the picnic basket onto the blanket they shared: overstuffed sandwiches, deviled eggs, macaroni salad, pickles, and potato chips.

"At least your parents are proud of your accomplishments," Al said. "The Honorable Robert S. Bartlett won't let up about promising boys who fritter away their talent. My father takes every opportunity to point out I didn't finish my studies in four years but must return for a fifth year in the School of Engineering."

"My mother thinks I am a failure because I accepted a teaching position," Lulu said.

"And I am not graduating at all," Roy pouted. He would return in the fall to complete the classwork he had missed after his accident.

"A lot of fun you all are." Ted uncorked a bottle of champagne. "This is a celebration." He held up his glass. "Stop your moaning and groaning, and let's make a toast to our glorious future."

Annabelle held up her glass. "To our glorious future."

85

Annabelle was reeling from the excitement of appearing in the senior class play, *Gloriana*, the night before. Although the play's producer had not selected her to play the lead, she had received a standing ovation for her portrayal of Kathy, the loyal maid.

Roy, penitent for what he now called his "nervous collapse," escorted her to the opening. In the play's afterglow, he told her he hoped to write plays himself one day. She assured him his talents as a poet would serve him well in the theatrical arts.

A playwright and an actress. Wouldn't they be a glorious couple? Now that Lulu was giving him the cold shoulder, Annabelle finally had Roy to herself. The accident, and subsequent hardships, had made him a man. Although he required an occasional drop of laudanum for his chronic pain, Roy assured her he was stronger now despite his physical appearance. No longer content to be the dandy arriving at the theater with two women on his arm, he had developed a leading man's presence. While helping her rehearse her lines, he had encouraged her to toughen up.

"You're playing a maid," he said. "Not an innocent schoolgirl. Quit simpering." She dug deeper to erase his surly scowl.

She credited Roy with her success.

Truth be told, she agreed with Lulu's mother. *A woman's success depended on her ability to catch a good man.*

Lulu held up her glass: "To a glorious future."

Clarissa Carson had convinced Mr. Staub, the Dean of Literature, to hire Lulu for the upcoming fall term. He had been skeptical, well aware of Lulu's relationship with Al.

"We need a serious scholar to fill the position," he told Clarissa. "Someone committed to the discipline."

"Lulu is the finest we have," Dean Carson had replied. "An exceptional student." She recounted the conversation to her protégée on a late spring afternoon, seated in her sunny office. "He was certain you would get married and run out on us."

Lulu replied, without flinching, "My mother thinks I will become a fallen woman if I graduate without a husband."

The dean laughed. "Worse things could happen to you."

"I am so grateful for your support," Lulu said. "I won't let you down."

"We women need to stick together. I began my career as a college instructor; I understand it's not always easy to prove one's seriousness." A gentle smile spread across the professor's face. "How is Al?"

"Still suffering from his father's disapproval."

"Good for him. You are lucky to have a friend who knows his own mind. He is more likely to appreciate that quality in you."

A friend? Lulu held her glass up to Al, and he returned her toast.

"To a glorious future," Al echoed.

Women do not need dainty commencement dresses to exude femininity, he thought, as he looked into Lulu's blue eyes. The courage of Lulu's convictions was more attractive than any tailored dress. It relieved him that, by accepting a position in the Department of Literature, she was content to remain in Eugene until he finished his studies. She had accepted the gold bracelet graciously, wearing it instead of the ring he had given her. The fact that neither of their parents understood the decisions they had made brought them closer than ever.

Al, too, had benefited from a mentor in his department. This summer he would join Dean McAllister, preparing a survey on the water power of the McKenzie and Santiam Rivers. McAllister had selected a team of his favorite students to collect the data needed to determine the most effective and economical methods of capturing power from the two rivers.

Al loved the assignment, loved being on the cusp of something new. He couldn't believe his luck. Oregon was the perfect place to pursue his passions. Oregon City's Willamette Falls was the source of the world's first high-tension power line, a fourteen-mile stretch of six copper lines carrying four-thousand watts of direct current across the river and up to Portland. Electrical engineers in Oregon, Dean McAllister assured him, would show the entire nation how to wire the countryside. They were inventing the modern city.

Now that was a glorious future. One day, even his father might understand.

For now, he had Lulu, and that was worth celebrating.

"To a glorious future." Roy found it difficult to summon his legendary magic. To speak with the bravura that was his calling card.

He didn't belong here, among his friends. After all, he wasn't graduating. As Vesta clumsily pointed out, he had not been with them in the beginning, and he would not be with them in the end.

If it had not been for Annabelle's insistence, he would have spent the afternoon lying on his bed in the dormitory. The hubbub around campus annoyed him. He had been trying to write a poem that reflected the depths of his despair for days, but the words wouldn't come.

So here he was, on his back, a drop of laudanum making the afternoon bearable. As Reverend Rose said, the darkest days are for counting our blessings. As he made his toast, he set out to list them silently to himself:

Lithe Annabelle's bright eyes, reminding him of his sister Jessie.

The advantage his seniority would give him over the underclassmen on the staff of the *Webfoot* when he assumed the editorship next year.

His gratitude that Lulu would remain on campus while he completed his studies.

He was getting stronger every day now, able now to walk the length of campus without losing his breath. His victory in debate buoyed his confidence. Condor Water and Power remained beholden to him. Their ever-increasing wealth ensured payment of his college fees and secured his mother's employment.

Why did he continue to feel as if the scar on his belly concealed an insatiable hunger? Anger festered even as the rays of spring sunshine danced among the pale green leaves. He once believed poetry would save him.

Draining his glass, Roy fixed his good eye on Annabelle, who smiled in return.

"Roy, when you escort me to graduation tomorrow, please put in your eye?" The others watched Roy think through his response. They sensed a shift, a liaison revealed by Annabelle's request.

"Sure thing, sugar," he said.

The governor was not a pessimist. He assured his captive audience that he honestly believed that by arousing the American people, he could drive dishonest, unfaithful public servants into obscurity.

In their rented robes, Lulu, Al, Ted, Annabelle, and Vesta scanned the crowd as his speech droned on.

Lulu's father, seated in the fourth row in a spiffy suit he had purchased in Manhattan, didn't appear to be listening. Lulu noted her father had not taken the seat next to Kitty. Lizzie separated her parents, holding a bouquet of white lilies for Lulu in her lap.

The judge sat in the first row among the regents. He maintained an expression of dignified attention, but his condescending expression made it clear he found the governor's reasoning simplistic and naïve.

Roy twitched with impatience in the back row.

Ted ducked out of the ceremony before the annoying musical numbers. To Vesta's delight, he had invited her to join him at the Alumni Ball. It would take place that evening at the Armory, one last university bash.

Chapter 6 Postgraduates

Portland, Oregon, Summer 1904

Lizzie tripped up the stairs, her skirts held high, red ribbons securing the braids bouncing on her back. "Lulu, where are you?" She darted through the parlor to the back of the house, where Lulu sat at a small pine desk near the window, a pile of books in front of her and a pen in her hand. Lulu had resolved to spend the summer preparing for her new job as an instructor in the Department of English, but she was panicking. Although she had completed her BA with honors, her knowledge of English literature didn't seem sufficient for the task.

"There you are!" Lizzie said. "Come now. You have a phone call." On her way home from the library, Lizzie had passed Mr. Simpson in front of the Western Union office. Waving his smoking cigar in the air, he had instructed her to "Fetch your sister. Someone is trying to call her from Seattle." The Cleavers, like most of their neighbors, were on the waiting list for a party line. Their only access to Ma Bell was via the Western Union office. Mr. Simpson, better than a ringing bell, used passersby at random to alert neighbors to incoming calls.

Lulu couldn't imagine who might have placed the call. Setting Hawthorne aside, she pulled on a shawl and followed her skipping sister down the block to the Western Union office.

"The lady will call back in fifteen minutes," the proprietor informed them, showing Lulu to a seat in front of the impressive wooden box phone whose two bells stared back at her like huge bug eyes. "Two long rings and one short, that'll be yours." Simpson sat down on a wooden stool; Lizzie hopped from foot to foot beside Lulu. Whatever the call, before long the entire neighborhood would know her business. The possibilities were alarming—her father so far away, Al off surveying a river, Roy still recovering. Lulu stared at the black ear horn, braced to grab it. *Ring, phone, ring.*

Two long rings, one short. "Pick it up," Lizzie squealed.

At first, static. Then she heard Vesta's voice swimming across the line.

"Lulu, Ted and I are married!!" The background noise was lively. Through the hubbub of a hotel lobby, Lulu tried to catch the basics: a drunken evening in Portland, something about belly buttons and bicycles, Ted in a brewery on his knees, a train ride, a justice of the peace, and a ruined dress.

"Congratulations!" Lulu said when at last there was a break in the tale. "Of course, I want to hear everything." As their time ran out, she suggested they meet in Portland when the newlyweds returned. "Annabelle will want to hear the complete story."

Friday, they agreed. "Lunch at my mother's house," Lulu said. Bidding her friend goodbye through the mouthpiece, she sent her best to Ted and turned to Lizzie and Mr. Simpson, who were dying to hear the news.

* * *

Kitty baked bread. Lulu sliced fresh fruit for a salad. Lizzie asked if she could stay once Lulu's classmates arrived. Lulu suggested confidentiality might be in order.

Vesta was radiant when she arrived, flashing a diamond ring that Ted had purchased in Seattle. She kissed Lulu on the cheek and repeated her news. "We eloped."

Annabelle put down her teacup and embraced her friend. "Tell us everything," she said. After a dramatic pause, Vesta told her story.

"Graduation night was a blur," Vesta began. The ceremony followed by the Alumni Ball. Dance after dance. Ted sharing his flask of dark ale. Before she knew what was happening, Ted pulled her across campus, his eyes bright with excitement, intent on taking the crowded commercial stagecoach to Portland.

They boarded the coach in front of Renfrew Tavern. Throughout the jostling ride to Portland, they sang "Sweet Adeline" at the top of their lungs, oblivious to the other travelers napping on the wicker benches.

"You know the song," Vesta said, beginning to sing. Annabelle joined in.

For you, I pine, Vesta sang. (*For you, I pine,* Annabelle harmonized.)

Lulu made another pot of tea. Together, her friends sang:

In all my dreams. (*In all my dreams.*)

"Our fellow passengers sang too," Vesta said, although Ted had to rescue her from a gnarly miner who joined the chorus, waving filthy fingernails in front of her face.

Lulu placed the fruit salad on the table, but Vesta paid no attention to her efforts.

In Portland's Liberty Brewery, the party continued. "We sang 'Bedelia' and the hilarious 'I Can't Do My Bally Bottom Button Up.'"

"I love that one!" Annabelle hooted. Again, the two girls sang.

> "*What's the use of buttoning the other bally buttons?*
> *When the bally bottom button's undone.*"

This time, Lulu couldn't escape their high spirits. With each repetition, the song's lyrics seemed funnier and funnier, the challenge of enunciation more difficult.

Vesta said she had never laughed so hard.

Between verses, Ted lectured the bar's patrons on the history of hops. "He knows everything!" Vesta squealed. In 1852, seven years before Oregon was a state, a German immigrant named Henry Saxer opened the Liberty Brewery.

"Ted told everyone, 'Did you know scientists began experimenting with planting hops on the OSU campus in 1893?'"

Each time Ted ordered a beer, he tossed loose change into a tip tray embossed with the image of Otto Bismarck in red epaulets and a golden sash. Vesta sipped the pale beer, thinking it more ladylike.

When Ted could no longer contain his excitement, he pulled Vesta to her feet. They strutted the length of the bar. "Bally," he sputtered. "Bottom," he spit. Soon the other patrons paraded behind him like a family of babbling ducks. Ted insisted Vesta lead them all.

After the dance, he introduced her to the proprietor of the bar.

"M'dear," he puffed, out of breath but exultant, "I would like you to meet Paul Wessinter, son-in-law of the late, great Henry Weinhard, who purchased the Liberty Bar from none other than Henry Saxer, the granddaddy of hops."

"I did not know who he was talking about," Vesta said.

Paul, a large, debonair man with a mustache and a deep laugh, extended a beefy hand. "Charmed to meet you. Your boyfriend is one fine fellow."

It all boiled down to this: Paul and Ted were opening a restaurant together. The two men had plans for the upcoming Lewis and Clark Exposition. "A grand expansion of the Brewery," Ted said, waving his hands to show the enormity of his ambition.

No matter how much Ted drank, she assured them, he remained on his feet. He glad-handed his fellow drinkers as if he already owned the establishment. Paul kept refilling their glasses, congratulating them on their graduation.

Somewhere between "Bally Bottom Button Up" and midnight, Ted changed his tune.

Dropping to his knee, he crooned:

"Daisy, Daisy, give me your answer do."

This time, Vesta sang along, letting the words sink in. And then he said, "Why should we wait? Let's get married tonight."

"And I said 'yes'!"

When the bar closed, Paul drove the couple to Union Station in his grand buggy trimmed in red.

"I stood there waiting for the train's arrival beneath the station's clock tower, thinking, 'Tonight is the last night I will ever be a virgin.'"

"Oh, Vesta," Annabelle said, her reaction difficult to read.

It took all of Lulu's resolve to keep a straight face.

Who could have guessed? Vesta and the class president, Ted Steiger, had eloped. Al and Lulu were not the only ones in their gang that had tied the knot.

* * *

In the fall after they graduated, Al continued to maintain his room at Sigma Nu. If Willard and Geoffrey noticed their roommate was around less, they didn't comment. Al still sneaked into Lulu's room above the department store whenever he had the chance, but, given their busy schedules and academic responsibilities, this occurred less often than the couple would have liked.

Life had a way of moving along. "You're my best friend," Lulu said, whenever Al complained that they never spent any time together. Al spent most of his days tinkering in the Engineering building. Between teaching and class preparation, Lulu didn't have a moment to herself. When she did, she honed her teaching skills in the privacy of her office in the English department.

Ted and Vesta had left for Portland, where Ted tied his future to the Liberty Brewery Company, while Vesta practiced the fine art of being a wife. When Roy and Lulu's paths crossed in the corridors of Deady Hall, Lulu nodded but didn't stop to talk. She had resolved to treat him with the same cordiality she would any of her students. It relieved her to see his color had returned and he had regained the weight he lost after his accident. Roy was once again at the helm of the school literary magazine. She heard via the grapevine that he and Annabelle were campus royalty now, a glamorous couple envied by the younger students. Although Annabelle had enrolled at the Academy of Music in Portland, she returned to Eugene on the weekends to stroll the campus on her beau's arm.

Lulu had struggled to teach Hawthorne as a TA, but now she moved on to the Transcendentalists. Her students found Thoreau much more palatable. She lectured with passion on his treatise of self-reliance, inviting her students to challenge the assumptions they had inherited from their parents. In her meetings with Clarissa Carson, she shared the thrill of her students' discoveries. "I truly believe I am widening their horizons."

In her mentor's office, she steered the conversation away from her personal life, seldom mentioning Al.

In December, Dr. Staub observed Lulu teaching a class. To her delight, after pacing the back of the room the entire time she lectured, he complimented her on achieving the goals she had submitted in the lesson plan: "Good English must search for principles and eternal things and find the enduring, underlying framework of thought."

"A worthy goal," he said. "One you seem to have well in hand."

Clarissa congratulated Lulu on winning over the skeptical department head. Empowered by her mentor's praise, Lulu suggested the names of several women students who, if asked, would gladly join the two women at the next meeting of the Federation. The nascent university women's group had kicked into high gear as the chapter prepared to join women from across the state at the Lewis and Clark Exposition, which was to take place in Portland the following summer. Eager students in tow, Clarissa and Lulu became vocal leaders of the local group. Excited that Oregon had enacted referendum voting, they rallied the membership to collect voter signatures for women's suffrage on the Eugene ballot.

"Until recently," Carson reminded her, "women have contributed to social reform through charitable activities. But social reforms, such as coeducational universities, are changing the playing field."

In their rare moments together, Lulu regaled Al with the passion she had discovered in the movement. Women who had shown little interest in the vote now saw the importance of suffrage. "With enfranchisement," she said, "we will soon realize our goal of social reform."

Al, always a good listener, supported Lulu in her campaign, delighted to see her engaged and happy. When not engrossed in the completion of his thesis, he applied for jobs in his field. Scorning Condor Water and Power, which he continued to hold responsible for Roy's accident, he widened the geographic area in which he might consider offers of employment. He hinted that Portland might offer the best opportunities. Portland Railway, Light and Power Company was consolidating transportation and power generation utilities between Vancouver, Washington, and Salem, Oregon. "It will be the biggest merger in Oregon's history, absorbing every electric light, power, and transportation company in the Lower Willamette Valley," he told her. "How would you feel about moving to Portland once I am certified?" he asked.

"One step at a time," Lulu replied. "First, let me prove my value as an educator." Her days at the university might be numbered, but her success as an instructor and Al's support had restored her self-confidence. "We'll figure out the rest when the time comes."

Lulu had a lot on her mind. If they moved to Portland at the end of the school year, she could join the suffragettes in their march on the exposition. Clarissa might respect that choice, if not the other one she had yet to reveal. For the time being, life was good. The day would come soon enough when her colleagues would learn that she and Al had secretly married.

* * *

The first spring bulbs butted their tender heads through winter's relentless mud. Soon, crew teams would be back on the river, the coordinated strokes of their oars beating like the wings of insects struggling to stay afloat.

How quickly the winter had passed. The endless tasks of teaching, the stolen moments with Al. There were never enough hours in the day. In her English department office, Lulu stacked the last of her graded papers. She had spent the prior evening correcting grammar and responding to her students' flailing efforts to put half-formed philosophies into correct English. Whether her students had made significant progress over the course of the school year, she was not sure. But assisting them on the journey had been satisfying. There was still so much more she would have liked to teach them.

Lost in rumination, she didn't hear the tentative knock on her door. A second, more assertive, rapping caught her attention.

"Come in," she snapped. *What now?*

"Hey, teach," Roy sauntered in, "could you give me a hand?" His smile was as bright as the old days, laced with mischief and innuendo. *He looked good,* Lulu thought, already flustered by his presence.

"Twelve students on the magazine staff and not a line editor among them." Roy flung the copy for the school literary magazine on her desk. As if it were not out of the ordinary, he flopped into the chair reserved for student consultations.

Lulu was at a loss for words. A list of inappropriate comments occurred to her: *how dare you, we mustn't, I've missed you.* Instead, she fell back on the mundane. "How are you, Roy?"

"Fit as a fiddle," he said. His black hair, clean and shiny, was parted down the middle. He wore a red bow tie as cheery as a cherry pie. His black eyes, both of them, sparkled.

"You look well."

"Kicked the stuff," he said. "Learned my lesson, if you know what I mean."

She did.

"Annabelle's got me on the straight and narrow. Reverend Rose saved me. Everything would be peachy keen if I knew someone who was an ace editor. Got me to thinking. Who do I know who could school the kids in good English?"

All loose limbs and ease. In five minutes, he talked her back two years.

"Roy, it's good to see you. How is Annabelle?"

"As silly as cotton candy, and just as sweet. Determined to make a splash on Broadway."

"I miss her. I've missed both of you."

"So don't be a stranger," he said. Closing that chapter as if it were that easy.

They spent the afternoon editing copy. He had put in his time; the kids were in excellent hands. He had even contributed a new piece of his own. He said the poem was his apology to Annabelle.

"A Defense

Man should love where'er he goes.
Love is sweet, and lives are few,
So I feel in loving you
I am like the honey bee,
Working out divinity."

She complimented him on his exquisite turn of phrase, nothing more. When they came to the bottom of the pile, he sat back in his chair, examining her. "How is the golden couple?" he asked.

"Married." She regretted her confession the moment it left her lips. It was none of his business. She had sworn Al to secrecy, and in telling Roy, she was the first one to break their vow of silence.

"We're moving to Portland once the semester is over," she inserted distance as a defense.

"I hadn't heard."

"No one has. I want to keep my job."

"I have my own irons in the fire," he said. "One of these days I might even graduate."

"With highest honors, I'm sure," she said.

"My days of milking Condor Water and Power are kaput. Self-reliance, isn't that all the rage?" he asked. After his collapse, he had withdrawn from her American Literature class, but, evidently, he had read the syllabus.

Roy showed her two glossy brochures advertising land deals in eastern Oregon. "Since your father extended the railway east, land parcels are practically being given away. I've been buying them up as fast as they come on the market. By the time I graduate, I will have banked enough money reselling the land to suckers back East to buy my mother a house."

He was trying too hard. She knew that. But then, he always had. It was part of his charm.

"But what would you care? I'm sure the engineer will provide for you now that you have joined one of Oregon's illustrious families. The judge must adore you."

"He doesn't know," Lulu said, alarms ringing in her ears.

Roy raised his eyebrows. "Are you afraid that he, too, might fire you?"

"It is none of your concern," she said, struggling to mute her defensiveness. "Marriage is between two people. It's a private matter."

"Not if you ask Vesta," he let her off the hook. "For our friend, marriage is something she wants to celebrate with the world."

"How is Ted?"

"Peachy. Ted is angling to make a living off hops. At least, he is doing his best to consume as many as he can. When you move to Portland, I'm sure he will show you a grand time. I hear he has a promising job there."

"Roy, I need you to respect my confidence. No one must know about my marriage until the term ends."

"Sweetheart, you can trust me." Roy said this as if she had no reason to question his devotion. He spoke with the conviction of the closing line of one of his crowd-pleasing speeches, the ringing truth at the end of a sermon. He'd come there to patch things up. The reason he was there had nothing to do with his student's manuscripts. They did not require editing. Roy always did know how to lay out a top-notch magazine, and the work he'd laid out before her demonstrated his growing expertise.

She could forgive him. But would Al give his old friend a second chance? Roy didn't broach the subject, leaving it up to her. Scooping up the proofs, he thanked her for her editing prowess.

"See you later," he waved goodbye.

"Give my love to Annabelle," she said. For the first time that spring afternoon, a ray of sun lit the subtle mesh of scars on his face. His glass eye went vacant.

With Roy, nothing was as simple as his confident manner suggested. Beneath his bravado, there were layers she couldn't fathom.

After he shut the door, she realized she had accomplished nothing that afternoon. She needed to record her students' grades before she returned the papers in class tomorrow. She worked feverishly through the dinner hour.

The sun disappeared into the river as she walked back to her room. A rosy glow lingered, as if not quite done with the day. She would need to tell Al she had spoken with Roy. Instead of heading downtown to her own room, she returned to the Sigma Nu fraternity house, hoping Al would be there.

Geoffrey and Willard were playing a game of touch football in the dying light. She asked Al, who was watching from the sidelines, to walk her home. After he said goodbye to his friends, she recounted the afternoon visit. She had done nothing more than help a colleague in the English department. The discomfort she felt was disproportionate to the act. By the time she and Al arrived at Cupid's sign, anger had taken over. *How dare Roy stroll back into her life as if he had never left?*

"I know I shouldn't have said anything, but I needed him to know that we were together," she said. "That all that foolishness is behind us now."

"We've kept this secret long enough," Al said.

"But what about my job?" she asked.

"You knew this was coming."

She did, but she wanted to finish the term. How foolish she had been. What if Roy told Annabelle? Annabelle might keep her confidence, but she would surely tell Vesta, and then their secret would be out.

"Maybe this is a good thing," Al comforted her. His composure surprised her, but then he added he had received an offer from the Portland Light and Electric Company in the day's mail. "The term is almost over. Give your notice now before they decide for you."

"I've made a commitment," she said. "I'm going to stick with it." But as she kissed him good night, she had to admit the prospect of moving to Portland looked better all the time.

After much consideration, Al and Lulu drafted an item for the fraternity newsletter:

Alton R. Bartlett, Sigma Nu, and Miss Lulu Cleaver were married at the home of the bride's grandmother in Baker City, Oregon, on Feb. 22. This wedding, together with several others of

Gamma Zeta Chapter, was the culmination of a romance developed in the shady walks and winding streams of the University of Oregon. Mr. and Mrs. Bartlett will make their home in Portland, where he has accepted a position as a salesman with the Portland Light and Electric Company.

A week after the newsletter arrived in the mail, the Eugene paper picked up the item.

* * *

"Dr. Staub needs to speak with you." Clara, the English department secretary, avoided looking directly at Lulu. She shuffled the papers on her desk. Given any opening, she usually engaged Lulu in a discussion of departmental politics or whined about the students' perceived lack of respect.

Lulu, carrying a pile of corrected essays in her hand, was running late. "My students are waiting. Can I catch him after class?"

"He says he wants to see you. Now." Lulu looked up. The calculating squint of Clara's eyes suggested she knew more than she let on.

Lulu sighed and set the stack of papers down. "Could you drop these off in my classroom and let the students know I will be there shortly?"

"Certainly, Miss Cleaver. Or maybe I shouldn't call you Miss anymore?"

Damn. Lulu froze, her sense of urgency deflated by the implication of Clara's words. *Clara knew. And if Clara knew, it meant news of her marriage had reached Staub. Did Roy spill the beans? It didn't matter now.*

"Thank you, dear," she said, struggling to maintain her composure. She refused to acknowledge the women's impudence. She took a deep breath and smoothed her skirt. When she knocked on Dr. Staub's door, her heart hammered out a warning.

He was waiting for her, pipe in hand. His long mustache made it difficult to read his expression, but his raised eyebrows challenged her. He was all business.

"Take a seat, Miss Cleaver," he told her, a captive to his consternation, as he tamped tobacco into his pipe. He struck a match, puffed on the pipe, and watched the tobacco flare. When he exhaled, it was with a long, disappointed, I-knew-this-was-coming sigh.

"I believe there is news you have neglected to share with the university?" he asked, and then inhaled again, looking out the window as he waited for her reply.

"Sir?" *He expected this,* she thought. *Hadn't he told Dean Carson that women didn't belong in the workplace? Insisted their proper role was that of wife and mother? Now he waited for her to confirm his deep-seated conviction.*

She sat up straighter. "Dr. Staub, I'm unaware of any dissatisfaction with my job performance." She was careful to keep her voice steady.

Another sigh. Another round of puffing. He cleared his throat. "I thought I made myself perfectly clear when I offered you this job. You signed a contract."

Lulu felt her face grow warm. She clenched her fists. "Dr. Staub, may I remind you I have met or exceeded every professional goal we discussed when you hired me. My priority has always been my students. I consider it an honor to instruct them. Have you received any complaints about my comportment as an instructor? I sincerely doubt you have, given the recent performance review I received."

"Dear," his condescending tone dismissed her argument without consideration, "the university's policy is, and always has been, women instructors must remain single. A married woman has no place in front of a classroom."

"With due respect, sir, shouldn't my job performance be the most important criteria?" By now, she knew her face was red. There was no way she could choke back her anger. "I ask you again, have you received any complaints in that regard?"

"There are rules, Mrs. Bartlett." With a meaningful glance in her direction, he brought the discussion to a close. "And reasons for those rules. You violated your contract."

"Al and I are moving to Portland at the end of term." Her voice wavered, further undermining her confidence. "What harm is there in letting me finish what I started? I promise you, sir, I will adhere to the highest standards. My personal life has never compromised my obligations to the university, and it will not now."

"That is not your decision to make." He set the pipe in his ashtray. "And speaking of judgment, I conferred this morning with Judge Bartlett on this matter and discovered that he, too, was kept in the dark. A regent, I remind you, of the university. Quite a scandal, young lady, I assure you. The rumors that have circulated about your shenanigans with his son are shameful enough, but a secret marriage is a violation that I must immediately address."

"A violation! Shenanigans!" Lulu stood up, placing her hands on his desk to stop them from shaking. "I have—we have—done nothing to be ashamed of." Lulu searched for a defense that would not further alienate Staub. *The role of the modern university. The changing expectations of women in the twentieth century. Her dedication. Al's sterling reputation.*

What could she possibly say?

"Control yourself, young lady," Staub said. "I must ask you to act with decorum. A university is no place for a woman's hysteria. Please do not touch my desk." He shivered with repulsion. "Please clean out your desk by the end of the day." With these words, their meeting and her career at the university ended.

"Control yourself." How dare he treat her like an emotional child? How utterly and unbearably unfair! She stormed out of his office, passing Clara without a backward glance. With every step, she thought of another argument. Despite their marriage, she was certain the faculty would continue to treat Al with respect. *His job was not in jeopardy. For that matter, hadn't the university tolerated Roy's unstable behavior, welcoming him back time and time again with warmth and compassion? The hypocrisy! How, in good conscience, could Staub disregard such a blatant double standard?*

Worse yet, he had the audacity to tell the judge! If the judge had been humiliated, as Staub seemed to believe, it was only because he refused to accept his son's right to make his own decisions. Al chose her and not his father's illustrious path. How did that choice have any relevance to her job as an instructor?

She stormed past the classroom where she was no longer welcome. At the end of the corridor, Clarissa's door was open. Her mentor stood waiting for her, arms extended.

"Dear," she said, "I'm so very sorry. Was it awful?" The older woman shut the door and embraced her as she sobbed.

"I'm sorry," Lulu said. "I never meant to deceive you."

"It's all right, sweetheart. Have a cry if you must. Just be sure that awful man doesn't see."

In Clarissa's sympathetic arms, Lulu did just that. Tears ran down her face as she repeated Staub's condescending dismissal. The older woman patted her back and clucked her tongue. "The cow. He couldn't write a comprehensive sentence if he tried."

"And he told Al's father!"

"So, I heard. Your love life is quite the hot topic in the faculty lounge." Clarissa handed her a lace handkerchief. Lulu blew her nose.

"If I owe anyone an apology, it is you. You have always been in my corner. I'm so sorry to disappoint you." Lulu's tears slowed as she realized she had thrown a childish tantrum in the office of the woman she admired more than anybody else in the world. *Would the day's humiliations never end?*

"Lulu, you're young still. You'll have plenty of chances to prove yourself. Your career doesn't have to end here. Who knows what opportunities await you in Portland?"

Lulu sniffed, calmer now.

"I'd be happy to write you a letter of recommendation. Several inspiring suffragettes I know live in the city. I'd be happy to also provide you with letters of introduction."

By the time Clarissa had completed her list, Lulu had reconciled herself to the fact that it was time to move on. She returned the sodden handkerchief. The two women embraced once more, and then Lulu headed out to find Al.

Part II: Portland

Chapter 7 Marriage

Portland, Oregon, 1905

Lulu unpacked the box labeled "kitchen." Her mother had labeled each box, thrilled to help her daughter set up housekeeping. Pulling out a linen tablecloth, Lulu spread it on the wooden floor. Al unwrapped sandwiches from the German delicatessen on the corner. Lulu put "The Shade of the Old Apple Tree" on the gramophone.

Al and Lulu had known each other since they were children. Eight years in preparatory school. Five years at the university. For the first time, they were alone, in a space they could share. In this unfurnished apartment on a busy Portland street, they were now, at last, a husband and wife at home. No parents to judge their actions. No longer children, role models for their friends, or obliging students.

It was just them now. A man and a woman. Adults.

Al had ordered rye bread, her favorite, asking the counterman to leave off the mustard she despised.

Lulu wore a slip and a pair of fuzzy slippers. Al stripped down to his underpants and, for a touch of whimsy, a pair of suspenders. And his eyeglasses, of course. He chose roast beef, piled high on pumpernickel bread.

A small lamp with an ivory shade, their first joint purchase, provided the only light. They had deliberated for hours on its purchase. Al said buying the light was appropriate, since they had moved to Portland so that he could begin his job at Portland Light and Electric.

"Do you think we'll miss the slinking about?" he asked.

"Tiptoeing late at night to my room above the department store?" She knew she would.

"The annoying streetlight humming outside your window?"

All that was behind them now. They left the lamp on when it became apparent that neither was hungry.

Al put down his sandwich and swallowed. "Do I have mustard on my mouth?"

Lulu licked his bottom lip. "Spicy." They had never laughed while making love; secrecy had been the priority. Now they tried it, giggling at their clumsy attempts to get comfortable on the hard floor. Were they behaving like the more sanctimonious of their friends had suspected all along? Lulu playing the part of a loose woman and Al her defiler. But it didn't feel like that, not for a moment.

"Mr. and Mrs. Bartlett," the newspaper article said. But of course, to them, Mr. and Mrs. Bartlett described the judge and saintly Cornelia. They were Al and Lulu, campus sweethearts no more.

Lulu pulled her slip over her head. Al blushed. Lulu stood in the sunlight until he crooked his finger, ready to pull her into his embrace. Tonight, they were tongue-tied, shy of each other in their new surroundings. Careful not to misspeak. Soon Al would chat about electrical upgrades and Lulu would opine on a woman's right to vote. But today, none of that mattered. Far from friends and family, they were naked together at last.

They made love in the light of day, with the window shades open.

When they finished, they recited their vows. As Lulu had wanted all along, without an audience. This once, only them. These were the vows that mattered.

"I, Al Bartlett, take you Lulu Cleaver as my wife."

"I, Lulu Cleaver, take you Al Bartlett as my husband."

They had made love dozens of times before. Eager love. Sneaky love. Weary and respectful love. But never like this. Two nudes in the afternoon sunshine, half-eaten sandwiches cast aside, the flimsy tablecloth in bunches under their sweaty backs, the unfurnished apartment filled with Al's groans and Lulu's whimpers, rising and falling like the static of the record still twirling on the gramophone.

In November, the marriage ceremony changed nothing.

In May, their vows had become common knowledge. Although embarrassing, this, too, changed nothing.

But tonight. Everything reset tonight with the ability to start over. To have, to be. Him and her. Husband and wife. *This*, he thought, *is marriage. Worth every painful revelation that preceded it.*

They made love again. At last, they had that luxury. Lulu said, "I could do this forever."

Al said, "Maybe wait until the bed arrives."

As dusk settled in, they sat side by side, knees drawn up, wrapped in the tablecloth. The wood floor bruised Al's knees and Lulu ran a finger over the darkening skin. "I don't want to hurt you," she said.

"I know," Al said. "But it's worth it." They lay down on the wood floor, rolled over, and turned out the light.

* * *

"Portland's most wealthy and powerful men pulled this together. Henry himself invested $10,000." Ted led the way across the exposition's park-like grounds as if he personally had planned and staged the Lewis and Clark Centennial. Henry Weinhard was Ted's boss.

Beside him, an exultant Vesta narrated the history of the exposition. "Without Henry's support, Guild's Lake would still be a swamp."

Two years of landscaping had turned Guild's Lake, a marshy slough surrounded by dairies and truck farms, into building sites and terraces that led to a sparkling lake. Exhibition halls, whitewashed buildings set against green hills, dotted the bluff and a peninsula accessed by the Bridge of Nations.

"Like diamonds set in a coronet of emeralds," Vesta said, quoting Mayor Williams and flashing her sparkling ring to punctuate her point.

"See this?" Al interrupted to point out a pipe entering the lake. "A constant flow of water is being pumped from the Willamette River to refresh the lake." Two weeks on the job, and already he recited the accomplishments of the Portland Light and Electric Company as if they were his own. The power company's presence, illuminated by a 30-by-110-foot sign with the number 1905, was everywhere at the fair. The company's president, Henry W. Goode, was the exposition president. "We provide the electricity for the one hundred thousand lamps that outline the fair buildings, streets, and walkways," Al said. "We even built a steam-generation plant in 1902 near 21st Avenue and Nicolai Street, specifically to deliver power to the exposition." As they started walking again, he pointed out electrical transformers hidden in underground pits and buildings.

Lulu surveyed the grounds. "Vesta, do you know where the Oregon Building is?" Tomorrow she planned to join her Federation sisters at a reception for Susan B. Anthony. She was still reeling from the impassioned speeches she had heard that afternoon at the annual National American Woman Suffrage Association Convention. Although the association had scheduled their convention to coincide with the exposition, the day's activities had taken place at the First Congregation Church.

"Why do you ask?" Vesta put her arm through Lulu's.

"Abigail Scott Duniway, the president of the Women's Club, is urging all women at the fair to attend the upcoming dedication of the bronze statue of Sacagawea by the Denver artist Alice Cooper. We are to meet at the Oregon Building." Lulu couldn't wait. "Perhaps you would you like to join me there?"

Before Vesta answered, Ted swung open the door of the Bismarck Café. "Dinner is on us," he said. The Weinhard Brewery, involved in every step of planning the expo, sponsored the German restaurant. They entered the dark-paneled saloon custom-built by the St. Louis company.

"Ted's company," Vesta said, "provides the dark lager called Kaiser Beer that is showcased here at the café."

"Don't you worry," Ted assured his guests, "we have an ample supply of this fine gold-medal brew."

As they entered the brewery, Al grabbed Lulu's hand. "What are they doing here?"

Lulu followed his gaze.

"Surprise!" Vesta said. "I invited Roy and Annabelle to join us tonight."

The dashing couple awaited them at the bar, Roy chatting up a dark-haired barmaid and Annabelle in an exquisite red velvet gown. Lulu locked eyes with Annabelle. Roy leaped up and gave Al an enthusiastic handshake. "You rascal, marrying the university's most accomplished maiden on the sly." Roy patted a stool and gestured for Al to sit down beside him.

Lulu greeted Annabelle, kissing her on the cheek. She didn't know what to expect.

"Look what the duck dragged in," Annabelle said. Her hand quickly reclaimed Roy's knee.

"A party!" Vesta squealed. "You didn't think we'd let the two of you get married without a celebration, did you?" Ted, his voice booming across the room, told the barmaids to keep the lager flowing. Platters of cold cuts and slices of pumpernickel and rye bread appeared on the long mahogany bar. "Drinks on the house!" Ted proclaimed. "In celebration of the union of my two dear, dear friends."

Vesta was in her element, the bar's unofficial hostess. She flitted between Lulu and Annabelle. "Isn't the fair marvelous?" she asked. "Have you seen the fountain?" she asked a patron at their side.

"Roy tells me you spent the afternoon with the suffragettes?" Annabelle shook her golden hair and strolled over to Lulu. Even as she asked, she did not take her eyes off Roy.

"The convention is more than just rousing speeches," Lulu said. "Today's program opened with music by the Lake Quartet."

Turning to Roy, she said, "There was even a poem, though not one I admired, by a poetess from New York." When the barmaid filled their glasses, Annabelle returned to Roy's side to cover his. He rolled his eyes and pouted but did not protest.

"Not one musician exhibited a shred of talent comparable to yours, Annabelle," Lulu said.

Roy and Annabelle made an attractive couple. They were clearly used to being the life of the party.

"Yes, won't you sing for us, Annabelle?" Vesta jumped in, seizing the opening. She didn't need to ask her friend twice. Draining her glass of beer, Annabelle launched into the chorus of "My Merry Oldsmobile."

"Come away with me, Lucille
In my merry Oldsmobile
Down the road of life we'll fly
Automobubbling, you and I"

"Al, that's your song for sure!" Annabelle perched on the bar, her long legs swinging to the beat. "To the church, we'll swiftly steal," she sang, "then our wedding bells will peal."

"Automobubbling, it is," Vesta said, ordering a bottle of champagne for a toast.

"All together now," Ted conducted.

Al, flushed with liquor by now, wrapped his arms around Lulu and swayed as he sang, only slightly off-key. "You can go as far as you like with me in my merry Oldsmobile."

"Should we buy a car, then?" he asked her, slurring his words. "We could tootle around town, explore the city."

Lulu smiled but didn't sing along. As the party became noisier and the guests drunker, she settled at Roy's side, preferring to watch the festivities but not take part.

Waiters in lederhosen and waitresses in dirndls served them dinner. Annabelle remained on the bar. Through the thick lashes of her lowered eyes, she struck a dramatic pose and crooned the entire song again, vamping it up for the crowd. After the meal, Ted and Vesta danced, and Roy, unsupervised, sipped Annabelle's wine.

Roy ignored Lulu, instead focusing his charismatic charm on Al, who, unaccustomed to late nights, was already yawning.

As the party wound down, Annabelle blew kisses to the crowd and returned to a bar stool next to Roy, who was pitching a land deal to the inebriated cluster of men. He even tried to convince Al, the most unlikely of investors. "Here's your chance to get in on the ground floor," he urged.

114

Ted and Vesta had already bought over a hundred acres, he said. Ted added an endorsement of their dear friend to anyone still listening. "Look at the expo," Ted said. "Oregon is on the move. Its population has grown by 3,000% over the last 50 years. The timber industry is exploding. With three transcontinental railways using the city as their Pacific terminus, Portland is destined for greatness."

Lulu rescued Al, who squirmed under Roy's intense glare. "We should go," she told her friends. "Al has work in the morning." Vesta embraced them both, urging them to stay a while longer. Fortified by the enthusiastic reception to her impromptu performance, Annabelle returned Lulu's tentative embrace. Roy shook both of their hands, reiterating his congratulations.

As they retraced their steps across the luminous fairgrounds, a hot-air balloon drifted across the starry sky.

"Roy is full of crap, as always," Al said. "But I have to admit, it was good to see him."

Two weeks later, Lulu stood with Vesta among a teeming throng of women on Lakeview Terrace. She had invited her friend to join her for the unveiling of the "Bird Woman" statue. The animated buzz of women's voices drowned out the opening notes of De Caprio's band. The crowd had settled down by the time Charles Cutter delivered the address of the day. But it was Abigail Scott Duniway's remarks that silenced the crowd.

"The pioneer mother who trudged across the almost untracked continent with her babe in arms never gave a passing thought to her own heroism. Whether she was engaged in the domestic pursuits of peace or defending her rude domicile from wild beasts or wilder savages, she was equal with any man.

"Little did the pioneer mothers of Oregon imagine, nor did Sacajawea think, that the day would come when womanhood would be honored. No man imagined, one hundred or even fifty years ago, that way out here, hard by the surging shores of the sundown seas, there would be erected, by women, in enduring bronze, a statue to celebrate another of their sex."

A young mother, two children in tow, cheered with a hoot worthy of an ardent fan, while a gray-haired matron sat on the stone wall lost in meditation. Lulu studied the faces of the surrounding women, moved by the women's enthusiasm. Vesta yawned, unimpressed by the work-a-day outfits sported by many of the women in the audience.

The speaker's words reminded Lulu of the many challenges faced by the women in her life. Kitty's unwavering loyalty to the husband who supported her but did not keep her company. Cornelia attending to the judge like a slave. Roy's mother teaching in a rural schoolhouse in western Oregon.

Despite the lofty words, the dedication provided no useful guidance for how to proceed, only inspiration that Lulu did not know how to put to good use. She missed Clarissa's clear-headed commentary, envied her ability to steer clear of sentiment. Clarissa would have known how to fit in with the strangers who now surrounded her. Instead, like the artificial lake manufactured for the exposition, Lulu feared the day's celebration would prove nothing more than a temporary illusion.

"My turn," Vesta said. "I sat through your boring dedication. Now let's do something fun." A week before, the first nickelodeon had opened in Philadelphia. Vesta was crazy to see what all the hubbub was about. Spouting Hollywood gossip, she dragged Lulu across the fairgrounds, arriving just in time to see a screening of the expo's free motion picture.

The one-hour film, *New York in a Blizzard*, was enchanting, Lulu had to admit. After the lights came on, Vesta also showed her the Singer sewing machine exhibit, where she purchased a souvenir postcard. When both agreed that they had they had their fill of the fair's delights, they walked toward the trolley arm in arm.

Al was still at work when Lulu returned home. As she prepared a simple supper in the small apartment's kitchen, she read through the evening paper, concentrating on the coverage of the day's dedication. It concluded with the closing line of Duniway's speech:

"In honoring Sacajawea, we pay homage to thousands of uncrowned heroines, whose quiet endurance and patient effort have made possible the achievements of the world's great men whom they loved and served."

There it was again. The article ended with a tribute to great men and not the intended heroine, Sacajawea. Lulu tossed aside the paper in disgust. In her closing words, Duniway had lauded Sacajawea's greatness in terms of its usefulness to men. *What would a woman have to do to be celebrated for her own accomplishments?* Lulu fumed, stomping around the room instead of setting the table. In her fury, she forgot all about the pan of hamburger frying on the stove until its acrid odor filled the room. The evening's meal went up in flames. Using the newspaper as a fan, she threw open the kitchen window. *Damn it.* With any luck, she could air out the room out before Al returned.

* * *

Al's face brightened when he saw the Eugene postmark on the envelope. After news of their wedding got out, Al and Lulu had received a printed wedding card acknowledging their marriage. Inside, Cornelia had signed, *the Judge and Mrs. Bartlett.* No love. No note. Not even a pro forma phrase of congratulations. Al had thrown the card in the trash. "The judge has rendered his verdict," Al said. "It's official. My father has written me off."

"He'll come around," Lulu said. But Al's face, a battleground of anger, hurt, and disappointment, had lingered in her memory for days. *How cold of his parents to respond in such a disaffected manner. How could they treat their son this way?*

Now Al ripped open the mail, and Lulu realized how much he still longed for his parents' blessing. Lulu watched his face as he unfolded the letter, knowing his expression would reflect its contents. At first, he furrowed his brow. Then a resigned smile replaced his frown.

"Who is it from?" Lulu asked.

"Ernest. He's moved into my old room at Sigma Nu."

"That boy's a hoot," Lulu said.

"He wants to visit us this weekend, Al said. "It would be grand to see him."

"He'll be our first houseguest."

Several days later, they welcomed the long-legged college student to their apartment.

"You'll have to sleep on the couch," Lulu said apologetically, realizing it was too short for the lad.

"I've done worse."

Al encouraged him to share news of home.

"Sigma Nu hosted a fizzing end-of-summer dance last night in Turner's Hall." Ernest was not only taller than Al, but considerably more outgoing. "The band was top-notch. You can't imagine the crazy dances going around." He demonstrated the Grizzly Bear, the Duck Waddle, and the Turkey Trot, each of which involved trotting or swaying across the room, imitating the particular animal. He bounced off the walls of their small apartment but didn't seem to mind. "Four new students joined the fraternity before the night was over."

Lulu hadn't heard Al laugh so hard in months. These days, her husband's favorite topic of conversation was his career. How refreshing to watch the two brothers share news of the fraternity, tripping over their words. Lulu kept the beer steins filled with Ted's Kaiser Beer. The afternoon passed pleasantly enough until Ernest turned to his brother. His grin gone, he slurred, "You know, you broke Mother's heart." In a somber tone, he described Cornelia's plaintive cry when she received the news of Al's elopement. "She declared she had lost a son."

Al's face went white. His smile disappeared.

"I don't understand. Why she doesn't she stand up to your father?" Lulu looked first at Ernest and then at Al. "We did nothing wrong."

Instead of responding, Ernest let his brother answer.

"Don't be fooled," Al explained to her. "Propriety is as important to Mother as it is to Father." He drained his stein and then turned to his brother with a defiant glare. "We moved to Portland to begin a life of our own. Lulu and I will not abide Father passing judgment on our life together." He put his arm around Lulu.

"Your parents should be proud of Al." Lulu patted his hand reassuringly. "His career is taking off. Why, next week he is presenting a paper at a regional engineering meeting. It's quite an honor." Lulu could not remember either the name of the meeting or the subject of the paper.

"Yes, the Institute of Electrical and Electronic Engineers has asked me to present at their annual meeting. I'll be discussing the development of the new transmission dynamometer." This time, it was Lulu who laughed. Ernest rolled his eyes.

"Tell us what it does, Al," Lulu insisted.

"A dynamometer measures the horsepower produced by an engine."

Ernest asked for another stein of beer.

"But why?" Lulu asked, filling Ernest's stein.

Al started to answer, but Ernest knocked over the glass as he reached for it. Lulu jumped up and headed to the kitchen for a rag.

Over dinner at Ted's restaurant, Ernest showed little more interest when Lulu described her involvement with the Portland suffragette movement. Ernest may have visited his brother to convey an indirect message from his mother, but, in the end, his visit showed them how far from home they had traveled.

"Why do I feel a need to explain myself every time I meet a ·member of your family?" Lulu asked Al that night as they prepared for bed.

"Don't be dramatic," Al replied, laying out his suit for the next day.

"I wish your mother had inherited a little more of her father's compassion." Lulu spoke to his reflection in the bedroom mirror as she brushed her hair.

"She is the judge's wife."

"Well, that's her loss. Your grandfather is the only member of your family with a heart."

The next morning, after Ernest left, Al headed off early to work, leaving Lulu to restore order to their cramped apartment. Straightening up the bedroom, she skimmed the agenda for the engineering meeting, which Al had left spread out on his bureau. The presentations included "A Unique Belt Conveyor, Offsetting Cylinders in Single-action Engines" and "Small Steam Turbines."

Why on earth did I marry this man? She chuckled. One year ago, she had embarked on what she hoped would be an illustrious career, teaching at the university. Since arriving in Portland, she read the classified ads daily in the *Morning Oregonian*, searching for teaching jobs or positions as a writer. "Editors," she had been told dozens of times by recruiters who looked her up and down and dismissed her resume unread, "are usually men." How many doors would she need to knock on, always without success?

Now, the best she could hope for was to sit in the audience watching other suffragettes and be inspired by other women's speeches. Al's words reverberated as she straightened the sheets on their bed. "She is the judge's wife." Cornelia's choice to marry Judge Bartlett had forever altered the course of her life. What would be the lasting impact of Lulu's decision to marry Cornelia's son?

* * *

Al reviewed his notes as he entered the convention hall. His stomach churned, his morning coffee not sitting well. In the lobby, he spotted C.H. Leadbetter holding court as usual, surrounded by a cluster of businessmen. *How could Lulu understand? Electricity was his obsession, not hers. She had never held a job outside of academia.* Still, it hurt when Ernest rolled his eyes and Lulu joined his brother in laughing at him. *Why should they care that the electrical industry was growing at the rate of one hundred percent every five years? That every day he went to work, he contributed to that progress?*

The rapid development of new technologies, the promotion provided by the Lewis & Clark Exposition, and the continuing improvements in lighting and home appliances such as toasters and heaters had created an increasing demand for electricity. Companies like Portland Light and Electric and the Portland Railway Company, backed by eastern capital, were under constant pressure to expand. Smaller firms struggled for funds to compete. Men like Leadbetter smelled money and were on the prowl for new investments.

Al spotted several coworkers among the seats reserved for the Portland section of the Institute of Electrical and Electronic Engineers. Before he had a chance to join them, Chairman O.B.

Caldwell and local railway officials took their seats on the stage. Al grabbed a seat on the aisle, and the editor of the *Portland Telegram* tapped on the microphone, asking for order and welcoming the guests on behalf of the city of Portland.

Al kept remembering items he had forgotten to include in his paper. He tried not to rustle his papers as he pulled out his notes, reading them over to be sure that he had everything there. Although he had gone over and over the paper, looking for logical flaws or unclear conclusions, his hands were sweaty each time he returned his notes to his briefcase.

If only he had Roy's talent for oration. The best he could hope to achieve was a clear delivery before a sympathetic audience. Public speaking wasn't his forte. But when his boss at Portland Electric had asked him to present the results of his work, he immediately agreed. The request was an honor, a sign that his career was on track, and he had come to the notice of the company's upper management.

The transmission dynamometer was his baby. It had been a mistake to try to explain the use of the tool to Ernest and Lulu.

Lulu hadn't even tried to understand.

That misstep shook him. Today, he needed to summarize his data succinctly.

His transmission dynamometer improved on the old-fashioned Prony brake. The significance of his developments had to be made clear to his colleagues. Leave Lulu to her suffragettes, he preferred to discuss technical matters with a roomful of engineers any day.

After lunch, he took his turn behind the dais. Almost two-thirds of the eighteen folding chairs in the seminar room were occupied. He cleared his throat before speaking, thinking of Roy's elaborate pre-speech routines. Maybe if he had worn a bow tie, his knees would not be shaking as he rose to speak.

"My name is Al Bartlett. I am in engineer with Portland Light and Electric." He cleared his throat.

"The old Prony brake," he began, "develops mechanical friction on the periphery of a rotating pulley by means of brake blocks." Looking up, he saw the audience was with him.

This might not be a church packed with adoring students, but he had his colleague's attention. He spoke with increasing confidence.

"By using my mathematical model of motor and drive system performance, we can measure the horsepower of an automobile's engine without decreasing its power." He concluded, "with this tool, our industry will grow and prosper."

Exhaling a sigh of relief, he headed for his seat. Once seated, he heard the applause.

"Great job." His boss gave him a thumbs-up from across the room, where he was hobnobbing with the mayor.

C.H. Leadbetter stopped him on the way out to shake his hand. The pompous man, who Al had last seen in Roy's hospital room, recognized him only as an opportunity. A reporter for the *Morning Register* asked for additional information on his project's applications. Soon, his coworkers surrounded him, eager to talk about their role in the project. Still clutching his papers, Al basked in their attention, already thinking of new applications for his work.

Chapter 8 Life in Portland

Lulu rinsed the breakfast dishes and sat down with a cup of tea to read the *Woman's Tribune*, a national suffrage weekly published in Portland. The news was discouraging. Despite the enthusiasm engendered by the Exhibition and the unveiling of Sacajawea's statue, the 1906 campaign for women's right to vote had failed. When all the votes were counted, the liquor industry and business interests prevailed, using the press, public relations, and their wealth to defeat the measure.

Lulu folded the paper in frustration. *What right did businesses have to control the lives of women? Why were powerful men so determined to keep women in a subsidiary role?* She eyed the dust accumulating on the sill of the apartment's only window, over the kitchen sink. The cabinets, half filled with castoffs from her mother, needed a coat of paint. Their apartment was small and sparsely furnished. A couch and desk in the windowless living room. The bed unmade in their bedroom. *I'm a lousy housewife, she thought, but I really don't care.*

Any other Monday, she might have attended the regular gathering of the suffragettes, who convened in the basement of the Methodist Church. But the bill's defeat was only the latest disappointment in the women's campaign for equality. Increasingly, the meetings were acrimonious. While Duniway advocated new legislation that would grant all taxpayers the right to vote, the more progressive women among her followers argued that her proposal was class-based and favored property owners.

She tied on her rain bonnet, deciding a walk outside would do her good. Lulu passed the church without stopping. She would spend the day on her own, maybe pick up some things for the apartment. She headed downtown, studying her reflection in the store windows, trying to see herself from the outside, determining whether she fit in this bustling city.

Her feet throbbed. Her high-heeled boots were all wrong for the mud and blocks of pavement. When she could no longer bear the discomfort, she plopped down on a bench in front of a narrow pet store, listening to the parakeets' songs through the open door. With nothing better to do, she entered the store.

The poorly lit wooden floors were dusty, the walls cluttered with shallow shelves and glass display cases filled with small, unidentifiable goods. Lulu dodged the signs that hung from the ceiling every few feet advertising dog collars, nail clippers, and birds for sale. Advertisements blocked dangling light fixtures with exposed bulbs. The store was so narrow that there was only a cluttered path through the middle of the merchandise.

A large sign over the cash register read "Ask Hiram" and boasted that the store stocked pet squids (for the whole family), songbirds, goldfish, and medicines for "every known pet." A placard offered free advice, parrots, dogs, cats, squirrels, and poultry supplies.

Lulu gravitated to the songbirds; their cheerful songs unmuted by the dusty darkness of the store. A yellow-green parakeet tilted its head and fixed its beady black eye on her before letting loose a waterfall of chirping delight; a song of pure joy.

"I would recommend you clip her wings." The solicitous proprietor appeared behind her.

"Whatever for?"

"A parakeet's mature feathers allow it to fly high and fast. In a moment of panic, a pet bird can hurt itself."

The bird cocked its head to listen.

"Well, I would encourage my bird to fly."

Sensing a sale, Hiram replied, "Oh, don't. Clipping the wings will assure the bird's safety and make it easier for you to get her back into her cage. Her inability to fly will encourage her dependency on you." Soon Hiram was showing Lulu ornate cages with wooden swings, ladders, and colorful perches.

Lulu, determined to rescue the bird from the salesman's offensive clippers, purchased bird food as the man wrapped her other purchases in brown paper. The parakeet hopped onto the shopkeeper's burly finger as he transferred it into a small box for the trip home. Hiram asked one last time, "Are you sure you don't want me to clip her wings?"

Inside the wooden box, the bird stopped singing. Lulu replied, "Absolutely not."

When Lulu arrived home, she picked up the breakfast plates and wiped down the oilcloth, which was littered with toast crumbs. Al arrived right behind her, carrying a copy of the alumni newsletter that had arrived in the mail.

"Are we listed?" Lulu watched as he scanned the newsletter.

"Among the proud graduates." Al pointed to the column listing alumni accomplishments.

Alton Scott Bartlett, B.S., 1904. Portland, Ore. Electrical Inspector, Portland Light & Electricity, Portland, Ore.

Lulu Cleaver Bartlett (Mrs.), B.A., 1904. At Home.

"Is that a bird I hear singing?" Al asked.

Lulu slapped the paper on the table and unwrapped her packages in a flurry of activity. She set the ornate cage on the counter and hung the swings without responding. Sliding open the wooden box, she held a shaking finger out for the frightened bird.

"A parakeet. How delightful."

Lulu transferred the bird to the cage and closed the wire door before turning to face her husband, her face a thunderous red.

"At home?!" Her lips trembled at the insult.

"Lulu, what's wrong?"

"At home? That's my status? Nothing more?" In the light of the kitchen window, the bird sang, a sad trill of uncertainty. "I might as well line the cage with this damn newspaper; let the bird crap on my worthless life."

Al's mouth fell open. Lulu folded the newsletter. Sliding out the floor of the parakeet cage as Hiram had instructed her, she positioned the paper so that the alumni news was directly under the perch and then returned the tray to the cage, wiping tears from her cheeks.

The bird skittered across its perch. It puffed up and then pooped, the white drop landing precisely on the offending article.

Lulu turned both faucets on and rinsed the breakfast dishes.

"Is home really that bad?" Al asked. If Lulu heard him, she didn't bother answering.

Lulu named the parakeet Sacajawea. From sunup to sundown, the cheerful bird sang.

"My project is going well." Al had returned from the regional meeting convinced he could play a crucial role in the upcoming electrification of the burgeoning city.

"That's nice," Lulu said. She barely looked up when he told her. The suffragettes, she explained, were preparing brochures they would distribute on street corners downtown the following day.

In large black letters, she wrote:

WOMEN HAVE FULL SUFFRAGE IN: Australia, Norway, the Isle of Man, New Zealand, Finland, and Tasmania.

"By the way, I've invited some of my friends over this evening."

"I've come up with a layman's explanation of my work. Maybe I can try it out on them."

"Not now, sweetheart. I want to get this wording right." That evening, she would prove that "at home" did not mean without vocation. "I really don't think these ladies will be interested."

"In that case, I might be home late," Al said. "Things are hectic at the office. Enjoy your little get-together." He kissed the top of her head. "Nice," he said, tapping the copy.

She added:

WHY NOT OREGON?

That night, in their small, cluttered living room, a dozen women Lulu had met at the NAWSA meetings spoke freely of their aspirations outside the constraints of the national organization.

"We need to build a coalition," Lulu advocated, pouring beer as well as tea. "Appeal to the masses through advertisements, leaflets, and theater presentations."

In the days that followed, Lulu reached out to the artists she had met at the exposition. When she handed out her brochures, she engaged men and women and asked them to attend her soirees. She assiduously rounded up like-minded people she met in coffee shops and the public library. The gatherings that resulted were a motley bunch, but what they lacked in style, they made up for in enthusiasm. Night after night, her guests made themselves at home on her couch and on the floor, surrounded by brochures planning the next demonstration.

"We must appeal," she said, "to women working without salaries, to women employed on the family farm, to wage earners in the professions, and to wives and mothers everywhere. We must work with men," she smiled at a poet with a dark beard and mustache, "and with senators, merchants, and mechanics."

Unlike Duniway, whose speech had been so impressive at the expo but relied on dogmatic rhetoric, Lulu argued that women of wealth or in prominent positions should not be the only ones fighting the battle for women's equality, despite their having the means to underwrite the campaign.

Al returned from the office long after the sun had set. He had to pick his way through brochures stacked and stored away in boxes for the next day's distribution. Animated women and men filled their small apartment, smoking and interrupting one another. Lulu ignored Al's late arrival; her eyes ablaze as she proclaimed the need for independence.

"Don't mind if I do," her artists said, accepting another bottle of beer as Al tossed and turned in bed, envisioning his next invention. While the suffragettes puffed on cigarettes, he covered his head with a pillow.

Despite her appeal for inclusion, Lulu knew these intellectuals, painters, and newspaper reporters who now gathered around her held little interest for her engineer husband.

"It's like living in a beehive and you're the queen bee," he said to her in the morning. "But it's good to see that sparkle back in your eye."

"You're a love," Lulu said. She hadn't prepared him breakfast but placed a box of day-old pastries on the kitchen table. Her husband didn't complain. She owed him that much.

Day after day, strangers arrived with offerings in hand. Soon, trays of foreign foods littered the apartment; exotic aromas filled the uncleaned kitchen. For breakfast, she left croissants and leftovers, smelly cheeses, and rich, aromatic coffee on the sticky kitchen table.

Al worked late at the office more often. Lulu seldom stirred until long after he'd left for work, briefcase in hand. Through it all, the parakeet sang in her cage, flapping her wings. Sacajawea never got the chance to stretch them out. Lulu totally forgot her intention of giving the bird the chance to fly.

* * *

Al arrived home, soaked to the skin by the never-ending rain and bleary-eyed from a long day reading schematics. The kitchen light was on, but Lulu was nowhere to be found. Dirty dishes filled the sink. Outside the apartment's window, he could hear the steady beat of rain, but, over the mountain of bowls and plates, he couldn't see the clouds in the sky.

He shed his wet coat and cleared a spot on the cluttered table for his briefcase. Only by chance, he discovered her note. "Rally downtown. Hope to be back by eight."

Of course, Lulu hadn't bothered to prepare any dinner for him. He should have stopped at the delicatessen on the corner on his way home, but he hadn't thought of it. He rooted through the exotic leftovers in the icebox, avoiding anything he could not identify, and finally settled on a piece of not too stinky cheese. *It would have to do.*

Damn it. What was the point of being married when you didn't even share your life with your wife? These days, they were like strangers passing each other on the street. At least there would be no salon that night. On the days Lulu marched with her suffragettes, she abandoned her role as hostess.

Al toasted a piece of bread and spread on the cheese. Then he rinsed off the dishes. He missed the days when they had shared everything. He tried to imagine how Lulu, no longer a student and unemployed, spent her days. *Certainly not as a housewife. She neither cleaned nor cooked.* He supposed she had no better idea of how he spent his days. *When was the last time she had asked him about his work?* He was mulling this over and drying the last plate when Lulu breezed in.

"You're home early," she said.

"Hardly."

"What time is it?"

"Almost nine. Have you eaten?"

"Enough." Lulu hung up her raincoat, oblivious to the pool of water that quickly accumulated on the floor below it, and gave him a perfunctory hug. "My nose tells me you ate up the limburger cheese for dinner."

"It was all I could find." He waited for Lulu to register the clean dishes in the drainer.

"I'm sorry. I had no idea I would be so late."

Not really an apology. Did she even care? At least she was home now, and he had her attention.

He considered asking her about her day, but he knew he would get an earful. He wouldn't have minded, if only she would then ask about his. But it wouldn't occur to her, he knew that by now. Even unemployed, his wife was a whirlwind of activity, but those activities did not include him.

"Lulu, can we talk?"

She raised her eyebrows, curious but not concerned. He plunged in before the clutter on the table could distract her.

"Why don't you come by the office for lunch tomorrow? My colleagues have never had the chance to meet you." He followed her into the bedroom and watched as she folded her blouse and skirt. She didn't turn around until she had covered herself with a long robe, cinched around her slender waist.

Lulu frowned. "It's a long trolley ride across town."

"I know, but I make the trip every day. I'll make it worth your while," he wheedled, keeping his tone playful. "The project we're working on these days is revolutionary. Any day now, partly due to our efforts, electricity will light up the entire city. It's been a while since I've had a chance to share my work with you."

He kept things simple. He debated explaining to her that alternating current technology would soon allow his company to link small, competing companies in a unified power grid, but decided to keep it light, not wanting to give away how much her support would mean to him. Nor did he tell her that he would be delighted to show her off to his coworkers.

"I have wondered how on earth you spend your days." Lulu picked up the box of brochures piled on the table, and he held his breath. "I'll drop these off at the Methodist Church in the morning and let the ladies know I'll be unavailable for the rest of the day. Shall I meet you for lunch?"

"That would be great. I'll give you the grand tour."

Late the next morning, Lulu strolled into his office, preceded by Nora, the office secretary, who opened the door for her, a dramatic entrance for his beautiful wife. Al stood there, beaming, as Lulu introduced herself to his coworkers. She shook their hands and asked Timothy the origins of his Lithuanian surname. She allowed Leo to explain, in agonizing detail, his role in the undertaking. The men were awed, and Al couldn't help but appreciate Lulu's display of the social skills she had mastered winning over her poets and lady friends to the cause of women's suffrage. Al ceded the spotlight, content to be in her shadow, optimistic that after meeting his colleagues, Lulu would show more interest in his career.

He should have known better.

After the "grand tour," he had taken her hand as they left the office, grateful that she had made the effort. The sun had come out and danced in the puddles, and he relived the animated conversations between Lulu and his coworkers as they hopped over them. *Timothy, usually so shy and withdrawn, had become almost verbose under her attention. Leo hadn't taken his eyes off her all afternoon. How satisfying it had been to walk through the office with her at his side.* It seemed only right that the sun had decided to emerge from the clouds that afternoon.

The trolley was idling at the stop, and he leapt aboard still holding her hand. They took a seat at the rear of the car. When the bell clanged, Lulu sighed and removed her hand from his.

"What a dark, dreary office," Lulu muttered to herself, but she might as well have yelled.

"Lulu, what did you say?" He held out hope that he had misheard her.

"I don't know how you can bear to spend so much time in such stale and dusty air."

And like that, the sun ducked behind a cloud. The warm glow that had warmed Al all afternoon dissipated. He clasped his hands so hard the blood ran out of his fingers.

"And those men... I scarcely understood a word they said. If the project you are all working on is so significant, you would think they would learn how to talk about it."

"Are you through?" He knew he sounded surly, but she might as well have stabbed him in the heart. *What was she thinking? Was Lulu oblivious to the cruelty in her words?*

"Oh Al, I didn't mean to hurt your feelings," Lulu said, as if her apology could take the sting out. "It's just I can't imagine a more depressing place. One window for fifteen men? No wonder you talk about light incessantly."

Every time the trolley stopped, he considered jumping out.

One block. Two blocks. They made their way through the dusky darkness. He glared out the window, watching the crowds jostling at the street corner, everyone out for themselves. *The worst of it was being misunderstood. He had only wanted to share his passion.* He chose his words carefully.

"Lulu, it's not like you to be so shortsighted." He struggled to keep his voice even, but the trembling gave him away. "The work these men are doing will change life in the city as you know it. They are some of those most brilliant fellows I've ever known."

"Oh, I'm sure they are." But obviously, that didn't impress her.

"Your lack of perspective floors me." The heat of his anger flared up again. "Do you know how superficial you sound?" *He had put up with her artists and suffragettes. He lived like a stranger in his own apartment and what did he get in return? Even after an afternoon in his world, she refused to acknowledge his accomplishments.* He pounded his clenched fist on the trolley window, his jaw clamped. The driver turned around with a look of alarm.

Lulu waved the driver away with an apologetic smile. She turned back to Al. "I didn't mean to hurt your feelings."

"Those 'sad little men' are my friends, Lulu. And they're every bit as brilliant as the characters you drag home night after night."

"I know. I'm sorry Al. I've been unkind. Please forgive me."

For the rest of the ride, they sat staring out the trolley's rain-streaked windows. When a sharp turn caused Lulu to slide onto Al's lap, she asked him to describe alternative current, and Al, lighter for having blown off some steam, explained the function of the power grid. "We're almost there. When they finish installing the wiring, everything will be connected," Al said.

"I am proud of the work you are doing," Lulu said. "But when those men look at me, all they see is a wife. It makes me cranky. I didn't mean to take it out on you."

Al put his arm around her. "When those men look at you, they see a beautiful and accomplished woman."

She rested her head on his shoulder. "You're a dear. Thank you for putting up with me. I suppose I have been awfully self-absorbed of late, but I so want to do something of value."

"And that, my dear, is a goal we share. Something that should bring us together, not tear us apart."

But by the time Al came home the next day, a new mountain of dirty dishes filled the sink, resembling a volcano on the verge of an explosion.

"The guys asked about you today," Al said, balancing his dinner plate on a pile of envelopes.

Lulu smiled, but her attention was elsewhere.

Al sighed, carrying his dirty plate to the sink. He returned to the table and spread open the newspaper.

"Honey, can I ask you a favor?" Lulu pulled down the paper so he could see her face. "The Suffrage Special is going to arrive at King Street Station in Seattle this weekend. There are two hundred fifty leaders of the National Organization of Woman Suffragettes on board. I'd really like to be there to greet them."

"There's no way I can get away this weekend."

"Oh, that's not a problem. I'm fine travelling on my own." She disappeared into the bedroom and reemerged with her bag, already packed. As she spoke, she attached a bright red ribbon to her wide-brimmed hat.

Al looked up from his paper. This wasn't a request.

"Darling, are you sure this is wise? Why just the other day, hooligans murdered a woman on the streets of Everett. See here," he pointed at an article on the front page, hoping he could slow her down. "Hecklers threw rocks at her as well as her compatriots."

"I read the paper too," Lulu said. "But I refuse to be afraid."

"And I suppose you don't have the time to clean up this mess before you leave?" He gestured at the dirty dishes.

"The only train I could book leaves in an hour. Let it be for now. I promise that when I return, I'll be a better wife. In the meantime, I'd love it if you could accompany me to the train station. It would give us some time together."

Al sighed but put on his hat.

They strolled the last blocks to the station. Lulu told him she had stayed up all night, completing an application for a state teaching certificate. "After visiting your office, I've decided it's about time I get serious about a career," she said.

While not the result he had intended, at least her visit to the office had inspired that much. As she disappeared into the train, Al followed her progress down the aisle. Lulu was easy to spot among the passengers, her hat and red ribbon held high on a head filled with new resolve.

From that day forward, Al kept his work life and home life separate. When, in early 1907, Portland Light and Electric announced a merger with the railroad, he kept the news to himself. The merger, which provided access to capital and the promise of improved service, would be of no interest to Lulu. He simply told her he would be working late for the next few months. She nodded and told him dinner would be ready when he got home, whatever the hour.

She was trying, he could see that. After the disastrous visit to his office, she had stocked their pantry and, with Kitty's help, restored some order to the kitchen. Kitty hung cheery curtains in the kitchen window, and the parakeet's cage was clean more often than not, though whether Lulu cleaned it, or her mother did, Al was never sure. At least now when he opened the apartment door, he did not have to brace himself for what he might discover. And since the merger, he was busier than ever. By the time he got home, he was content to eat Lulu's cold leftovers and grab a good night's sleep, easier now that Lulu had agreed to limit her salons to once a week.

So, when Nora approached his desk and told him Parker Morey wanted to see him, Al didn't bother to leave a message telling Lulu he would be delayed. Instead, he followed the secretary to his boss's office, his heart pounding with equal parts apprehension and excitement. He entered the paneled office and took a seat across from the president of the new conglomerate, a quiet, white-haired man who wielded his power from behind closed doors. Al waited while Morey shuffled through a pile of official-looking papers, carefully restraining his foot, which badly wanted to jiggle. When Morey looked up, he cleared his throat and then, in a matter-of-fact manner, asked Al if he was ready for a challenge.

"Always," Al said.

"We're thinking of putting put you in charge of developing the Faraday Powerhouse on the Clackamas River. And if you're interested, we'd like you to oversee the new interurban line from Portland to Estacada. Do you think you could handle these projects?"

"Yes, sir. I am ready for the challenge." Al wished he could leap from the chair. Do a little jig. Given the opportunity, he would have demonstrated the dance steps his brother had taught him. *Holy cow! They were offering him a promotion and a significant raise.*

But he simple nodded, and the two men shook hands. "Superb," Morey said. "We'll get back to you with the details."

Al didn't stop to discuss the news with his colleagues. He grabbed his briefcase and hurried home, like a magnet drawn to metal. Now Lulu would see the payoff for all his hard work. Hell, his father might even appreciate the important role the company had offered. But when he swung open the front door, Lulu was out once again. *Undoubtedly planning another demonstration with the suffragettes,* he thought. *Why couldn't she have been here, if only today?*

Sacajawea showed no interest in his news, so he poured himself a glass of water and sat down at the kitchen table with a piece of paper and a pen. He would write a letter to his parents and share his good news.

"Today, PLE offered me a management position," he started writing, and then sat with the pen in his hand. No matter how many times he searched for words to describe the opportunity he had been offered, he failed. He could only come up with hackneyed phrases like "honor" and "responsibility," which his father already owned. Over and over, he crossed out bumbling attempts. Finally, in frustration, he pushed the paper aside. *No one cared. Not his father. These days, not even Lulu, who had always been his staunchest defender. Who had he been kidding? No matter how grand his accomplishments, in their eyes he would always be an engineer, an uninteresting man whose passions they did not appreciate or even understand.*

It was midnight before Lulu flung open the door and made her grand announcement. "Sorry I'm so late. We had envelopes that needed addressing. But that isn't my news. Al, I found a job today!"

* * *

Lulu had answered an advertisement for an editor of a magazine called the *Bonville's Western Monthly*. "The publisher responded almost immediately," she told Al. "Finally, somebody was willing to consider a woman for a publishing position. At least, that was a start."

More than a start. By the end of the day, she had a job.

She had been interviewed by Frank Bonville himself that very morning at his office in the Marquam Building downtown. The building, an impressive eight-story brick, sandstone, and terra-cotta Romanesque Revival building, was right in the center of things.

As she had entered the ornate lobby, she had been a bundle of nerves, patting her hair and checked the pins in her hat. When she left, she was an editor.

"Have you heard of my 'Ninety-Nine-Year System'?" Bonville asked before she even sat down. "A square deal that promises unlimited success. My lectures sell out in days." The burly man rested his elbows on his desk, his shirtsleeves smudgy with ink. He interlaced his chunky fingers and balanced his double chin on the hassock of his hands.

Five minutes into the meeting, she determined that the magazine, like Bonville's system, didn't exist. This guy was one slick operator.

Roy, she thought, would love him.

"Also," Bonville said, "I'm launching a magazine."

He read her resume as she sat in front of him. "Hmm," he said. She circled her ankle. "A university gal. Classy." His idea for a magazine seemed sound. A monthly periodical promoting the West. They would distribute it to hotels up and down the West Coast. The money would come from the advertising.

Despite the small office, Bonville pointed out that the Marquam Building was Portland's first skyscraper, every bit a modern office building, next door to the Marquam Grand Opera House. The man had plans.

"I'm looking for good English. Somebody steady."

"I'm your gal," she replied, thinking maybe she had a chance. He hired her on the spot, even before they discussed salary.

Bonville bragged he had already sold an ad to Frederick Kribs' Pacific Coast Timber Lands.

"There are greater profits to be made in magazine publishing than in any other legitimate business in America. Advertisers spend seventy-five million dollars every year on advertising space and copies of American magazines."

All Lulu needed to do was nod in agreement.

"Take *Munsey's*," he said. "Why, its yearly revenue is about one million, six hundred thousand dollars. *Bonville's Western Monthly* may yet be a figment of my imagination, but I intend for it to win a place among the great publications of our country. The day is not far distant when Bonville's will rival *Everybody's* and *Munsey's*."

It wasn't the prospect of prosperity that excited Lulu. The lure for her was Bonville's statement that he "would leave the literary crap to you." He suggested a few engaging travelogues, some high-brow fiction, drawings, and poetry. "Catchy stuff that'll keep 'em reading." She assured him she would not disappoint him.

Editor, now wasn't that something? He was leaving it up to her.

"I'm offering you the opportunity of a lifetime," Bonville said, exhaling a plume of blue smoke.

"And you won't regret it," Lulu said.

"We are looking for investors." His eyes narrowed. "To secure the funds to carry on our extensive business, we are offering stock to the public at such liberal rates anyone can make a safe and profitable investment." He examined her fingers, which she had crossed in her lap. She saw him register the modest gold ring. "Perhaps your husband would be interested?"

Lulu, already laying out the magazine in her mind, realized he expected a response when he cleared his throat.

"My husband is a lowly engineer," she said, putting on her most engaging smile. "Every dollar he earns is spoken for, but I will convey your offer to him."

Bonville snorted. "This opportunity may never come again."

"And I look forward to assisting you in publishing a magazine that will make us both proud." Lulu extended her hand, hoping for a businesslike shake but instead enduring a slimy kiss on the knuckles.

* * *

On her first day on the job, Lulu drafted a classified ad for the Portland papers. It read:

"Bonville's Western Monthly magazine is in the market for short and serial stories for which it will pay fair rates. Though a new publication, it is one of promise. Its editor seeks literary works by men and women who will shape the modern world's thinking."

Before long, the tiny desk in the corner of the office that Frank Bonville had assigned to Lulu was piled high with poems, essays, and other submissions. Mr. Bonville was frequently out of the office, speaking to civic groups about his Ninety-Nine-Year System and drumming up funds for his publishing company.

Lulu familiarized herself with the magazines that her boss cited in his pitch, reading late into the night long after Al was snoring at her side. She wanted to put together a publication with articles for everyone: Western-oriented literature that would show Oregon at its finest with a table of contents that included both male and female authors—established writers and talented young people. In the smoke-filled office, she read everything she received: verses, medical treatises, stories, and spiritualistic tracts. Political analysis and contemporary history. Sports, of course, and comics. No matter how many manuscripts she received, she wasn't satisfied. The submissions lacked the quality needed to produce a credible literary magazine. She sorted through the mail, concerned that she might have gotten in over her head.

Every morning Al and Lulu left the apartment together, briefcases in hand. "You wouldn't believe the garbage I receive," Lulu told Al as they headed for the trolley. Or he chatted about the electric company, and she deprecated the poor grammar of contemporary writers.

"You'll sort it all out. I'm confident you'll put together a magazine that exceeds your publisher's expectations." If his wife was happy, Al was happy.

"But there's just not a lot of excellent writing out there."

"Have you thought about contacting some of your suffragette friends? You've always praised their rhetoric so highly."

Lulu thanked him for his suggestion and asked what time he would be home for supper. Their life finally settled into a pleasing rhythm, as busy as the city streets, and as productive.

If only she could find a source for the quality literature the magazine required.

Preoccupied with her new job, Lulu entertained less. She seldom had time to go to the rousing speeches of her friends. They were still waging a vigorous campaign to pass a bill granting women the right to vote. NAWSA had contributed $18,000 to the effort, and President Anna Howard Shaw and other national organizers were in Oregon for the campaign. When Clara Colby came to Portland to publish her *Woman's Tribune*, a weekly national suffrage newspaper, Lulu attended the speech, but now she saw the woman through a new lens. She had dreams of publishing her own newspaper once she honed her skills. There would always be battles to fight. But right now, she had more pressing matters on her mind.

One May morning, two months after he hired her, Bonville announced he had raised enough money to publish by summer. He had a couple of hot leads. One hundred pages, say? He used *Munsey's* as his model for everything; he did not know how to publish a magazine.

One hundred pages by summer? Lulu panicked. She needed content, and she needed it now.

"Congratulations, dear." On the other end of the telephone line, Clarissa Carson granted the benediction she had not given when Lulu informed her Al and she had wed. "An editorship, quite an accomplishment."

"Thank you, Clarissa. Coming from you, that is high praise."

In a late-night moment of inspiration, Lulu had decided to take advantage of her university connections. The next morning, she placed a call to the dean.

"I always knew you had it in you." The dean's voice was warm.

"How are things in the English department?" Lulu asked.

"Humming along. I've nominated three women this year for instructor positions. I'm determined not to let Professor Staub get my goat."

"Bully for you. I hope the lucky ladies aren't planning to marry."

"One day, that will change," Clarissa said. "But I'm delighted to hear you have landed on your feet."

"I do hope so, but there is a reason for my call. I've never put a magazine together before. I was hoping you could provide me with some guidance. I know you maintain contact with many of your students after they graduate. By any chance, would any of them have manuscripts they want to publish? I desperately need some quality material for the magazine."

"I'd be happy to help out in any way I can," Carson said. "Let me see what I can do."

"What about your current students? I'd love to use the magazine as a vehicle for talented young writers." How lovely it was to speak with Clarissa as a peer! "Maybe you would consider contributing a piece yourself; perhaps something on the poets of Oregon?"

"Have you spoken to Roy Bacon?" Clarissa asked. "He's doing a magnificent job with the literary magazine. He'd know which students are writing publishable work. And his experience might be of use to you."

Lulu dismissed the recommendation, not ready to stir up *that* beehive, but the dean's support invigorated her. Submissions continued to pour in. A few of them, though not many, were closer to her requirements. The piles on her desk grew as the days passed and her deadline neared.

If only she had a clue how to convert the pile of manuscripts into a magazine. When he was in town, Bonville observed her work with increasing concern.

"Tick, tock, Mrs. Bartlett," he said, tapping his watch. His laugh was less than convincing. She assured him her work was going grand. Then one pile of manuscripts toppled to the floor, the numbered pages shuffling like a deck of cards. As Lulu fell to her knees, scooping them up under Mr. Bonville's skeptical gaze, she could no longer deny she needed help.

Remembering Clarissa Carson's recommendation, she telephoned Roy, who, according to Vesta, was dawdling through the second of his senior years. What harm was there in reaching out to an old friend? As soon as Roy recognized her voice, Lulu spilled everything. Told him about the magazine she was editing and the opportunity it afforded, if only she could put together a superior product.

"One of your poems would be perfect for the maiden issue. A majestic ode to the grandeur of eastern Oregon?"

Roy, talking from the hall phone of the university dormitory, did not reply immediately.

"I haven't been writing much," he said at last. "My land deals require frequent travel to eastern Oregon."

Vesta had mentioned that Roy had multiple irons in the fire, to Annabelle's consternation.

"Aren't we the harried professionals?" Lulu laughed. "Certainly, you could find time for a worthy undertaking?"

He didn't respond.

"It's not just the poetry. You could run an ad in our magazine. I'd do it for free," she coaxed, surprised at how much she wanted him to agree to help her out. "Mr. Bonville has sold subscriptions to eleven hotels, up and down the coast. Think of the exposure that would give your land business."

That got his attention.

"I would like to see my poetry in print," he said, his tone warmer now.

"And I desperately need your expertise. When we worked together on the school magazine, you made laying out the magazine seem so easy. I haven't a clue how to pull this thing together."

They agreed to meet on Friday, in front of the Marquam Grand Opera House. Roy offered to review what she had so far and collect contributions from his classmates in the meantime. As Lulu hung up the phone, she let out a sigh of relief. She needed another set of eyes. Someone who knew what they were doing.

Chapter 9 The Conflagration

Al slid the ivory envelope across the table. "Another letter from Eugene," he said, his tone measured. His face was like a flag signaling caution. "But this time, it's not from my brother."

Lulu examined the envelope. The stationery was of the highest quality, the paper the color of fine linen. The return address, written in elegant calligraphy, was that of the Judge and Mrs. Bartlett.

Now what? Whatever was inside, the timing couldn't be worse.

She studied Al's face, but he gave nothing away. She slid open the envelope and extracted a formal invitation.

> *The Honorable Judge Robert S. Bartlett*
> *and his wife*
> *request the honor of your presence at a reception in honor of the*
> *marriage of*
> *their son, Alton R. Bartlett*
> *April 22, 1906, at 2 p.m.*

The party would take place at the Bartlett's home during the university's Easter holiday. In an accompanying handwritten note, Cornelia explained the intimate gathering would be a tasteful get-together as befit the son of the Chief Justice of the Oregon Supreme Court. "We've realized that, as the judge's reputation grows," his mother wrote, "his legacy by all rights should include his bright and industrious issue."

Lulu set down the envelope. Blood pulsed in her temples. Al scrutinized her every move, as if she were a zoo animal and he the keeper responsible for taming her.

"His bright and industrious issue? I suppose by that she means you?"

Al didn't answer. Instead, his eyes pleaded with hers.

He might as well have been holding her back with a raised chair. At least a tiger in a zoo could express its dissatisfaction. When a caged animal roared, spectators applauded.

"And I suppose I shouldn't take offense at the omission of my name? I see Cornelia is equally nameless."

"Darling, don't you see? It's an overture." Al spoke calmly, as if in doing so he could set the tone of their conversation. "As close to an apology as we'll ever receive. Mother is trying to make us feel welcome."

"This isn't an invitation, it's a summons." Lulu paced the dining room floor, unable to sit still as her fury grew. "We weren't even consulted before the invitation was mailed!"

"They are offering to accept you into the family at last." Al removed his glasses, polishing the lenses as he defended his parents' request.

"I, for one, refuse to be a part of this sham. Your parents didn't bother to acknowledge our marriage after Dr. Staub fired me. Now they expect us to come running when they call?" Lulu held up her hands, her fingers tense, nails ready to scratch.

"Take some time, think it over. I really do believe they mean well. I would appreciate it if you would consider attending. You would not be doing it for them. You would be doing it for me."

"I can't believe you even ask." Lulu walked over to the kitchen window and looked down at the teeming city below. "We have our own lives to consider. I have no interest in becoming a footnote in your father's legacy."

When she turned to face him, Al put his glasses back on as if hoping to see her more clearly.

But Lulu wasn't done. "I have a career now, as do you. I can't just drop everything to appear in a familial tableau." She picked up the pen that was never far from her hands and held it up like a weapon. "I refuse to be chattel owned by your illustrious family." She spat out "chattel," delivered "illustrious" with scorn.

"Just this once, darling. Just this once. For me." In response to Lulu's tirade, Al's face transformed into that of a child's quivering before an angry parent.

But didn't he understand? A keeper who allows a lion to sense his fear risks being attacked.

Lulu glared at him, daring him to repeat "For me." Disturbed by their argument, the green and yellow parakeet shrieked in the sunshine of their kitchen window. Lulu swept up her briefcase and stormed out of the room.

She landed briefly at her desk, but the tornado of her emotions made it impossible to sit still.

She stood up, knocking the chair to the floor. Tears she wasn't about to let him see ran down her cheeks. She brushed them away and pivoted back to the door of the kitchen, where she braced herself against the doorframe.

"If you make me go," she said, "I will never forgive you."

Al wouldn't let it go. Night after night, they argued. He pleaded. She ignored him. He sulked. She told him he was better than that.

Kitty finally put an end to it. "Go, darling," she said. "He is you husband. They are your family now."

Lulu's father sent a note expressing his displeasure. "The Judge's invitation is an honor. Please respect your wifely duties. It's bad enough that you have disappointed me, but I refuse to let you break your mother's heart and humiliate your husband. We raised your better." Her parents planned to attend the reception in Eugene, and they expected her to be there.

Lulu had no trouble standing up to Al, but her father had never questioned her choices before. His stern words stung. At least her mother didn't suggest she wear the bridal suit still hanging in her bedchamber's closet. She'd do this, but there would be a price.

"I hope your grandfather will be there. He is the only person in your family I look forward to seeing."

They traveled with her parents to Eugene. Al's parents welcomed them, if somewhat icily, as a maid took their coats at the front door. The judge explained, in his inimitable pedagogic style, that a few carefully chosen faculty members would attend, eager to meet Al's "new" wife. His brothers greeted them with apologetic smiles. Robert explained he had taken the rare break from his responsibilities at the hospital. Ernest fought to keep the smirk on his face under control.

Before the guests arrived, the entire family was to sit for a portrait to commemorate the occasion. As a hired photographer fiddled with his equipment, the judge posed in front of the oak wainscoting of the parlor, his expression serious, his mouth framed by a drooping walrus mustache, his bald pate shiny. He wore a white vest and dark suit. He instructed Cornelia to stand to the right of him, which she did, her back ramrod straight and her head held high. The photographer suggested the three sons squeeze in around their parents. Lulu noted that all three sons wore matching dark suits and wondered if they had coordinated their attire. Their ties matched the judge's. Each had parted their hair down the center. They stood woodenly at their father's side, their mouths expressionless straight lines. Only when she examined them closer did she spot the differences between them—Robert's scowl of concentration, the cleft in Ernest's chin.

Lulu lingered at the edge of the room, waiting for the family to ask her to join them. But, satisfied with their position, the photographer covered his head with a black cloth and squinted through his camera's lens. Then there was a puff of flash powder, and with a flourish, he announced he was done. This portrait, which would finally, formally, recognize Al and Lulu's marriage, did not include her. Lulu fumed, watching from the sidelines as the judge begrudgingly declared his oldest son's "new" status as a married man.

Her mother tiptoed her way around the room, careful to attract no attention, and placed a cautionary hand on Lulu's arm. Her father pulled his stopwatch out of his pocket and pretended to check the time. Their expressions warned her now was not the time.

Lulu searched the attendees, looking for Al's benevolent grandfather and his long white beard. "I'm looking forward to meeting Professor Scott again," she whispered to Cornelia as they formed a reception line in the front hallway.

"Unfortunately, my father will not be in attendance. The judge and I wanted an intimate gathering and so invited only immediate family and the judge's closest colleagues."

An intimate gathering? Lulu watched the judge greet the guests as they arrived. What he wanted was the limelight.

Lulu shook off the snub, determined to maintain her dignity. Holding her head high, she greeted the arriving guests, introducing herself because neither the judge nor Al did so. She flirted and bamboozled the judge's colleagues. The trill of her laughter filled the Bartletts' parlor as the guests gathered around the crystal punch bowl. She discussed the upcoming elections with the politicians and smiled graciously at her father when he joined them. She looked blushing professors in the eye, daring them to bring up the past. While the judge discussed the finer points of his judicial philosophy with those who aspired to be his peers, she drank champagne and accepted toasts to the union. "Don't mind if I do," she chirped as the elderly guests vied for her attention, winking at Al, who had heard the line many times before in their Portland living room.

The judge's mouth pursed every time she entered the room. She ignored him, choosing instead to entertain Al's brothers, recounting the fiery speeches of her favorite suffragettes. She found them a willing audience. Cornelia watched her warily, stepping lightly around the fraying carpet of their family.

But as the guests began to thin out, Lulu found herself alone in the library with Al's mother. "Did you hear?" the nervous woman asked, "Johns Hopkins Medical School accepted Robert into their residency program. It is a quite an honor." Cornelia pulled a few cherished albums of family clippings from the shelves, each one labeled and dated. Lulu flipped through the albums. Cornelia had documented every aspect of her husband's career, underlining

147

passages that described Bartlett as honest and steadfast in purpose. "The judge works late every night honing his judicial opinion. I worry about his eyes," she said. Lulu supposed she wanted sympathy.

Lulu closed the album and planned her escape.

"And your father? I hope he is in good health?"

Cornelia looked at her blankly. Her father, apparently, was not included in her script.

"Welcome to the family, my dear," Cornelia said at last. The entreaty in her eyes mirrored the expression Al had adopted ever since they had received his parents' invitation.

"I don't pretend to understand Al's choice of vocation, but my father assures me he has every chance of success."

"Well, there you are," Lulu said. "Professor Scott's encouragement of Al's career meant a lot to him. Your father is a magnanimous man."

This time, Cornelia's face registered Lulu's discontent.

"Dear, I hope you appreciate the important role a wife plays in supporting her husband." She hesitated, as jumpy as Sacajawea on her perch.

"Please excuse me," Lulu said. If she heard one more word about the judge, she was certain she would explode.

Al had retreated into the parlor, shielded from his father's colleagues by his amiable brothers.

"Ah, the bright and industrious issue," Lulu said, taking him by the arm.

Ernest chuckled, and Robert bowed. "I believe you've married a firecracker, brother. Lulu will be an inspiration to your children." Perhaps the physician-to-be meant this as a compliment, but Lulu didn't appreciate his comment. She and Al had never discussed children. It was a subject she avoided, certain they would never agree. She tugged at Al's tie, winked at his brother, and then pulled her blushing husband in closer. "Get me out of here," she said, "or I will make a scene."

If he had said "Pay him no mind," she might have believed Al loved her more than his family.

If he had said "Feel free," she might have laughed and rejoined the party. Flirted a little longer with the elderly lawyers.

If he had introduced her as a writer or editor, she might have discussed poetry with the professors.

But he had not refused to have his picture taken without her by his side.

That omission said it all. She had arrived in a fit of pique, but she left with an icy resolve. She would not let her marriage to Al determine her fate.

Al fetched their coats, explaining to his parents that they had a train to catch. Her father, who had finally made his way to the judge's side, didn't notice when the two of them slipped out the front door. Her mother probably did, but Lulu couldn't have cared less.

On the train ride home, Al showed her an advanced copy of the article that his mother had submitted to the *Morning Register*. The brief item, undoubtedly dictated by the judge, stated that the groom had been the manager of the university's indoor baseball team. The article mentioned neither Al's position with the electric company nor Lulu's graduation from the university. As always, his father's reputation took precedence over his son's identity.

"Can you believe it?" Having survived the reception, Al was more relaxed that he had been in weeks.

"What did you expect?"

"They staged the entire event just to produce another article for my mother's collection," Al said.

"You gave her the opening," Lulu snapped. "You have only yourself to blame."

* * *

Lulu returned to Portland prepared to throw herself into her job. Instead, the first task Mr. Bonville gave her was to place an ad in the *St. John's Review* informing the public that he was putting his lecture series on hold. The copy read:

"Mr. Bonville's proposed lecture tour, scheduled to begin the first of the coming year and to extend from Portland to the Atlantic Coast, is postponed. Matters of importance connected with the

Ninety-Nine-Year System make it expedient for him to remain in Portland."

"The magazine is my priority," he told Lulu, looking over her shoulder as she dusted cigar ash off a stack of submissions, afraid it would go up in smoke. "How soon will you be ready?"

Lulu was unclear what matters of importance caused him to cancel the scheduled lecture series. In fact, she never had quite figured out what comprised his Ninety-Nine-Year System. But whatever had changed, it put him in a foul mood.

His breath was rancid. He hung over her. His shadow made it impossible to read. When he asked her again when he would see the final proofs, she assured him she had it under control. "I've asked a talented editor from Eugene to help me out," she said.

Roy arrived just in time. Not only was he able to help her assemble an impressive selection of material for publication, but his presence in the office kept Bonville at bay. The two men took to each other at first sight. As she edited copy, Roy and Bonville discussed the Ninety-Nine-Year System. Roy described the lucrative land deals he had offered to inexperienced East Coast investors who did not know how lucky they were. Each was sure their deal was better than the other's, but even so, Bonville offered Roy a discount rate to run multiple ads in the first edition of the *Bonville's Western Monthly.* The very next day, Roy handed Lulu an ad for Calumet-Buena Vista Mines:

"TO THE INVESTING PUBLIC!

The first block of this stock is now being offered for the sum of 5 cents per share. This stock soon will be worth many dollars per share.

A few dollars invested in this company may return thousands!!!"

"I thought you were selling land," she said.

"That too," Roy answered.

With more time, perhaps she might have questioned him further, but Bonville put a calendar on the wall, counting down the number of days until the manuscript had to be at the printers. He offered to put Roy up in a local hotel, but Roy, determined to graduate at last, agreed to travel to Portland once a week to help with the magazine.

If they completed the manuscript by June, they could publish by July. Bonville told her he had promised the investors copies would go on sale by July 1. This was the first she heard of his promise.

Lulu knew she should tell Al that Roy was in Portland. She knew she ought to keep things aboveboard, but, like her, Al spent most of his evenings at the office. When he did come home, his mind was on the electric company. There never seemed a right moment to tell him that Roy's contribution was crucial and strictly professional.

After an evening with Roy, going home to Al was a letdown. Her husband seemed as washed-out as his fellow engineers, a cog in a well-oiled machine, happy to perform the same routine work day after day. How much she missed the spark of Roy's inspiration, the energy that filled a room when he entered.

"What are you reading?" she asked Al one night as they both put on their bed clothes.

"Nothing that interests you," Al answered. She supposed she deserved that. She had, after all, laughed when he tried to describe the Prony brake, unable to feign interest in his invention.

"What are you writing?" he asked. She covered her mouth, trying to put together a few well-chosen words that would satisfy Al's expectations. She could hardly expect him to understand the passion she and Roy invested in the magazine. Getting it out absorbed her every waking hour. Instead, she told him she was struggling to finish her own contribution, an essay titled "Personal Reminiscences of West Coast Poets," written under the pseudonym of W.W. Fisher, a necessary subterfuge to cover her lack of experience.

Telling Al about Roy required too much effort when her work at the magazine required every drop of energy she had. *I'll do it,* she thought, *as soon as the final proofs are on Bonville's desk. I'll do it when I can give Al the attention he deserves.*

Working with Roy, in contrast, was effortless. He could look at a manuscript and assess its value in no time. He loved poetry with all his heart and yet could talk business with the publisher while line editing at the same time. The University of Oregon's literary magazine had won three awards under his tutelage, and he wasn't shy about telling Bonville to butt out if he wanted comparable commendations for the new publication. Working together, the three of them performed like a flawless machine.

They made the deadline with three days to spare. The first edition of the *Bonville's Western Monthly* arrived from the printers in July 1908, one month after Roy had graduated at last. On the cover, a golden-haired beauty looked out sloe-eyed through long black lashes. Solemn and dignified, she wore a large-brimmed and feathered hat tilted to one side, revealing one ear and a jeweled earring. The photograph, Roy said, was a humdinger. Lulu thought it resembled Annabelle at her most glamorous.

* * *

Fifteen cents an issue. Paid-up subscriptions in every hotel in eleven states. Classified advertisements one dollar a month.

Frank Bonville was so pleased with the success of the first issue of the magazine that he offered Roy the position of general manager. Roy came up with the idea of offering a free pen with every new subscription. Bonville thought his idea brilliant.

Roy stepped up when they needed him. Lulu and Roy made the perfect editorial team. Lulu was as proud of the magazine's success as her fast-talking boss was. Surely Al would understand that. But she dreaded the day he saw Roy's name on the masthead.

She resolved to tell him before the second issue bearing his name as general manager appeared on newsstands. As soon as they completed the content for the second edition of the magazine. Bonville had promised a monthly magazine, and if they were going to meet that deadline, they needed to pick up the pace of their work. In the meantime, she told Al not to count on her for supper.

It was only a matter of time before Al discovered that she and Roy had become business partners. Vesta had sent her a note insisting that Al and Lulu simply must drop by before their baby arrived.

When Lulu called Vesta to tell her they could not get together until July, Vesta sighed. "I'll be as big as a house by then."

It would be just like Vesta to spill the beans.

"Poor Annabelle," Vesta said. "Did you hear? Roy's left her high and dry."

Lulu bit her tongue, filled with a sense of foreboding. Annabelle had caused all the hoopla last time around. If she was furious that Roy, before moving to Portland, had split with her for good, this was not a sentiment she would keep to herself.

Yes, she had better tell Al that she and Roy were colleagues. The sooner the better.

"I'll tell him Bonville hired you for your business acumen." She tested her explanation on Roy one evening as they sat amid a pile of manuscripts they had been editing. "That I had nothing to do with the decision."

"Yeah, I'm sure he'll buy that day-old fish. If there is one thing you can say about Al, it's that he's one smart cookie."

Roy's resilience amazed her. Over cold hot dogs, he confided that, after his collapse that night at the First Christian Church, the doctors diagnosed a breakdown. To wean him from the opioids, they prescribed a new regimen. He would never be free of the aches and pains from that long-ago explosion, and, from time to time, he craved relief from the headaches that resulted from the strain on his damaged eye. But whenever he felt himself fading, when he craved medication's power, they suggested he try a pinch of cocaine. It snapped everything right back into place.

"Vesta tells me you've broken it off with Annabelle."

"The girl is nice enough, sings like a songbird, and is easy on the eye, but..." Lulu, head filled with bad poetry, registered the change in his attitude toward Annabelle. How easily he dismissed her, as if they had been a couple of convenience. She was quite certain Annabelle did not see their relationship the same way.

This was the first time they discussed his "breakdown." His casual reference to the evening in the rectory surprised Lulu. They had never spoken about it. She admired his honesty. The fortitude required by his recovery seemed almost superhuman, and yet he talked about it with as little effort as Al rewired a flickering light.

Roy, she was learning, ran deep. She had never given him credit for that. The ease with which he excelled at so many things distracted her. For the first time (*was it the first time?*) since they'd started working together, Lulu noticed the taut energy of his body, the intensity of his attention. Lulu reread the poem in front of her, incapable of determining its value.

> *"Ah, what shall be the song of her*
> *Who rocks a babe upon her breast*
> *Unnamed, unblest."*

"Too dramatic?" she asked.

"Very Dickensian," he said. "People love babies."

She sighed. "I suppose. Do you?"

"Lord, no," he said. "There is too much I want to do in life to be tied down by a child."

"I couldn't agree more." They accepted the poem, but more importantly, he reaffirmed her world view. His ambition, her determination to succeed. There were days they hardly spoke, their decisions aligned so closely.

Roy, she knew, wanted more from life. He wanted sunsets and shooting stars, the images he captured so magnificently in his poetry.

He wanted a grand romance.

Didn't they all?

"At this rate, we'll be here until midnight," he said. "Al will think you have deserted him."

Roy didn't seem concerned at the prospect. They fell back into the rhythm of their work. Three piles: rejects, to be considered, and ta-da! Each had a final say on rejections and acceptances, but the "to be considered" pile they reconsidered together.

When that third pile dwindled, Roy sat back and closed his eyes.

"You're tired," she said. "These can wait until tomorrow." She studied his face. His scars added a new dignity to his weathered face, making him more handsome, more striking than the shallow boy he had once been. He had aged well.

He opened his eyes and took in her gaze.

"To be considered," he said, without changing his tone. "You are the love of my life."

She tidied the pile, pinned down by his intense gaze, that flash of black eyes that attracted all the girls back in college.

"I'm married," she said.

"You got married because I kissed you," he said. "If I kissed you again, will you get divorced?"

Roy sat in Bonville's desk chair with its ample, upholstered back, rocking gently on its padded seat with his thighs spread, his sleeves rolled up, and his hands tucked expansively behind his head. He waited for her to answer. In no hurry, he raised his eyebrows expectantly. She was certain an embarrassing blush gave her away and waited for its heat to recede before she sputtered her response.

"Why would you say that to me?"

His good eye never blinked. That dark pool mesmerized her. Sometimes she was afraid she might drown in it.

"Come over here."

"We're not done yet." Lulu shuffled the papers on her desk.

"Kiss me, Lulu, and then tell me this isn't what you've wanted all along." He patted his lap.

"This isn't the time. And besides, I am a married woman."

"There will never be a good time."

She opened her mouth but couldn't come up with words sufficient for the moment. She felt the pull of his gaze, the reverberation of his words in the dead air of the office.

"Roy, we shouldn't..."

When she didn't finish her sentence, he wheeled the chair across the creaky wood floor, propelling himself with a push of shiny black shoes. He faced her, grinning. Their knees touched, separated only by the scratchy wool of her skirt and the shiny fabric of his slacks.

He opened his arms expectantly, smiling when she hesitated. "Don't be like that. I don't bite. I won't pass out on you this time." He framed her face with his long fingers, ink-stained, warm on her flushed cheeks. She wondered if they left a stain. If he had already left his mark.

"God, you're beautiful." He brushed a strand of hair off her cheek and tucked it behind her ear.

"What do you want, Roy?"

"You know what I want. I want what you want." She waited for him to make the first move, her heart pounding so loudly she was certain he could hear. Blood rushed to her head. He entangled his fingers in her hair, massaging her scalp, oblivious to the bobby pins popping off in protest. Her head tingled at his touch. Sparks danced down her spine.

"I'm waiting," he said.

He knew he had her now. What else could explain the satisfied grin that spread across his face?

"One kiss. Then tell me this wasn't meant to be."

Tears sprung to her eyes when she bent forward, her quivering lips drawn to his, her body no longer willing to wait while she sorted things out. She closed her eyes, refusing to see the inevitable. He pulled her closer, spreading her thighs gently as he pulled her into his lap. One leg dangling on each side, she straddled him as if riding face forward. His tongue wheedled its way into her mouth. Where one kiss ended, the next began. Between each, she inhaled deeply as if coming up for air.

They rocked in Bonville's chair for what seemed like forever, two bodies magnetized. Through his trousers, she felt his manhood nudge her, but still he rocked, back and forth, back and forth, until she was no longer conscious of his desire, but was overwhelmed by her own, a feral heat that spread between her legs like a hot liquid spilled in her lap.

"What do you want, Lulu?" Roy whispered in her ear, his breath damp and hot. "Tell me what you want."

The dusty air seemed filled with static. Her body strained to defy the space that even now divided them. *Isn't this what she had always wanted? To live freely? To take lovers and explore her passion, unfettered by the strictures of society?*

"Tell me, Lulu." His words, spoken as if to a wayward child, were more persuasive than his most bombastic speech. He said them again. "What do you want?" His voice was inside her head now; her body throbbed in response.

"I want you." Although she answered under her breath, it seemed the only answer, the only possible line to end the poem they had worked so hard on together. The electricity that coursed through her veins was unlike any sensation she had experienced. It overwhelmed her, split her open, left her sobbing and vulnerable. He cupped his hands below her bottom and raised her up into the dancing air, using his thumbs to peel down her panties. Greedy flames danced into a conflagration. Every nerve ending in her body a light, straining for him, craving him. She sighed, impatient, while he unfastened his belt. His pants fell with a whoosh to the floor.

In their boss's chair, which stunk of cigars, they crossed the line. Disheveled, unrepentant. They dared. He asked her to repeat the words over and over.

"I want you." Each time she said it, he pulled her closer, burrowing deeper inside her. All she could think was that she didn't want this to stop. Not now. Never. If these were the words that made him continue, she would say them over and over.

But he didn't stop. "What else, Lulu?" he asked. He stopped rocking and waited for her to answer. Desire swept over her. A tidal wave capable of destroying everything that stood in its way. "Tell me what you need, my beautiful girl. If you prefer your engineer, I'll stop right now."

But it was already too late. This time it was she who had come undone.

"Tell me what you need," he repeated.

"I need you, Roy." Her words came out as a sob because this was all she had ever wanted, and he knew it. Had always known it. And in the end, what choice did she have?

Nobody walked in on them this time. There were no excuses. Roy was neither ill nor out of control. Lulu was not a victim.

In the dark office, they didn't worry about being discovered. They took their time. Roy explored every inch of her body as if mining it for gold. She ran her fingers along his scars as if memorizing his wounds.

"Don't leave me," he said.

"Don't make me regret this," she said.

Chapter 10 I Never Wanted to Hurt You

She opened the front door. Al was sitting at the kitchen table. "I'm leaving you," she said. After her night with Roy, she was disheveled, red-eyed, and incapable of covering up the raw emotions that had consumed her.

Al took off his glasses and rubbed his eyes. It was impossible to tell whether he was laughing or crying.

"It's him, isn't it?" Al asked.

Her silence gave her away.

"Why was he here in Portland in the first place?"

Lulu squirmed, unsure of what to say. "I was floundering. Roy knew how to put together a magazine. Bonville hired him as his general manager."

"That charlatan must be ecstatic. The two of them running the crap circus together. If I were you, I'd watch my back." He put his glasses back on and looked at her, shaking his head in disapproval. "But then, when did you ever listen to my advice?"

Lulu opened her mouth to respond but thought better of it.

"Just tell me one thing. Did you ever love me?"

"I never wanted to hurt you," Lulu said.

"Well, it didn't show. All those evenings you strutted in front of your suffragette friends. Lord forbid they discover that you didn't know what you were doing. So instead of working hard like the rest of us, like a princess you summoned your prince to come to your rescue. A fairytale ending. Screw the husband."

"Al, that's not fair."

"Not fair!" he thundered. "I gave you a second chance."

He didn't call her a whore. That might have made the humiliation easier to take. If he had railed against the injustice, told her he had trusted her, reminded her of the nights they had spent in each other's arms, she might have tried to explain. Instead, he said they could get divorced at a Utah divorce mill. He opened his briefcase and took out an advertisement from the local paper. The mill offered public transportation, pleasant hotels, good food, accommodating lawyers, and a cooperative court system. He would make all the arrangements. They could get the deed done that weekend if she desired.

She held the advertisement in her hand, bewildered.

"Divorce is a profitable business, I'm told," he said with a tinge of uncharacteristic bitterness.

"Why do you have this?" she asked, holding up the paper. His composure caught her by surprise. *Had he been planning to leave her all along?*

"Lulu, do you really think I didn't know you were unhappy? You never have kept your emotions, not to mention your ambitions, to yourself. No matter how hard I tried, you made me feel invisible. And you haven't exactly been the devoted wife since we returned from my parents' reception."

He had done the required research. "I hoped it wouldn't be necessary, but..."

Trust Al to be prepared.

Even then, he was a gentleman. She knew she had let him down, and the way she had treated him was unforgivable. He didn't deserve it. He deserved loyalty, a devoted wife who would make him a home and raise his children. A woman like her mother who valued his steadfast nature and stability and didn't aspire to more. Who shared his life and his bed. She was capable of none of these things.

He deserved a woman who would say she was sorry. But Lulu would never be that woman. Instead, as Al prepared to sleep on the couch, Lulu fell into the bed they had shared, relieved to be free of him.

Their marriage had been a mistake, entered into for the wrong reasons. Now she had taken the reins. Now it was over.

Al was gone when she woke the next morning. The shades were drawn, the room dark. By the light of the lamp on the bureau, she used a cloth to wash herself. Filling a bowl with warm, soapy water, she washed her face first, then scrubbed her body. She was raw, sore, and disoriented by the turn her life had taken. Pulling her suitcase out from under the bed, she opened it and stared at the empty space inside. From the bureau, she lifted a pile of neatly folded white blouses and placed them in the satchel, next came her pragmatic black skirts, and then a warm crocheted shawl. She combed her hair and tied it up in a loose chignon, as always, settling for the simplest style. Today, she felt the tug of Roy's fingers as she combed her hair. Surveying the room, she collected the few items she would need to take with her, a favorite book, the necklace her father had given her at high school graduation. She left behind the bracelet Al had bought for her in college and her wedding ring.

She closed the bedroom door behind her.

The kitchen was bright with morning sun. Sacajawea rocked on her perch, her breast swollen with incipient song as if she had been holding it back, waiting for Lulu to join her.

"Sacajawea," Lulu said, "you've brightened up this dreary home." Loss lodged in her breast. The bird cocked its yellow-green head and hopped onto her outstretched hand, its claws wrapping around her index finger.

Lulu had never clipped the bird's wings. The bird spread them wide now, each feather poised to fly.

Opening the kitchen window, Lulu extended her arm. The parakeet hopped to the windowsill and scurried from one end to the other as if measuring the distance. She pecked at the dust that had settled there from the bustling city. Finding it of little interest, she looked up at the clear, blue sky.

Lulu held her breath, willing the bird to escape, but wanting it to choose its own freedom. The summer breeze ruffled the kitchen curtains. The bird tilted its head one more time and then flapped its wings, trying them out before heading toward a tree on the opposite side of the courtyard.

Lulu left the window open as she made her breakfast, but Sacajawea didn't return. Before leaving for the office, she removed the soiled newspaper from the bottom of the cage and cleaned the perches. The empty cage remained on the counter.

She hoped the parakeet would enjoy her freedom.

If it occurred to her that the bird was in danger, she pushed the thought out of her head. She was consumed by the physical memory of the passionate evening that had changed the trajectory of her life. The parakeet disappeared into a bright blue sky, but Lulu's feet remained on the ground, and they carried her to him, to the only man who had brought her to her knees.

* * *

Ted poured Al another stein of beer. "Fickle dame," he said, "thinks she's better than the rest of us."

Al sipped the dark brew. "It's not like there weren't warning signs." Having never discussed his personal life with his friends, he had no idea how much they knew. Ted and Vesta danced into marriage, singing popular tunes, amazed at their good fortune. Even now, Ted couldn't quite squelch the satisfied smile on his face.

"Did you know Roy was in town?" Al asked.

Ted looked down at his beer. "We knew he had broken it off with Annabelle. She called Vesta from the conservatory one night in tears, saying she couldn't go on without him. Vesta stayed the night in her apartment downtown, holding her hand."

"Lulu never said a thing to me. Only Bonville this and Bonville that. She let me think it was all about the magazine."

Ted refilled their glasses.

"She took everything but the parakeet cage. Lord knows what she did with the bird."

"You're better off without her."

"That bird made a racket."

"Tell me about it. My wife never stops singing."

"What drives me crazy is that my father told me this would happen. Said she didn't have it in her to be a wife." Al popped a peanut in his mouth. "And I didn't care. She convinced me we had this newfangled relationship. Equals, careers, and interests of our own. Even when she filled our apartment with women who railed against men, I believed in her. Supported her every step of the way." He set his stein down hard on the bar, startled by the slam of glass on the oak surface, the beer splashing drops like tears on his lenses. "Roy always had a thing for Lulu, you know."

"He is a slippery guy. A poet," Ted scoffed, "looking for a muse. After his accident, I thought he might have been content to walk the earth with us mere mortals, but he always had his eyes on the heavens."

"Or so he says."

"Selling land these days, I'm told," Ted said, "besides his job at the magazine."

"Another scam, if you ask me," Al replied. "The man will never be satisfied. I'm ready to wash my hands of the both of them."

They drank for a while in silence. Ted put it all on his tab.

"She broke my heart," Al said.

"I know." Ted ordered another round.

Al drank his beer. *Had he said too much? But who else could he confide in?* The men in his family discussed sports and their jobs, never their emotions. His coworkers couldn't believe he had let his beautiful wife go. From time to time, he started to say something more and then sighed without uttering a word and returned to his beer. Ted signaled to the bartender to keep their glasses full, raising his eyebrows to signal his friend's distress.

But Ted could never be still for long. "How's life at the electric company?" he asked.

"Good." Al looked up. His face brightened. "Something new every day."

"You landed at the right place at the right time. Everything is electric now." Encouraged by Ted's interest, Al described his presentation at the conference, and Ted congratulated him on his success.

"I never imagined you a successful businessman," Al admitted. "With a wife and a baby on the way, no less."

"And I never doubted you would succeed at anything you set your mind to."

By the end of the evening, the two men walked out of the restaurant arm in arm. Friends forever.

The strange part was that Al wasn't putting up a brave front. Sure, he was furious: Lulu had made a fool of him. He had raged for days after she left, even stomping on the parakeet's cage until it was nothing more than a ruined tangle of metal bars. First his father, then Lulu. He had always lived in someone else's shadow. But now he was free to pursue his career without apology. To step up at work, confident that he could be a leader. He tidied up the apartment and asked for an office with a window.

Ted was a good friend, loyal. Al had taken loyalty for granted, but now he had learned its value. Lulu and Roy might prefer the drama of their tumultuous lives. He preferred a quiet place to think. Besides, Lulu would get her comeuppance in the long run. He was sure about that.

* * *

After Lulu returned from Utah with a copy of her divorce papers, the *Bonville's Western Monthly* dominated her every waking hour. She spent twelve hours a day in the smoky office in the Marquam Building, drinking tea, sweet-talking authors, editing, pasting, and putting together the magazine. Roy assisted with editing when he wasn't sitting across from Bonville, feet on the boss's desk. He cheered on the owner's grandiose ideas every chance he got and added a few of his own.

In the evenings, she lay in Roy's arms in the shabby room he had rented in a nearby hotel. "We really need to find someplace nicer to live," she'd say. And then he would pull her closer, and she would remember why she was there.

"Why does it matter?" he teased, stroking her thighs. "Your eyes are always closed."

The man had a point, Lulu thought, as his hands continued their exploration. Besides, when her eyes were closed, she didn't think about what she had done.

Bonville loaded boxes six high on the trolley. He tried a seventh, but it caused the entire stack to fall. Lulu typed address labels. Each box, sealed and labelled, contained dozens of copies of the second issue of *Bonville's Western Monthly.* When Bonville left with a stack of them for the post office, Lulu sat at her desk, admiring a copy, as proud as any mother of her child. By tomorrow, there would be copies in California, Washington, and every town in Oregon. Any day now, Bonville said, the money would pour in.

Lulu straightened her desk, sharpened her pencils. She debated whether to call one of her suffragette friends to catch up on the news of NAWSA's latest campaign. Before she could decide who to call, Lizzie rapped on the office window.

"I thought you were in Eugene," Lulu said, letting her in. Her sister, a new member of the University of Oregon's Class of 1910, was wide-eyed, her lace blouse attempting an escape from her skirt. She appeared to have just run a footrace; perhaps she had taken the stairs. "What brings you into the city? I thought you moved into the women's dormitory on campus."

"I've got BIG problems," her sister announced, closing the door behind her. "Are you alone?"

"I am. Bonville is off to the post office." Lulu started to explain Roy's whereabouts—a sales call in eastern Oregon—but realized her sister might not know its relevance. Roy's sales ventures were still a mystery to her, and she wasn't sure they reflected the best side of him.

"I tried calling you at home, but no one ever answers the phone in your apartment building."

"About that," Lulu said. "How much has Mother told you?"

"About you and Al? Just that you two are on the rocks."

"Those rocks have rolled into the sea. Al and I should never have gotten married."

Lizzie's mouth formed a surprised "O." She flopped into the chair across from Lulu's desk, the one Roy usually occupied. "I want to hear all about it. But first, I have a favor to ask you."

"Shoot."

"Do you still use your Dutch cap?"

"Lizzie, I'm a married woman who doesn't want a child. What do you think?" *I was a married woman,* she thought. She'd have to explain that later, before Lizzie noticed she wasn't wearing her ring.

"Can you tell me how to get one? It's a bit of an emergency."

"An emergency?" Lulu raised her eyebrows. "Tell me more."

"There's this boy on campus..."

"There are plenty of boys on campus. What's the hurry?" Lulu smiled fondly at her sister, whose girlish energy filled the smoky room. Shiny and bright, just what she needed after weeks filled with days of frantic work and nights of startling sex. She couldn't wait to tell Roy this story. He would find it delightful.

"I told him I did it all the time."

"You told who you did it all the time."

"Hugh Smith. His father's a Mormon."

The last time Lulu laughed this hard, Vesta had just recounted her elopement. Lulu wiped away tears, struggling to regain her composure. "Well, you're going to have to tell him that he'll have to wait."

"Did you?" Lizzie asked. "When you fell in love with Al?"

"I think this discussion should take place over a cup of tea. Bonville will be back any minute now, and I don't think we should talk about our love lives in his presence."

"Hugh's the eighth child of a polygamous Mormon who operates a lumber mill outside of Seattle." Lizzie couldn't wait. As they walked to the nearest cafe, she described her paramour. "He enrolled in the university to escape the rigorous rules of his religion. His father is strict; a true believer." By the time the sisters had settled into their seats, Lizzie had described Hugh in agonizing detail. She had taken him on as a project, fascinated by his background.

"Did you know Mormons can't vote for or hold public office, even in Utah?" Lizzie asked. "The crusade against Mormon polygamy is merely a ploy to keep the states in the hands of the Democratic Party."

"Frankly, I know very little about the Mormons, although I did recently visit Utah," Lulu said. "But I still don't understand why you told him you were more experienced than you are."

"His father has four wives."

"I'm not sure I see the relevance."

Lulu ordered tea, but Lizzie insisted on coffee. "It keeps me awake."

"So, his father has four wives, and Hugh thinks you are a profligate?"

"Lulu, you're the one who raised me on stories of women who were free to love whomever they pleased. Certainly, married life hasn't soured you on the concept?"

"Hardly." Lulu took a long sip of her tea. It hadn't, but it had certainly taught her that nothing is that simple. "You know I divorced him, right?"

"Who? Al?" That silenced Lizzie. She put down her coffee.

"There's someone else." Lulu looked into her sister's eyes, gauging her reaction.

"Now I understand what Mother's been going on and on about. The thing you're going to regret for the rest of your life. But I never imagined…"

"It's complicated," Lulu said.

"Well, aren't we two women of the world," Lizzie responded.

I suppose I am, Lulu thought, unsure whether this was a good thing. Her sister's words brought it all back. Lulu's own first year at the university. The titillation of being on her own. She had been so sure she knew what she was doing at Lizzie's age. It had hardly mattered whether she had fallen in love with Al. She had an agenda and he fit right into it.

"Sweetie," she stirred her tea, "take your time. Be sure you know what you're doing. There will be other boys." Advice that, of course, she had not chosen to follow.

"But will you help me if I decide this is what I want?"

"Of course." Lulu sighed as she watched her sister pour more sugar into her coffee. "But..." *Was she in any position to offer counsel to her sister? What lessons could she offer?* "Be careful, Lizzie." She thought of Roy off selling who knows what to who knows who. *Why was it so much easier to give advice than follow it?*

"Lulu, are you all right?" Lizzie's eyes grew even larger.

"I will be, sweetheart. I will be."

They passed a pharmacy on the way back to Lulu's office. "If you decide this is what you want, I'll accompany you to the Society for Constructive Birth Control. They sell a contraceptive sponge made of rubber."

Lizzie made a face.

"Or you can ask Hugh to buy a condom. Just be sure he uses it."

When Lizzie's train arrived, they hugged each other goodbye. The frivolity of the afternoon had been a pleasant diversion from the intensity of the office, not to mention the exhaustion of night after passionate night with Roy in his airless hotel room. By the time she returned to her office, Bonville was at his desk, taping up another box. She offered to take it to the post office on her way back to Roy's shady abode.

Chapter 11 Life with Roy

Two weeks after Lulu left Al, Bonville insisted Roy accompany him on a business trip, leaving her behind to run the office alone. Bonville was oblivious to the change in his employees' relationship, but Lulu watched his increased interest in Roy with wary eyes. She hoped Bonville was not leading Roy astray and entangling him in his business shenanigans. When Roy returned from Los Angeles, he described long nights on the train listening to Bonville expound on his Ninety-Nine-Year System while polishing business plans and projecting balance sheets. Although Roy didn't smoke, his suits reeked of cigars.

When Roy was not traveling, they lay awake late into the night. Lulu asked him about his father; she wanted to know everything about his childhood. He showed her the gold nugget he still carried in his pants pocket, describing the long nights after his father had deserted them.

"My mother did the best she could to provide for us. But we were never sure where the next month's rent would come from. Night after night, my mother tossed and turned in her bed. Until my accident. After the explosion, C.H. Leadbetter cashed in on one of his connections and hooked her up with a teaching job in Willow Springs. The house she lives in was part of the deal. Blood money, if you ask me. To this day, Condor Water and Power carries the mortgage. Every time I visit her, I'm reminded that I'm in their debt."

Lulu ran her finger along the scar that crossed his face. "Your mother is an admirable woman," she said. "Despite tough times, she never gave up." She pulled him toward her, overwhelmed by a desire to comfort him. Cradling his slender body, she ran her hands over the sinewy strength of his muscles. She massaged his shoulders and felt the muscles respond to her touch.

"Put it in," he said, shoving her playfully away. She knew by now he meant her Dutch cap. Her insouciance when inserting it never failed to titillate him. "You remind me of the barmaids in Kennett. Tough on the surface, but generous to a fault." He watched her silently, an amused grin spreading across his face.

After another business trip, this time to Seattle, Roy stood in the doorway and observed the hotel room with fresh eyes. "Oh darling," he said. "I need to get you out of here." He proposed a visit to his mother, a brief vacation after they had sent the proofs to the printer. Some precious time for them to spend together.

That night, they recited poetry to each other. Works they had written but never shared. They read each other's diaries. When he came to the passages where she had recorded the loneliness of her first married days in Portland, he held her close and whispered, "If only you had called me then."

Lulu cherished every moment of their time together, but as they walked to work the following morning, Roy told her he might have to make a brief jaunt to the eastern part of the state. The Calumet-Buena Vista Mines ad he ran in the first issue of the magazine had attracted dozens of new inquiries from eager investors. The success of the campaign convinced him that, if he could close a few of these deals, he would have the funds necessary to buy back his mother's house from the Condor Water and Power Company. This last tie to the company's self-serving benevolence stuck in his craw.

"Since my father left us high and dry, my mother has depended on charity," he said. "The time has come to put an end to that."

So that was what motivated him. The salesman side of Roy had always made Lulu uncomfortable; it seemed somehow shady and crass. But now she had a window into what fueled his desire to raise a fast buck. She spent her childhood in a house on a hill, but he was still compensating for the deprivations of his youth.

"I'm sure Alice would be delighted to have a home of her own," she assured him. Perhaps his generous gesture would help him put his past behind him. As they approached the Marquam Building, she admired their reflection in the lobby window. What a handsome, professional couple they appeared, walking hand in hand down the bustling boulevard. She wanted to bring out the best in him.

"There were two things I resolved to do when I woke up in the hospital the morning after the explosion," he continued. "Marry you and take care of my mother. Two birds and all that."

"Whoa there, cowboy. I made that mistake once already." Lulu's pleasant reverie evaporated at the mention of marriage.

"Your mistake was not in marrying." Roy stopped dead outside the revolving doors, set down his briefcase, and placed his hands on her shoulders. "It was marrying the wrong man. Lulu," he said, looking into her eyes, "this was meant to be."

"But isn't it enough that we are together?" Lulu kept her tone light, raised her chin flirtatiously. "Sweetheart, it doesn't get any better than this." Ignoring the snarl of pedestrians pushing their way around them, she stood on her tiptoes to kiss him on the lips.

"Sure thing, sugar," he said. "You know you're stopping traffic here."

She handed him his briefcase. "Well then," she said, "we'd better get to work before Mr. Bonville sends out a search party."

But the issue of marriage would not go away. Roy fixated on it. That night, as they prepared for bed, he brought up the topic again.

"You married Al, whom you didn't even love. Why won't you marry me?"

She pulled her nightgown over her head. It didn't seem the right time to stand naked in front of him.

"I insist on it," he said, his dark eyes flashing.

"Insist?" she asked, raising her eyebrows, knowing how much he admired her haughty demeanor.

When that didn't work, he pouted. For the first time since she had moved into his hotel room, he rolled away from her instead of wrapping himself around her. He pulled the thin blanket up under his chin like a shield.

"Roy, don't be silly."

"There nothing comical about this conversation," he said.

Shivering in the drafty room, Lulu lay there wondering what to do. Roy's insecurities should not have surprised her. His tempestuous nature, the dark days that had haunted him—they were a part of his dramatic charm. Was she willing to sacrifice this grand passion to take a stand on principle?

With Al, she had been unwilling to surrender any of her high ideals. Where had that gotten her? This time around, she was wiser. She was prepared to sacrifice what didn't serve her, compromise when necessary. Roy had a point. She had given her hand to another man but was withholding the same commitment from him.

She rolled over and licked his ear. When he groaned, she knew he was awake.

"Roy? Can't we talk?"

As long as he couldn't be sure of her, she knew he would see Al as a rival. While she resented being cast as a prize, there was an element of flattery in his need to prove he had won her in the end.

"If it's so important to you..." She couldn't bring herself to say the word, but he knew what she meant.

"Tell me what you want." His wheedling tone demanded more. They'd been down this road before. He required proof.

"Roy, how could you possibly question how much I want to be with you?"

"More than any other man?"

"Only you." She whispered the words she knew he wanted to hear, the only words that filled the bottomless hole of his need. She hoped that would put an end to it.

"Show me how much you need me." He rolled onto his back. She could see he was feeling better.

"I need you, you sexy, exasperating man."

"Say it again."

And she did. They did. And everything was all right.

They decided they would take the trip to his mother's house that weekend. "We can do both things at once," he said as they got dressed for work the next morning. "Get married *and* take over the mortgage on my mother's house. Maybe we can spend Monday night on Mount Shasta while we're at it."

"Do we really need to get married?" Lulu asked. In the light of day, the institution still left an unpleasant taste in her mouth.

"I'm not letting you get away this time. It's just a piece of paper. Don't sweat it."

Because he had never really asked her to marry him, she figured she had never really said yes. She would learn how to steer around the shaky ground of his insecurities. For now, Lulu supposed, she was going to have to get married. Again.

* * *

Willow Springs

Roy and Lulu stood on the wooden steps of Alice's front porch, unannounced. Lulu took in the peeling paint, the weary facade of the rented house. The house needs work, she thought. Roy raised the knocker.

"Roy!" Alice swung open the front door, wiping her hands with a worn dishtowel. "What a wonderful surprise." She wrapped her son in a bear hug and then turned to Lulu. "It's lovely to see you, dear."

Roy beamed, carrying their carpet bags over the threshold.

Alice didn't bat an eye when Roy told her he had invited the justice of the peace for tea that very morning. "I would have preferred Reverend Rose, but he had commitments in Eugene, and we wanted an expeditious ceremony."

"Are you—?" Alice asked.

"—Lord, no," Lulu interrupted.

"It wouldn't matter to me, either way," Alice said.

To change the conversation, Lulu presented Alice with a copy of *Bonville's Western Monthly,* opening the volume to one of her favorite articles. Roy pointed out the full-page ads. As Alice looked on, they tripped over each other's words as they described the publisher's chaotic office, Frank Bonville's quixotic campaign, and the boxes of magazines piled up to the ceiling and about to topple. They laughed about the disorder, saying they hadn't the time for housekeeping.

Alice laughed at their tales; a teacher skilled in listening.

"Our wedding ceremony will have to be short," Roy said. "I have an appointment this afternoon."

"Well, at least let me bake a cake," Alice said, and Lulu offered to help. As Lulu sifted the flour, Alice broke eggs into a bowl. She didn't ask about Al, saying only that she regretted Jessie was away at school and not able to join them on this joyous occasion.

The justice performed the deed. Roy left on his errand soon after.

By early afternoon, Lulu sat on Alice's sofa, wondering how she had gotten there. *What had she done?* Fortunately, Alice didn't ask any uncomfortable questions. Instead, she asked Lulu if she would like to play cards. She was keen on a new card game called gin rummy. The two women settled in front of the fire with an ease Lulu never experienced with her own mother, whose opinions were always so close to the surface. Lulu appreciated the woman's quick wit and clever strategy in assembling melds and never blaming the luck of the draw. "Roy's father was a salesman, too," Alice said. "There were always highs and lows with that man. Roy didn't have an easy childhood, although I tried to shield him from the worst of it. I'm grateful he found you to steady him." She studied the cards in her hand, rearranging them over and over before declaring "Gin," for the third time in a row.

"He's doing a phenomenal job," Lulu said. "You can be proud of him." She dealt them each ten cards and then examined her hand. No runs, no matches, nothing but deadwood.

"I'll never forget how kind you were to him after the accident, you and..." Alice closed her eyes, swallowing the next word. "I wished then that Roy would bring home a sensible woman like you, not a coquette like that Annabelle, always giggling at his jokes at the wrong time. Maybe my son set his mind on you back then, but we just didn't know." She picked up the card that Lulu had thrown down and slipped it into the fan of cards in her hand with a gentle smile.

"That said, take care of yourself," she added. "Men like Roy and his father, they aren't easy. Don't convince yourself that you can depend on him."

Roy's mother was smarter than Lulu had given her credit for, and tough. She'd had to be.

"Enjoy the ride."

"I can take care of myself," Lulu said. "But my life is certainly more interesting now that Roy is in it."

"I'm sure it is."

Roy blew in around midnight, flashing a thumbs-up to show the success of his mission. Alice prepared a pot of tea, two teaspoons of sugar for her son, and they sat up for another hour. Roy reenacted with gut-splitting accuracy his rendezvous with a weasel of a man from Ohio who had arrived with a bag of cash and left, broke, but planning Oregon's first naturists' community. "At least you aren't doing business in the Crystal Saloon," his mother said.

"But the waitresses at the coffee shop in Willow Spring aren't half as beautiful as the barmaids in Kennett," Roy said. "The sacrifices I make to be a legitimate businessman." He winked at Lulu, who enjoyed watching mother and son sparring together, their rapport as comfortable as two siblings recalling their childhood.

The bank in Willow Springs was housed in a small, cluttered storefront next to the Silver Palace Dry-Good Emporium on Main, one of four stores on the intersection that comprised the downtown. Roy grasped Lulu's hand as a string of cowbells hung on the inside knob announced their entrance. He jovially greeted J.F., the head cashier, and his mousy sister Mae, barely visible behind the barred window and the high counter. "My friends," he bellowed, "have you met my charming wife, Lulu?" Mae giggled and said, "I'll get Mr. Litel. He's expecting you."

Mr. Litel, the bank's vice president, escorted them into his cluttered office, as smoke-filled and paper-pile-cluttered as Bonville's.

The agreeable man eyed the bag of cash that Roy placed on his desk and then methodically counted the bills, chatting all the while about the chinook salmon he'd caught on his last fishing expedition up the Rogue River. "God, I miss those days," Roy said, recollecting a trip the two had taken together as boys. "Remember the time I bet you I could catch more bass with a fly than you could with bait?"

Mr. Litel completed the paperwork, signed off on the deposit, and reviewed the terms of the mortgage. "Of course, the bank will hold on to the title until you pay off the house, but as of today, your mother's house is in your name. Congratulations." Shaking the banker's hand, Roy glowed, as exultant as a child on Christmas morning.

While they were out, Alice prepared her son's favorite meal, meatloaf and mashed potatoes. Lulu had seldom seen Roy eat with such an appetite. Never seen his cheeks so flushed, nor his face so relaxed. After they finished the meal, he stood up and, with a grand flourish, presented his mother with the deed.

Alice's usual stoic composure went all to hell. She took the deed from Roy's hands with trembling hands, set it on the counter, and kicked off her heels. Twirling and laughing, as tears rolled down her cheeks, she danced around the kitchen. Roy beamed with pride. On her second circuit of the room, Roy pulled Lulu from her chair. With one arm around her waist and the other holding on to his mother, they pranced around the house, which suddenly seemed cheerier. Alice's house!

When she finally stopped to catch her breath, Roy insisted Lulu join them in a high-stakes game of poker, two cents a hand. They competed fiercely until long after the sun set. Neither mother nor son let the other win. When midnight struck, Lulu pleaded exhaustion, and Roy escorted her to bed. Alice insisted they stay in her bedroom. She was content to camp out on Jessie's unoccupied bed.

"Must you leave so soon?" Alice asked when they came down to breakfast, flushed from the night's activities, clutching their carpet bags.

"I promised my love a night on Mount Shasta," Roy said, helping himself to a piece of homemade bread with jam. "I once wrote a poem to Lulu, but I couldn't tell her I'd written it for her. Now I want to sing it from the mountaintop."

"Perhaps you will join us in Portland for Christmas?" Lulu asked, thinking Alice might be a perfect foil. Her own mother had not spoken to her since the divorce.

"What a lovely invitation. We'll see." Alice hugged them both and handed them a lunch basket for their travels. *This woman is a stalwart,* Lulu thought. She was glad Roy had chosen his mother to be their witness.

After their visit to Mount Shasta, Roy began writing poetry again. He couldn't get the words down fast enough. He attributed his burst of creativity to the mountain air, but Lulu, who had a few story ideas of her own, knew better.

***

"It's about time the city council acknowledged the needs of young women in the city." Lulu showed Vesta a newspaper headline that said Lola Baldwin had been named Superintendent of the Women's Auxiliary to the Police Department for the Protection of Girls. She stepped around another stretch of brick sidewalk construction while Vesta maneuvered her twins' pram over a mud puddle, more concerned with damage to her exquisite gray suede boots than the pram's large white wheels. "The council earmarked $6,000 for the city dog pound and asked for half that annual amount to protect Portland's girls and women."

Lulu couldn't tell whether Vesta was listening. With reservations, she had agreed to meet Vesta for lunch and a shopping expedition to the Meier and Frank department store. "Ted buys all his suits there," Vesta suggested. "Now that Roy is doing so well, encourage him to dress better."

Vesta hadn't said a word about Lulu's own successful career. Instead, she chatted away about Charlie and Katie, the two tow-headed babies asleep in the pram. "Charlie is clever as all hell, but

Katie's going to be the beauty, no doubt about it. Isn't that right, my precious fuzzy monkey?"

Vesta angled the pram into the elevator when they entered the elegant, white terracotta five-story building. "Of course, you're downtown every day," she said as she parked the babies against the elevator's back wall, "but for a mother like me, lunching out is pure heaven. My life is baby, baby all the time." The subjects they couldn't discuss (Al, Annabelle, marriage, divorce) far outnumbered those they could.

Vesta picked at her Waldorf salad, bemoaning the difficulty of getting her figure back. Lulu looked at her watch, tried to steer the conversation back to issues that mattered to her, and finally gave up. With half an ear, she listened to Vesta moan and groan about the trials of motherhood. She doubted her friend had ever read a literary magazine.

Bonville's publishing company, like all of Portland, had fallen into a slump. All day long, Roy and Bonville commiserated about their inability to drum up enough advertising to keep their publication afloat. On the road, Roy compensated for the disappointing returns of the magazine, selling anything he could that would produce a profit: tickets to the Russian Symphony, flour and feed, and land grants. He would hock anything to flush out enough money to pay the rent on their small, still unfurnished apartment.

Lulu appreciated his effort but feared it would never be enough. Frank Bonville continued to lose interest in the magazine, which had not shown a profit after the first year of publication. He spent most of his time promoting his book on the Ninety-Nine-Year System. Too often he asked Roy to accompany him. If Lulu hadn't been feeling itchy and abandoned, she would never have accepted Vesta's invitation. But the excitement of the never-ending piles of manuscripts had long ago paled, and she had foolishly looked forward to a foray outside of the office. She had news of her own to share.

"Roy is doing brilliantly these days," Lulu tried one last time. "Did you see the piece in the *Capital-Journal*?" The article had complimented a poem Roy had published in *New West* magazine, calling it "a blood and thunder take-offlet on the Rubaiyat style of poetry," and Roy "a genius of the Wallace Irwin type."

New West magazine, one of several rags Bonville insisted on spawning, was one of Lulu's newer responsibilities. He'd handed it over to her like a piece of discarded furniture left on the curb. "It's not worth my time," he'd said. Her time, of course, was of no value to him. "This magazine racket is draining my coffers," he complained. "The only thing I did right was to put it in the hands of a woman and cut my losses."

Roy's contributions to the magazine were the best thing about it. Roy assured her their boss hadn't meant what he said. "The fellow says whatever crosses his mind. Stick to your guns." Of course, Roy had been on a high ever since the article in the *Capital-Journal*. How often does a writer get called a genius?

Vesta, unimpressed, cooed as she adjusted the pale-yellow blanket covering the babies. "We've been seeing Roy's ads all over the papers," she said. "Do tell, what's the scoop? Ted is always on the lookout for an inside line."

The scoop—which Lulu wasn't about to confide now—was that she and Roy were considering moving south in the fall. Lulu had applied to attend Riverside School of Library Science in southern California. If accepted, she would study to become a librarian, a career that would make her secure for life, no longer dependent on Roy or any man. A field in which one day she might be the boss. Roy supported her application. He was ready for a change, brimming with ideas for a movie script, and convinced that Hollywood was about to become all the rage. Moving would put him right in the middle of things. But she wasn't about to justify their plans to Vesta, who, keen on visiting the hat department, wasn't listening to her anyway.

"Dear," Vesta said, "I hate to say it, but your hat is frightfully outdated." This was the final blow. Lulu begged off, citing a deadline.

"Splendid," Roy said.

Lulu had presented the letter with a flourish. Roy's face lit up when he read the first line.

The acceptance letter from Riverside School came just in time. Every sign seemed to tell them to go.

When the Marquam Building was placed in foreclosure, Bonville announced he was closing the office by the end of the year. The blowhard had already rescheduled his long-deferred lecture tour, and the next issue of the *Bonville's Western Monthly* was to be its last. Roy had returned from his last two business trips in a foul, defeated mood. Lulu suspected that his frequents "toots" of cocaine had less to do with his disabilities than with a fear of failure. The magazine had lost its luster, and lately disappointment seemed to have settled on his shoulders like a heavy weight.

"Time to make tracks from this ole cowboy town," he said, handing her back the letter. "Giddy up!" He slapped her behind with an abandoned tie and pranced around the room like a man possessed. Lulu waited him out, relieved to see him smiling again, but miffed that he viewed her successful application through his own distorted lens. A simple "congratulations" would have satisfied her more. Better yet, a hug acknowledging the professional possibilities that were now opening up for her.

"California sunshine is just what the doctor ordered," she said, tucking the letter back into its envelope for safekeeping.

They gave notice the very next day. As soon as the magazine's final issue left for the printers (even then, Lulu would not abandon work half-done, Frank Bonville be damned), they would leave rainy Oregon behind.

"I'll be sorry to lose you," Bonville said to Roy when they told him their news. "I'd always thought one of these days you'd come up with a scheme that would make both of us rich."

Roy smirked and shook the man's hand. Lulu waited for the publisher to address her.

"Well, you gave it the old college try, my girl," he said. "Nothing ventured, nothing lost."

Wasn't the rest of the expression "nothing gained?" He dismissed two years of effort with a flick of his chubby wrist.

Bonville's goodbye present to Roy was a card embossed with the name of a business colleague in Riverside who could "fix you up good." Roy tucked the card into his pocket before cleaning out his desk. Watching the two men in cahoots, Lulu couldn't wait to get out of there.

They packed their things—what few belongings they had acquired—in boxes that they sent to Alice's for safekeeping. They would travel light, Roy said. Make it an adventure. Who needed money when the entire world was out there for the taking?

But first, Lulu said, they should visit their mothers one last time. Who knows when they would return?

* * *

Lizzie, home from college, greeted them at the front door as usual, waving a notebook in which she had drafted her "masterpiece." "Perhaps you can take a look?" Lulu noted her sister's new bohemian dress, a lacy confection that stopped six inches above her ankles.

"Written for anyone in particular?" Lulu asked.

Kitty had prepared two separate bedrooms for their visit. Lizzie rolled her eyes, but Lulu's mother insisted on propriety. Two years in, she still refused to acknowledge Roy and Lulu's relationship. Roy, having none of it, pulled out his eye patch and fell back on the pirate patter of his early recovery, lurching about the house like a madman, with Lizzie egging him on. Lulu had hoped that her plan for postgraduate studies might defuse her mother's condemnation, but Kitty's judgment ran deep. Lulu's father, now settled in Boston full-time, had offered to help with Lulu's tuition, which, while convenient, only fueled her mother's resentment.

Over a tense dinner of overcooked spaghetti, Kitty blamed her youngest daughter's flightiness on Lulu's poor example. "If only she had more stable role models, say, for example, an engineer whose career," she looked at Lulu to be sure she understood her intent, "was above approach and is still on track."

Despite what her mother called "the unfortunate troubles in your marriage," Kitty refused to give up on Al. "I'm sure the judge is proud of that poor boy at last. He's a hard worker. Any woman would be glad to have him."

Lulu pushed the food around her plate, afraid to look up at Roy. "Drop it, Mom." Roy and Lizzie giggled. With a pirate's brogue, Roy recited poetry, spilling a glass of water when he emphasized an inappropriate line with a dramatic gesture. He had stopped listening to her mother when she refused to kiss him when they walked in the door.

"This will take time," Lulu told him when her mother left the room.

"Why bother?" he replied.

Lulu cleaned up the mess, happy for any distraction, and then joined him in the spare bedroom, where they spent the night reading Lizzie's novel and listening for footsteps outside the door. The novel, the story of a rebellious Mormon, was well written, if somewhat melodramatic.

They left first thing in the morning. If she'd had any doubts, the visit convinced Lulu that leaving Portland was one of the best decisions of her life.

In Willow Springs, Roy's mother welcomed them with open arms and an aromatic apple pie. She promised to guard their possessions with her life. Honeysuckle now covered the latticework of her covered porch. Hummingbirds sucked nectar from the bee balm blooming in the front flower bed. Inside, Alice had painted the kitchen a welcoming yellow. The pie cooled on the windowsill.

Roy surprised them both by hiring a horse and carriage for an excursion to Ashland Canyon Park. The discovery of lithia water near Emigrant Lake had inspired the recent opening of a mineral spa at the park. The late summer day was ideal for lolling about in the springs in their bathing suits, discussing their plans. Alice, who found teaching a most rewarding profession, extolled the opportunities that would be available to Lulu once she had received her library degree. Roy shared his vision of writing for the film industry. "The technology is ready," he said. "All they need is talent." Roy, more relaxed than

Lulu had seen in him in months, kicked his pasty white feet, stirring up bubbles in the warm water.

On the way back to Alice's house, Roy and Lulu sang "California, here I come" at the top of their lungs.

Mother and son headed straight to bed, Alice yawning and Roy complaining of a headache. Lulu lingered in the swing on the honeysuckle-covered porch. Watching the moon climb into the sky, she thought of everything she was about to leave behind. Friends, family, her career as an editor. None of them entirely satisfactory, but the only life she had ever known.

She had thrown her lot in with Roy. She had no illusions; her choice of library school had been pragmatic, not romantic. Roy's mother had warned her. She couldn't count on him. But that was all right. Finally, she would be the master of her own fate.

She doodled in her notebook. The list of things she would miss morphed into a melancholy verse. By the light of the full moon, she realized this might be the last night she would sleep in the state of her birth.

"Frost, the weaver's hand,
And the red and yellow and brown and green.
Shimmer and blend and merge in one
Like the Orient gleam
Of a prayer rug, done.

Small need is mine to roam
Who has the world at home."

She woke up to a chilly morning, her neck stiff and her legs covered by a red and green plaid wool blanket. She pulled the thick blanket up under her chin. The swing's rusty chain creaked, startling wrens in the bushes along the front of the house. The birds flew off in a panic, their song laced with a warning. As her eyes followed their flight, she noticed Roy standing at the bottom of the steps, watching the sunrise. When he turned to her, he held her journal in his hand.

"You were the one who applied to school in California." For a moment, she didn't understand his words, and then the verse came back to her, her late-night melancholy.

"The moon's lyrics, not mine," she said, patting the seat beside her.

"If you don't want to go, we can take our boxes right now and turn around."

"Not on your life."

The trees came alive with the first rays of morning sunshine.

"We're in this together?" Roy asked.

"Forever," she said. "What we have, our life together, can't be altered by a moment of melancholy."

"In that case, may I compliment you on your elegant verse?" he said, his salesman's smile back. This was, she realized, the first poem she had written in years.

"Worthy of the *Bonville's Western Monthly*?"

"Better than that. I suggest you submit it to *Sunset*. We're moving up in the world." Roy said. "Stick with me. Life will always be an adventure."

She tucked her notebook under her arm, and they walked into his mother's house arm in arm. For the moment, there was no place on earth she would rather be.

Part III: California

Chapter 12 Riverside

Riverside, California, 1910

The first thing Lulu noticed as their train pulled into Riverside, California, was that the town was everything Portland was not. Portland was rainy and lush. Riverside was dry and prickly, dotted with palm trees and covered with lifeless, brown grass. Portland was hilly; Riverside was flat. Portland was chilly, but Riverside was hot, so hot that before their train hissed to a stop at the station sixty miles east of Los Angeles, she removed her winter coat. Still, the heat rolled over her like an enervating wave. Thousands of navel orange trees stretched in tidy rows to the horizon. Through the heat's haze, Roy pointed out low mountains dusted with snow on the horizon.

Joseph Daniels, the wiry but energetic director of the Riverside Library Service School, greeted them as they entered the bustling station. "Mrs. Bacon, I am delighted you have arrived at last," he said. He shook Roy's hand but fixed his attention on Lulu, welcoming his newest student with the enthusiasm she would have expected from a younger man.

"I've reserved a room for you at a local boardinghouse," he said. "It's not much, but it's clean and quiet and not far from the library. One of the many old mansions in town that has been converted into lodging."

As he drove through town, he pointed out the mission revival style public library on the corner of Seventh and Orange Streets where Lulu would attend classes. His hands were pale, with meticulously manicured nails. *This was a man who lived inside,* Lulu thought. *A scholar.* "In 1901, Andrew Carnegie gave Riverside $20,000 for a library building with a capacity for twenty thousand volumes." he said. "Last year, we expanded with another Carnegie grant—a $15,000 project—and added a children's room." He exuded pride with every proclamation.

Roy yawned, unable, or unwilling, to mask his boredom after the long, tiring journey.

"I believe you will find our community welcoming." Daniels turned to Roy at last, noticing his discomfort. "Many easterners have moved here for our warm winter climate." When Roy didn't reply, he smiled sheepishly. "I'm sure you must be weary after your travels." Turning back to Lulu, he said, "Classes begin on Monday. You'll be working with the library staff on training projects before you know it. People are the key to any library, as I'm sure you already know. Books are only tools or containers."

They pulled up in front of a large, somewhat shabby, three-story home with a wraparound front porch. Two men—Japanese, maybe Chinese—sat on white rockers, squinting into the sun and smoking cigarettes. As Mr. Daniels unloaded their luggage, an overweight woman with short, coiled curls and wearing a Hawaiian-style muumuu waddled out the front door.

"Welcome, my friends," she said. "You must be the new librarian."

"And her husband," Roy added.

Daniels carried their suitcases onto the porch. "I'll leave you in Mrs. Shumway's capable hands," he said. With a tip of his fedora, he climbed back into his buggy, leaving Lulu and Roy behind.

"Such a lovely man," Mrs. Shumway said. The Asian men stood and bowed in their direction. "You must excuse your fellow tenants," the landlady whispered. "They don't speak much English." Al dipped his head, and Lulu followed his lead in what she hoped was an appropriate response. Their landlady turned to the men as they sat

188

down once more in their rocking chairs. Speaking loudly, she exaggerated her words and tapped her watch. "Dinner in twenty-five minutes." She held up fingers to translate the number.

Al and Lulu followed Mrs. Shumway into the entry hall of the house, where an overhead fan attempted to stir the steamy afternoon air. "Feel free to use the sitting room at any time," she said, indicating a small parlor with two worn armchairs. The fat on her arms swung back and forth as she pointed out the relevant rooms. "The dining room is in the rear, next to the kitchen. I put out breakfast by six in the morning. Fresh-squeezed orange juice if you arrive early enough. Your fellow tenants, four fine Japanese men who work in the orange groves, will undoubtedly eat before you. They leave early, often before sunrise. Supper is at six in the evening, and you are always welcome to join us for a nominal fee. Lately, Mr. Homma has been showing me how to prepare Japanese dishes using local produce. I think you will find the meals here quite a treat."

The gregarious woman stopped halfway up the stairs to catch her breath. The second-floor bedrooms, she explained, had been converted into rooms for rent. The two smaller rooms housed two Japanese farmworkers each. The largest bedroom would be theirs and had a lovely window looking out onto the backyard. "My room is upstairs, so I am always nearby if you need me."

"Will you be joining us for supper this evening?" she asked. Lulu, imagining the English-less farmworkers glaring at them as she ate what passed as their native cuisine, was relieved when Roy stepped in to reply. "We're bushed, but thanks so much for your warm welcome."

Mrs. Shumway clicked her tongue sympathetically and pointed out the bathroom at the end of the hall before wheezing her way up the narrow stairway.

Their room was stuffy, dusty, and hot. "Well, she's a bundle of fun," Roy said. "I bet she's dying to grill us." They could hear her lumbering footsteps over their heads as they placed their suitcases on the narrow bed and then turned to examine the plain wooden dresser and matching desk, the thin faded rug. Lulu opened the window into the pleasant backyard, but there was not even a smidgen of a breeze.

"Quite the cast of characters," Roy said. "Books are only tools or containers." He mocked Daniels, swinging his arms loosely and pretending to push glasses up his nose.

"It was very kind of him to find us a place to stay," Lulu protested. "His program is one of the best in the West." Why did Roy have to be so critical? It wouldn't cost him anything to appreciate Mr. Daniels's hospitality. And these accommodations were as nice as those they had in Portland. "Graduates of the school are among the finest professionals in the field."

Roy and Lulu stripped off their sweaty clothes and lay down on the lumpy bed in their underwear. Salty sweat caked Lulu's skin, but she was in no hurry to check out the shared bathing facilities. Instead, she turned her face to the open window. Roy gazed up at the ceiling. "Do you think her bed is right above ours?"

"I certainly hope not," Lulu said, though the springs creaking above them led to just that conclusion.

"Well, I'm for finding a decent coffee shop in the neighborhood and steering clear of our fellow tenants whenever we can. They give me the creeps," Roy said. "At least Hollywood isn't far from this dump." He rolled over and embraced her from behind, his hands cupping her breasts, his damp body sticking to hers. "Come to me, Miss Librarian," he said. "I want to check out a book."

Lulu, still smarting from Roy's imitation of her boss, pushed him away. "It's hot as blazes in here," she said. "Give me some air."

Roy rolled over in a huff.

The sky was beginning to turn red. "Hopefully, it will cool down now that the sun is setting," Lulu said.

"If you say so." His tone was cranky. The heat did that to him.

Lulu rolled over and licked the salt off his neck.

"Better?" she asked.

"Better," he conceded. He turned back to face her. "One hell of a sunset."

Two days later, Lulu started school. Roy headed into Hollywood with the card from Bonville's colleague tucked into his vest pocket. Lulu left the window open and allowed the aroma of orange blossoms to fill their room before leaving to explore the library stacks under Daniels's benevolent gaze.

Roy returned home wearing a short-sleeved shirt he had purchased during the day and a new bowler hat. He had removed his bow tie for good. "Meyers says Hollywood will soon be the capital of the whole damn industry."

Meyers, Lulu assumed, was Bonville's "colleague." That, in itself, was reason for concern.

"Did you know Thomas Edison's company in New Jersey owns ninety percent of all the motion picture patents?" Without waiting for her to respond, Roy continued, one word running into the next. "Edison has been suing filmmakers willy-nilly, making them stop mid-production. California judges have refused to enforce Edison's patents in California, so filmmakers are moving to southern California in droves."

Lulu hung up her work attire, pulling a lighter linen dress over her head. Even its skirt clung to her legs in the warm evening air, but she hated to add the extra layer of a petticoat.

"Meyers's office is smack dab in the thick of things on Hollywood Boulevard." Roy paced the small room, unable to sit still. "He's looking to buy up every stick of real estate, putting us into the driver's seat."

The "us" got Lulu's attention. Although her father had paid her thirty-five-dollar tuition, the couple had no money to spare. The plan had been that Roy would seek employment as soon as they arrived. "Did he offer you a job?" she asked. She had yet to get a word in about her first day at the library, but Roy excitedly recounted every moment of his day, his words a torrent of details.

* * *

"Look in the mirror."

Roy had watched as Meyers admired their reflection in the mirror behind the bar of the Hollywood Hotel. Meyers pronounced it "mirrah."

"Have you ever seen so much talent in one room?" The minute Meyers opened his mouth, Roy knew the man had to be from Brooklyn. "What a fabulous idear," the New Yorker effused after

Roy described his concept for a screenplay. Short and plump, with a waxed mustache, Meyers favored shiny suits and smoked hand-rolled Turkish cigarettes. His clothes reeked, and one never knew where his r's would land.

"A salesman, huh?" he asked Roy, who had introduced himself as the former general manager of the *Bonville's Western Monthly*.

"And writer," Roy replied.

"Writers are a dime a dozen," Meyers said. "Frank told me you could sell a swimming pool to a drowning man."

"Land," Roy corrected him. "I put together profitable land deals."

"Land deals," Meyers's cough, deep and phlegmy, filled the bar. "My official office is right around the corner, but I prefer to do my business here at the bar of the Hollywood Hotel." He pulled a crumpled handkerchief out of his pocket and wiped his mouth. "Tell me, Roy. Do you know a good investment when you see one?" The man's cigarette smoke irritated Roy's good eye, but he wasn't about to let his discomfort show.

"I've made a few." Roy flashed his gold nugget and beamed a winner's smile. "Need I say more?"

"Major motion picture companies are sniffing around here. The way I see things, if we buy up all the local real estate, that'll put us into the driver's seat." Hollywood would soon be the center of the burgeoning film industry, Meyers said, and land was at a premium. "You know how this town was named?"

Roy didn't, and he figured the story might be useful for his sales pitch.

"In 1886, a guy named Whitely stood on a hilltop overlooking the valley. Along comes a Chinaman in a wagon carrying wood. The man climbs off the wagon and bows. Whitely asks him what he's doing. The Chinaman says, 'I holly-wood.'" Meyers's raucous laugh ended in another cough. He wiped his mouth with the dirty handkerchief.

Roy joined in the laughter but looked away when Meyers spit into the rag.

"Your sales acumen might come in handy here." In the meantime, Meyers added, a small investment would secure Roy's interest in the new enterprise. "A couple thou?" he asked. "Surely, you can swing that much?"

"No problem," Roy answered.

At least, he thought, the cad is picking up the check. By the end of the day, Roy was a founding partner of Meyers, Baum, Bacon, and Associates. A few sales would replenish the money he borrowed from his Oregon savings account to buy his way in.

"Nothing ventured, nothing gained." Meyers offered a cigarette to seal the deal.

"I'd prefer an office of my own," Roy said, slapping Meyers on the back.

When Roy finished his account of his day, he turned his attention back to her.

"Creative talent—that's what they call us—is in high demand here. Don't you worry, sweetheart. In California, the sky's the limit."

"I hope you're right," Lulu replied.

* * *

Day by day, Lulu adjusted to the heat, casting aside her heavy woolen skirts and replacing them with garments made from light cotton fabrics. The brilliant sunshine tanned her pasty skin. Roy's complexion soon glowed with health, an attractive addition to his ubiquitous enthusiasm.

With Roy happily ensconced in Hollywood, Lulu finally had time to herself. Daniels's curriculum filled her days, but while Roy attended "business meetings" in the evening, she reworked the opening to a short story she had titled "The Path-Treader."

"I suppose, after all, it's people like Emily Briggs who keep the world going. People who live by the rules and do things the way their folks have always done them. So many senseless things—stupid, cruel, and funny things—are done every day, just to make life move along. And it is Emily and her kind that hold the rest from going off on a tangent and upsetting it all. Path-treaders they are, and not trail-

*breakers, but they keep down the weeds and make the landscape
tidy."*

Roy read an early draft. "Well, I, for one, intend to be a trailbreaker, always," he said. "That's why the movie business is perfect
for me." Lulu, however, was surprised how much she enjoyed the
structure of her librarian duties. For the first time in her life, she was
beginning to appreciate the value of path-treaders. Someone had to
keep things in order.

"Not much there for a screenplay," Roy said. "I have an idea for
a project of my own, but I'm not ready to share it. Yet."

After they changed out of their work clothes, they headed out in
search of an inexpensive restaurant. As they walked along the main
drag of Riverside, they tried to memorize the names on the street signs
and surveyed the windows of the local shops. When Roy had
exhausted his supply of tales, Lulu rehashed her day's work at the
library; the ambitious course of study that Daniels had laid out for
her.

They settled for a picnic along the Santa Ana River: fresh fruit—
available in great abundance—and slices of cheese from the deli. The
evening breeze was preferable to their stuffy room, and the price was
right.

* * *

Lulu soon became accustomed to the welcoming, if silent, bows
of the Japanese men who spent their evenings smoking, drinking
beer, and playing Mahjong on Mrs. Shumway's front porch. She even
joined them from time to time for dinner. Especially when Roy
worked late, and she was on her own.

The men were polite. Despite their lack of English, they
encouraged her, with gestures and shy smiles, to taste Mrs.
Shumway's somewhat baffling attempts to replicate their native
cuisine. Despite the strange salty sauce, the concoctions were a
pleasant change from the makeshift picnics that had become her and
Roy's usual fare. Nodding her approval, she slurped up noodles
before an audience of eager faces.

"They aren't much older than I am," she said to Mrs. Shumway. "I wonder why they don't have families."

"Oh, they do," Mrs. Shumway assured her. "But their families aren't welcome in town. That's why they rent rooms here during the harvest."

"What do you mean?" Lulu asked.

"Owning property in town would violate the California Alien Act," her landlady replied. "And their children are not welcome in our town's schools." Mrs. Shumway adjusted her considerable weight, causing the flimsy dining room chair to protest, before helping herself to a generous portion of soba noodles. "The Act was a godsend, if you ask me," she said. "During the harvest, I never have a vacancy now. And my tenants are well-behaved and quiet. They make their payments on time. That's more than I can say for some."

Lulu blushed, taking another bite so she wouldn't have to answer. When Roy was home, he certainly was not quiet. He was a practiced orator, and she knew his voice carried. With the summer nights so warm, they seldom closed their window. And the one thing that had not changed since they arrived in California was Roy's passion for lovemaking. Now she wondered who was listening when he, quoting his script-in-progress, asked her to "ride him home." She hated to think that Mrs. Shumway might have heard, not to mention the polite men now encouraging her to take a second serving of noodles and vegetable. And she would have to check with Roy to be sure he had paid the second month's rent.

She held up her hand to show she had eaten enough. Perhaps tomorrow she would look through the library's reference section for a book containing Japanese greetings and surprise them when she returned to the boardinghouse. In the meantime, she thanked Mrs. Shumway for the lovely meal, avoiding her gaze. She excused herself, retreating to what she had foolishly thought was the anonymity of her room.

The next morning, Lulu asked Mr. Daniels about the Alien Act. He explained that the law, recently passed by the California senate, discouraged immigration from Asia. They clearly intended it to create an inhospitable climate for immigrants already living in California.

"But who else would work twelve-hour days in the orchards?" she asked. "If you ask me, I say these men are providing a necessary service."

"Exactly," he said, "but anti-Chinese and anti-Japanese sentiment is rife these days in California. Recently, there have been a series of city ordinances passed, some right here in Riverside. One even outlaws laundry businesses."

"Those poor, poor men, separated from their families," Lulu replied.

"Ohayou gozaimasu." She made a note of the Japanese phrase meaning "good morning," resolving to use it when she greeted her neighbors.

That night, when Roy came home, she told him what she had learned.

"Babe," he said, "don't you have your hands full campaigning for women's rights? Sometimes, you have to pick your battles. Besides, one of the highest-paid actors in Hollywood is a Japanese immigrant named Sessue Hayakawa. Tom Ince paid him $500 a week to star in the film adaptation of *The Typhoon*." Roy had no interest in their fellow tenants, but he had immersed himself in Hollywood lore. "Of course, D.W. Griffith prefers to use white actors made up to look Asian. He recently cast Dick Barthelmess to play the leading role in *Broken Blossoms*. In *The Chink at Golden Gulch,* Charlie Lee starred, but the film's heroes were the white men who came to the rescue of a white woman in danger. After that portrayal of an Asian as the villain, I doubt he could hire a Japanese actor even if he wanted to."

None of these names meant anything to Lulu. But she stopped really listening when Roy mentioned the campaign for women's rights. As usual, he had a point. Since starting library school, she had yet to seek others committed to the campaign that most directly affected her. While Roy dived into his new life with total commitment, she had limited her activities to the library and her evenings to writing her stories in their room. Perhaps it was time for her to expand her horizons. Mr. Daniels's regimented schedule left her evenings wide open. In Oregon, she had pursued a role among the suffragettes. There was nothing keeping her from doing the same now.

Nevertheless, as she prepared for bed, she greeted the polite fellow who allowed her to precede him into their shared bathroom with the Japanese phrase for good evening. "Konbanwa." He echoed her words with a wide smile.

Ablution complete, she climbed into bed with Roy, putting a finger to her lips. "The walls have ears," she whispered. But when Roy jumped out of bed and cupped his hand to the wall, his eyes open in exaggerated concentration, her reservations quickly dissolved.

"Come here, you nincompoop," she said.

He lunged for her, landing on the squeaky bed with an actor's aplomb, one hand bracing his head while the other pulled her toward him. "Can Mrs. Shumway hear us now?" he asked as he unbuttoned her blouse. "Are her boarders listening now?" he asked, throwing kisses to the wall. The only way she could silence him was to kiss him back. He embraced her, and she no longer cared who heard.

The next morning, taking advantage of the library's extensive periodical collection, Lulu learned that the two active women's rights groups in southern California were the Political Equality League founded by Pasadena businessman John Hyde Braly and the Votes for Women Club** led by attorney Clara Shortridge Foltz. Reading through a schedule of upcoming events, she saw that Clara Foltz was speaking at the Riverside Woman's Club the very next week. She asked Daniels for the afternoon off.

The Woman's Club auditorium was packed. When Lulu entered the room, the club president was introducing the speaker. "Clara Foltz," the enthusiastic woman said, "is a legend in the local suffragette community, the first female lawyer admitted to the California Bar. In 1878, when Clara took the bar examination, California law permitted only white males to become members of the bar. Undeterred, Clara authored a bill to replace 'white male' with 'person' and passed the examination. When she decided to sharpen her skills by attending Hastings College of Law—which had denied her admission because of her sex—Foltz not only sued, but she also argued her own case. Once again, she won."

The audience applauded as a short, boxy woman approached the dais. The sixty-something-year-old exuded the energy of an adolescent. She sported a stylish gingham dress with puffy sleeves and wore her unruly curls piled on top of her head, secured with half a dozen bows and a large Mantilla comb decorated with glittery gold balls. Her deep voice commanded attention. "Because the Constitution states that 'all men are created equal,' the court ruled that we, as women, do not fall under its protection."

The audience booed.

"Balderdash, I say!" Foltz thundered now, her voice filling the large auditorium. The women rose to their feet. "Our day has come. California suffragettes, I need your support now more than ever. Taking advantage of a progressive Republican administration, we have successfully lobbied the state legislature to put the right to vote before the voters once more. We have eight months to organize our campaign. I'm calling for all hands on deck!"

After the lecture, Lulu joined a long line of women eager to meet the dynamic speaker. Foltz greeted each volunteer with a hearty handshake. When Lulu reached the front of the line, they shook hands. "I recently moved here from Portland, where I was the general editor of a magazine," Lulu said. "Now I'm a librarian. Perhaps you can use my skills in your campaign?"

"Portland, I know it well," Foltz effused. "Would you care to join me for a cup of coffee after the assembly?"

"I'd be honored."

While she waited, Lulu watched Foltz work the crowd, admiring the skilled organizer's ability to greet each woman as if she were the most important attendee. "I appeal to you as a mother," she would say, or grandmother or garment worker or teacher or nurse. When Lulu said she was a librarian, she received the same warm reception.

The woman's charisma rivaled Roy's in those early days when the young women at the university couldn't take their eyes off him.

"Call me Clara," she said, joining Lulu at last. "What brings you to California?"

Lulu cleared her throat. "I'm studying with Mr. Daniels at the Riverside Library. A second career, you might say. I'm still finding my way." She debated whether to mention her first marriage, but instead related the tale of Frank Bonville and his ill-fated magazine. "My husband is a writer and public speaker, although he prefers sermons to political rhetoric."

"I knew we were kindred spirits." Clara's fixed gaze never left Lulu's face as she took a seat in the auditorium's small kitchen. She groaned with pleasure, resting her boots on a folding chair. "I understand preachers," she said. "My father was a minister and a lawyer. He preferred the fervor of religion to the dry realities of the legal profession."

"Roy is trying his hand at screenwriting."

"I'm a divorcee myself," Clara declared, lighting a cigarette. "My Jeremiah was a poor provider at the best of times. When we moved to California, he made matters worse with frequent visits to Portland to visit the woman who became his second wife."

Lulu, sipping her coffee, choked.

"Are you okay, dear? I didn't mean to shock you. My marriage was not without reward. It blessed me with five children. When Jeremiah and I split up, I embarked on my first speaking tour. After some success, I became a lawyer. Who would have guessed they would appoint a divorced mother to the Los Angeles District Attorney's office? You never know where life might take you."

Lulu nodded in agreement. The story of her own marriage paled in contrast to the dynamic woman's tale.

"What can I do to help?" Lulu asked. Clara, not one to sit still, was already preparing to move on.

"We encourage suffragists to speak to voters wherever they meet them. In the street and in automobiles. In your case, the library. We're scheduling mass rallies, picnics, and more meetings like the one we held tonight. Lillian—did you meet Lillian? She's wearing the black silk automobile bonnet—that woman loves her automobile. Lillian is running workshops to produce pin-back buttons, pennants, and posters. With your background in publishing, you might try your hand at creating postcards. Maybe playing cards or shopping bags. I encourage you to be creative. Why, we are even planning electric signs, an eighty-foot-tall billboard, and lantern slides to carry our message." The woman spoke in exclamation points without ever seeming to lack sincerity.

"Absolutely! I'll help in any way I can." Lulu gave Clara the library's phone number. Life in California suddenly seemed more exciting. "Have Lillian call me."

Clara grabbed the number with one hand and waved goodbye with the other. "Welcome aboard, Lulu. You have joined our movement at a momentous time. I look forward to speaking with you again soon."

Clara's automobile idled outside, the driver smoking a cigarette as he waited. Lulu walked home in a daze, reliving the evening. Unlike the final contentious meeting she had attended in Portland, the California suffragettes exuded optimism. *This time*, she thought, *we might even win.*

* * *

While Lulu was finding community among the suffragettes of southern California, Roy was spending most of his evening at the Hollywood Hotel bar.

"Creative talent, that's what they call us," Roy reminded the barmaid.

He had placed his first property into escrow. David Horsley, a filmmaker from Canada, signed an Intent to Purchase on a lot behind the tavern on Sunset and Gower. Horsley, who had built a bicycle business and run a pool hall in Jersey, planned to build a motion picture stage on the lot, an abandoned orchard Meyers had purchased for resale.

"Horsley figures," Roy told Meyers when he sidled up to him at the bar, "that in California, the weather will allow him to film his movies all year round."

The sale's timing was fortuitous. Roy's mother's mortgage payment was coming due, and unless he returned the money he had withdrawn from his bank account, his check would bounce.

Meyers slapped him on the back. "Atta boy," he said, lighting another cigarette. "I knew you had it in you." Meyers had switched to Marlboros, foul-smelling pre-rolled cigarettes made from the bits and bobs left over from manufacturing other tobacco products. He smelled worse than ever.

No worries. Roy didn't plan to spend much more of his precious time selling vacant lots to out-of-towners. He'd pitched his spiel to four other aspiring movie moguls who were interested in purchasing land. Once he closed those deals, he could get out of the property business once and for all.

Roy and a few of the guys who hung out in the bar were brainstorming a script for a film based on Calamity Jane, the spunky frontierswoman. He had mentioned the idea to Horsley when they completed their transaction. Jane, known for her claim that she knew Wild Bill Hickok, fought Indians on her own, a great setup for a modern motion film.

"A resourceful gal," Roy said. He figured that, given his experience in Kennett and his intimate knowledge of the Wild West, he was the perfect man to write the script. "I was practically raised in the Crystal Saloon in gold country," he'd told the filmmaker. "I learned from the real thing."

"Talk to the guys at Biograph," Horsley said. "We buy all our scripts from them."

Chapter 13 Suffragettes

Lillian, the chairwoman of the Votes for Women workshop, called Lulu a week after her meeting with Clara Foltz and invited her to the group's next meeting. Lulu rode the trolley to the outskirts of Los Angeles. Across the street from the trolley stop, she rang the doorbell of Lillian's modest bungalow. Lillian swung open the door as if prepared to admit a stampede. She was a tightly strung woman who talked a mile a minute while adjusting the bobby pins that held her practical black bob back from her face.

Young and enthusiastic volunteers filled Lillian's living room, each engrossed in a task. A young woman with a coil of braids on the top of her head queried a group of women with books spread on their laps as she drafted a pamphlet on the history of women's failed attempts to get the vote. Another commandeered the dining room floor, where she painted posters with alarmingly red letters. With Lulu in tow, Lillian perambulated the perimeter, offering words of advice here, a caution there. She never remained still for more than a second.

After showing Lulu around, she looked her up and down. "Clara's thrilled you could join us. She said you're an editor? Just what we need to get our important message out!"

Lulu blushed, overwhelmed by the woman's enthusiasm. She had yet to get a word in. Lillian twirled around, and Lulu followed her to a slender young woman sitting alone at a small table. The girl had red curls and freckles spread across her nose. "Cassie here is in charge of our newsletter. Cassie, Lulu is an editor!"

Cassie looked up from her large stack of mimeographed sheets. "I-I-I..." Her stutter only intensified the startled look on her face.

"I'd be happy to help in whatever capacity I'm needed," Lulu jumped in, hoping to reassure the young woman that she had no intention of taking over her position. "Would you like me to fold these and address them?"

Lillian waved her hand in dismissal, her job done, and moved on to a cluster of women discussing the agenda for an upcoming rally. As soon as she left, Cassie relaxed. "Did you actually p-publish a magazine?" she asked.

"A failed one, yes," Lulu said. "It's harder than you might imagine. The layout is the hard part. But it looks as if you're doing an excellent job of that."

Cassie smiled and handed her the pile of newsletters. Lulu began folding. "Maybe we can work on the next issue together?"

"I'd like that," Cassie said.

"Anything to get the word out."

Lillian, overhearing their words from across the room, signaled her approval. "Excellent ladies," she said. "Excellent." Then she disappeared into the kitchen, where, Cassie told Lulu, another crew was baking cookies for a sale.

"That woman—" Cassie said.

"—is a whirlwind," Lulu finished her sentence. Both women smiled. For once, Lulu was happy to let someone else take the lead. It thrilled her simply to be a part of the movement.

* * *

Oregon seemed far away. An occasional letter from Vesta or Alice arrived in the mail. From time to time, her sister sent a postcard. Roy and Lulu had been in California a month, had scraped together their second month's rent, when the post also contained a letter from the Bank of Oregon. The official letter, signed by Mr. Litel, stated that the most recent payment on the loan Roy Bacon signed to buy his mother's house had bounced. If the bank did not receive payment within thirty days, they would file for foreclosure on Alice Bacon's house.

Lulu showed Roy the letter as soon as he arrived home that evening. He threw it to the floor with a dramatic flourish.

"That bastard," he said. "All his talk about our days fishing together and he has the nerve to treat me like any Tom, Dick, or Harry two days behind on their payment." Lulu could see that the businesslike tone of the letter had set him off, but he assured her the content didn't alarm him. "Nothing to worry about, sugar." He removed his tan jacket and hung it on the back of her desk chair. "Things are coming together now," he said. Making monthly payments would not be a problem. Certainly not Lulu's problem.

He picked up the letter and tucked it into his briefcase, saying he would take care of it the next day.

"Sweetheart," he said. "This is business, nothing more."

"I would hate to see your mother out in the cold."

"I would never let that happen." Roy stripped down to his underwear, his favorite attire at home these hot days.

"Calamity Jane," he said, announcing the subject of the screenplay he was writing. He had been promising to tell her for days, but she suspected he chose this moment partly to change the subject. "The woman was fearless but also admired for her compassion for the sick and needy. Her daredevil attitude set her apart, as did her habit of wearing men's clothing. What do you think?"

"They always say you should write about things you know." Lulu was still absorbing his choice of protagonist.

"You showed me the way. Your latest story is a winner."

All it took was few words of praise. Glowing from his compliment, Lulu opened to his brainstorm.

"And, Lord knows, I know the West. To tell you the truth, she reminds me of you."

Despite her earlier alarm, Lulu was touched. Even now, in the company of creative movie pioneers, he saw her as the powerful woman she aspired to be.

"Before this whole librarian thing," he added.

Lulu threw a pillow in his direction. She aimed at his head, but it landed on his stomach. The scar on his belly had faded. Like a white zipper, it stretched across his white skin as if sealing in the disorder of the organs inside.

"If you weren't so damn busy all the time," he said, "I'd invite you down to central casting to help me audition the cast. The sweet, young actresses in Hollywood are way too soft. I need to cast a real woman in this role."

Placated, Lulu struck a pose as a languid cowgirl, hands on her hips, her chin lifted in a proud but steely profile perfect for the movie's poster.

With him directing, she acted out the scene he was working on. Roy played the dashing pioneer; Lulu smoldered in the role of Calamity Jane, tough but compassionate, as strong and handsome as any man. "Well, Wild Bill," she said, "I believe the West is a more noble place with you in it as a scout."

"And I, my dear," Roy exaggerated his western twang, "would be lost without you."

Dressed only in her slip, she draped his jacket over her shoulders and stood in front of the window, dipping his bowler hat over one eye and aiming a broomstick as if it were a shotgun. Freeing her sandy hair from its usual prim bun, she let it hang unrestrained to her shoulders. "Don't you ever forget you said that, or I'll string you up like a pig."

"Librarian by day," Roy laughed, "but Calamity Jane by moonlight." They didn't sleep a wink that night, enacting the fantasy that held them together. The cowboy from nowhere clung to the tough woman, who did not give a damn. Together they conquered the frontier, fearless and forward, inspired by the open range and at home on a wild horse's back. Roy swore his script wrote itself after that night, Jane herself dictating the action. He was nothing more, he assured Lulu, than a lowly scribe recording the brave frontierswoman's words.

* * *

Lulu never told the dedicated women in the Votes for Women workshop about her evening enacting Calamity Jane, any more than the other women shared the quotidian details of their personal lives. What they shared was a higher purpose. That, and a fascination with the travels of "Two Gun" Nan Aspinwall.

All the women had heard of Aspinwall, the "Montana Girl" of Bill's Wild West Show and a star in Pawnee Bill's Great East troupe. But Lillian, their energetic leader, was the one who told them that Aspinwall had accepted a challenge from the two Bills to ride her horse across the entire country, solo.

"Bully for her," a demure white-bunned woman said without looking up from the lettering on a sign she was preparing for the following week's demonstration.

"Solo?" Cassie asked, her eyes wide.

"You betcha," Lillian replied.

The younger girl sat up taller, just imagining the woman traveling alone. Watching her, Lulu was reminded of those heady college days when she sat across from Clarissa Carson, inspired by her strength and emboldened by her support.

Here were women supporting one other. Cheering each other on.

The women followed Aspinwall's progress with the devotion of university students rooting for a baseball team. Lillian, the vigilant reporter, passed on crucial details about Aspinwall's progress as the women clustered in her kitchen, folding brochures. "That gal," she editorialized, "has enough gumption for us all."

Lillian's enthusiasm fired up the crowd.

Lulu joined their ranks the day Lillian informed them that Aspinwall refused to ride sidesaddle. Instead, along with her bright-red riding shirt, the horsewoman sported a split skirt, specially tailored to accommodate a front-facing saddle.

"Reporters are calling her ride a scandal." Lillian held up the *Los Angeles Times*, waving the newsprint in the air to stress her disdain. "Well, ladies, she's learnin' the men a thing or two."

"Bravo," Lulu said. "I gave up the sidesaddle years ago. Such foolishness. It only put women at a disadvantage."

"I knew you were one of us the first time I saw you," Lillian said, giving her shoulder an affectionate squeeze. In turn, Lulu told Cassie she'd teach her how to ride. "There's nothing more thrilling than watching the world from the back of a horse."

By the time the women mailed their brochures, Aspinwall's horse had gone through fourteen pairs of horseshoes. She had taken care of everything the horse required without any man's help.

As they addressed newsletters, Lulu told Cassie about her summer rides through the streets of Portland. How, by defying her mother, she had discovered the elixir of independence. And now she had found another home among this band of women, united in the goal of gaining independence for all women.

On July 11, 1911, "Two Gun" Nan arrived in New York City. In 180 days, she had traveled 4,496 miles. The *New York Tribune* announced her arrival: "Snappy Western Girl Rides Horse Clear Across Continent."

"Snappy, I like that," Lulu said. "Of all the adjectives used to describe a lady, snappy is going to be my favorite from now on. Let's be snappy, ladies."

Cassie laughed, delighted at Lulu's antics. Aspinwall's ride energized the group and reminded them of the goals underlying their work.

Six months to ride across the entire country. Without the aid of any man. They had eight months to convince the electorate of the value of their cause.

Swept up by their enthusiasm, Lulu thought, *We can do this.* But later, on the trolley ride home, sobered by the gentle rocking of the car, her feet were firmly on the ground. Cassie might never ride a horse. The streets were increasingly filled with motor cars. Even Lulu hadn't ridden since she had arrived in California. But she consoled herself, she had friends now. A community of peers. And, by studying for a profession, she was one step closer to self-reliance.

As if to prove her point, the next morning, Daniels led a cluster of potential donors from the Carnegie Foundation on a tour of the library. At the lending desk, Lulu cataloged books. Daniels introduced her and touted her background: "A graduate with honors from the University of Oregon, a skilled editor, and a published author."

Lulu listened to Daniels, proud of her accomplishments but aware that Daniels's speech was meant to impress the potential donors, to prove the value of his educational program. His popular but impoverished school was in constant need of more funds, especially since Daniels had alienated the California State Librarian, James Gillis, by publishing an editorial challenging Gillis's belief that library training belonged in a university setting. If Lulu's presence gave Daniels's program legitimacy, she was happy to help him out. In return, Daniels had taken her under his wing.

"Here," he said to his audience, "we train the very best. Before you, you see the paragon of a modern librarian."

* * *

A greeting card from Clarissa Carson arrived two days before Christmas. In a handwritten note, Clarissa wished them a joyous new year. "Your sister is my most promising student this year," she wrote in her spidery script. "Truly a breath of fresh air. I have great hopes for Lizzie." Clarissa added that there were now three women on the English department faculty: Miss Slater, Miss Bigelow, and Miss Woods. All unmarried. Lulu wondered what each had sacrificed to secure her position. She found it hard to imagine her spirited sister among them.

Two days later, she received a cryptic postcard from Lizzie. "Have lost my cap, with disastrous results."

"Oh Roy," Lulu said. "I think my sister is in trouble."

"Well then, we must come to her rescue." Roy's every word these days belonged in a Hollywood script. "Call her right now and tell her we are on our way."

Movie making has gone to his head, Lulu thought. *He thinks he's the hero in one of his screenplays.* But despite his drama, his heart was in the right place. When she asked him for change, he emptied his pockets, and they headed downstairs together.

The pay phone in the boardinghouse lobby wasn't the ideal location for a private call. Hopefully, the Japanese men could not understand their conversation, but Mrs. Shumway was all ears. She couldn't worry about that now. There was no time to waste. She placed a call to her mother's house despite the unwanted ears, knowing Lizzie would be home for the holiday break.

Unfortunately, her mother answered.

"Lulu, is that you?" Kitty yelled into the mouthpiece with eardrum-splitting intensity. She had yet to get used to the phone her husband had installed in the house. "Is something wrong, dear?"

"Merry Christmas to you, too, Mother," Lulu said.

"Thank you for the box of oranges you sent," her mother yelled.

"Thank you for the sweater." (A Butterick pattern, her mother had written on her Christmas card. Elegant, yet economical.) "Is Lizzie there?" Lulu waved Roy away. He made faces as she spoke, imitating Kitty's worried brow.

"Hold on a minute, I'll see." She heard the clatter of the receiver being placed on the sideboard, followed by the lilt of her mother calling Lizzie. A second call and then a muffled reply. This was costing them a fortune.

After she deposited two more nickels, Lizzie came on the line. "Lulu?" Lulu heard the trepidation in her sister's voice. Of course, this was not a discussion they could have in her mother's presence. Roy, in the meantime, was mugging again. Mouthing the words "Is that her?" and cupping his hands over his stomach.

"Lizzie, I received your postcard. Would you like to join us for New Year's? Southern California is practically tropical in December. It might be just what the doctor ordered."

"The doctor? Oh!" Lizzie must have shielded her mouth with her hand because the next words she spoke were muffled. "You wouldn't mind?"

"Sweetheart, I told you I would help if ever you needed me. Roy and I are here for you. Come on down. We'll work this out." In the background, Lulu heard her mother asking what she was saying.

"She invited me down for New Year's," Lizzie relayed the message to her mother. In the silence that followed, Lulu imagined her mother's familiar expression of disappointment. Kitty had probably been looking forward to her sister's visit for months.

"Let me know when you're arriving. We'll pick you up at the train station."

"Thanks, Sis." Her sister's voice sounded older. Lulu hoped she hadn't intervened too late.

* * *

Roy scooped up Lizzie's bags.

"So where is Hugh in all of this?" Lulu asked her sister.

"He transferred in December. His father will only pay his tuition if he attends Brigham Young."

"Does he know?"

Lizzie shook her head "no." Without her brilliant smile, she resembled their mother, the cares of the world on her shoulders. "He thought I used protection."

"That old story," Roy said. "Lulu here is a fanatic. She puts in her cap before I even know I'm horny." He laughed, quite pleased with himself.

"Nothing is a hundred percent," Lulu said. "This isn't entirely your fault." She placed her hands on her sister's shoulders. "I'm sorry if I misled you. In rhapsodizing about free love, I never considered the price some women have to pay."

"You always held Mary Shelley up as my role model. She could handle anything," Lizzie said.

"If only life were truly that simple."

Lulu had called her friend Lillian that morning, sure the dynamo would know where she could find help for Lizzie. Since the turn of the century, nearly every state had passed anti-abortion laws, including California, and yet she knew it was often a woman's only alternative. But instead of advice on how she might find an abortionist, Lillian, her tone laced with indignation, had given her an earful.

"Don't even ask me that," Lillian had snapped. "It serves no purpose to mow off the top of a noxious weed while the root remains. Whether it be for love of ease or a desire to save the unborn innocent from suffering, a woman is guilty who commits that deed. If your sister has an abortion, it will burden her conscience in life; it will burden her soul in death."

"But she is only nineteen, a promising student, and the man has deserted her."

"Even Clara Foltz bore five children," Lillian pointed out. "It did not keep her from becoming a lawyer."

"But if my sister has a child now, especially on her own, so many doors will close to her." Lulu, who had never faced this decision, felt the weight of her responsibility. The example she had set for her sister had led her right to this door.

"Let your conscience be your guide." Lillian had hung up.

Stunned into silence, Lulu hung up the phone.

Twenty years ago, one quarter of births ended in abortion, but now it was a crime.

Now, as Lizzie climbed the stairs to their room, Roy put his arm around her. "Don't you worry, little sister."

Lizzie slumped down on their bed, her head lowered.

"What you need is a trip to Hollywood Boulevard," Roy said. "We can find you what you need."

Lulu shot him a dark look.

"I know an actress who visits her midwife more often than she goes to the dentist," he said.

Lizzie looked confused. She turned to Lulu for guidance. Lulu shook her head at Roy. "Not now," she said. "This is not the time for your Hollywood tales." She sat down next to her sister. "Sweetie, tell me what you want."

"I want a life." Tears filled her sister's eyes. "I want to write a novel. I want to travel to India and meditate with the Buddhists. I want to climb Mount Fuji." She sobbed, long desperate cries she had undoubtedly held back for days.

Lulu rocked her. She had never seen her sister in so much pain.

"Can your actress friend give us her midwife's name?" Lulu asked Roy. Her voice was full of regret, laced with an unspoken anger. That her husband cavorted with actresses disturbed her; that he knew about their abortions was unacceptable. There was so much about

Roy's life in Hollywood that alarmed her, but her sister's welfare came first.

"Lizzie, are you sure this is what you want?" Lulu remembered Lillian's words. Lizzie would live with this for the rest of her life.

Lizzie nodded miserably. "I can't live with myself if I don't."

* * *

Roy and Lulu paced outside the shuttered storefront.

"She may never get over this," Lulu said.

"Pshaw. It happens all the time," Roy said.

The previous evening, he had watched Lizzie swallow the infusion of pennyroyal prescribed by her midwife with great curiosity. But when the nausea hit, when Lizzie's face went white and she clutched her stomach in agony, he had announced he needed some fresh air. Lulu had been the only one there to hold her sister's hair back when she vomited. To wrap her in a thick blanket when the shivering wouldn't stop.

They arrived at the office that morning before the midwife hung out her shingle. The dark-haired, middle-aged woman hadn't flinched at the site of blood running down Lizzie's legs. "Leave her with me," she said. "I'll put her right."

"I can't expect you to understand," Lulu said to Roy as they waited outside the woman's "office." "Men are not reared with the expectation of marriage and children. Nobody ever questions your right to put yourself first. Women are told our future lies in the hands of men."

Roy held his hand up in surrender. "Guilty as charged."

She wanted to wipe that smirk off his face.

"Churches and schools teach us birth is a miracle. As adolescents, we bleed, our bodies reminding us that our primary function is to reproduce."

"I get it, Lulu. I get it."

"What would you do if I got pregnant?"

"I would sing a joyful hymn to the heavens," Roy said. "Of course, only if the child were mine."

There it is, Lulu thought. *The unscalable chasm between a man and a woman.*

* * *

When Lizzie emerged from the midwife's office, she was pale. But despite the cramps that caused her to stop every few minutes, her step was lighter. She sat between them on the trolley back to Riverside.

At dinner that night, she was back to her old self. "Dean Carson asked me to write an article for the literary magazine," she said. "Roy, tell me more about Hollywood."

The aroma of oranges wafted through the air. A couple more days of sunshine, and Lizzie would be as good as new. Lulu watched Roy describe the protagonist of his script. His words brought Calamity Jane to life. Lizzie listened, transfixed by his animated gestures and the fire in his eyes.

"Jane was a woman to be reckoned with," Roy said.

"That's what I want to be," Lizzie said.

"Just like your sister." Roy said. Lulu looked up and their eyes met. In the wave of gratitude that swept over her, Lillian's harsh words of condemnation flew right out the window. After all, the woman was a spinster and knew nothing about love. In life, sometimes one simply has to follow one's heart.

Chapter 14 Tinsel Town

When Lulu completed four months at the library school, Daniels was so pleased with her progress, he offered her a small stipend for her work at the library. The normally shy man was practically effusive in his praise. "Your value to the library is immeasurable. Your knowledge and work ethic continue to impress me."

He shuffled the papers on his desk as he talked. It was always difficult for him to meet her gaze. "I do hope you'll choose to remain on staff after you complete the program."

"Mr. Daniels, that would be an honor," Lulu said. Unlike Frank Bonville's rants, Mr. Daniels's words had been carefully chosen and imbued with sincerity. His praise meant a lot to her, and the stipend he offered would come in handy. Maybe she could spruce up their room at last. Soon, she hoped, they might even begin to put money away for a house of their own.

On the walk home, Lulu perused shop windows, looking for a few items she might buy to cheer up their rented room. Since arriving in southern California, she and Roy hadn't had a dollar to spare. Any extra money they had, they had put aside to pay Roy's mother's mortgage. Now that would change. She could use a clock for her desk. The five-and-ten-cent store displayed a cheerful bedspread with a pattern of oranges and strawberries that evoked the fields outside their window. Passing the corner pet store, she heard lilting birdsong and stopped to enjoy the cheerful chorus. Remembering Sacajawea and those dark days in Portland, she thought of how far she had come. No longer "at home," now she had a career and a bright future. In the company of a committed group of suffragettes, she was helping women to achieve the elusive goal of earning the right to vote. In California, no metaphor need cover the bottom of a captive bird's cage. Like Daniels, she was proud of her accomplishments.

Roy was home when she opened the door to their room. He sat on the bed, hunched over, examining the day's mail. When he finally looked up and acknowledged her arrival, his face was red, his mouth an angry knot. Lulu spotted an open envelope from Litel's bank in Oregon on the bedspread. "What's that all about?" she asked.

"Nothing you need to be concerned about," he said, crumpling and tossing the letter into the trash can. "Litel has taken it upon himself to monitor the payments on my mother's mortgage."

"But why would he?" Lulu asked. She knew Roy made the payments on time. She licked the payment envelopes herself.

"That SOB doesn't have a clue. Never did have much on the ball. I have half a mind to write a letter of complaint to his boss and ask for a formal apology for his unethical intrusion in my personal affairs." Roy stood up and paced the small room like a gathering storm, his tone indignant. "Litel had the nerve to speak directly to my mother!" He slammed his clenched fist into the mattress. "He had no right to involve her in my business."

Lulu waited for him to calm down before she told him about the stipend Daniels had offered. Not that she didn't share his concern, if not his attribution of blame.

"Fabulous!" he said, his face brightening. He pulled her into a congratulatory hug and kissed her passionately on the lips. "Sweetheart, you are an amazing woman." His ability to change gears with lightning speed still startled Lulu. How, after his burst of anger, he could act as if he hadn't a care in the world.

"Excuse me a moment. I need to see a man about a horse." He rummaged through his dresser drawer for the small leather satchel that contained his shaving kit and headed down the hall to the bathroom.

When he returned, he was a new man, bright-eyed though still unshaven. Energized with a plan. "Lulu, it's time I introduce you to the wonders of Tinseltown. We're going to celebrate your promotion." He held up the crocheted sweater her mother had given her for Christmas. "It's party time. Tonight," he said, "will be all about you."

"Now?" she asked. "I just got home. I'm tired."

"No time like the nighttime," he said, dragging her from the room.

Lulu barely had time to wonder what he had in that shaving kit. Whatever it was, it had given him the strength of two men and the enthusiasm of a cheering squad. She'd take a look in the morning. If he was back on the laudanum, she would have to confront him before things spiraled out of control. But tonight, buoyed by his ebullient mood, she would celebrate her promotion.

On the Pacific Electric Red Car, he provided a running commentary. The private electric trolley was the "largest trolley system in the world." The Hollywood Hotel, where he proposed they have a drink, was "the most glamorous hotel in the city" and its bar "a magnet for land buyers and the wealthiest men in town." D.W. Griffith had conceived his notion for *In Old California* at the popular bar while sipping one of the most expensive bottles of whiskey that had ever been bottled.

"Hollywood's a mecca unmatched anywhere in the world," he practically bellowed. When they arrived at the hotel, Roy entered the bar like a returning hero and introduced her to his buddies. The cluster of lively men included the founders of Biograph, a collaborative company of screenwriters working for the moviemaking companies. "These men love my Calamity Jane script," he announced for all the bar's patrons to hear. "Any day now, they're going to put my movie into production. Ain't that so?"

His new friends grinned before resuming their conversation. Each time Roy excused himself to use the john, he returned with another story. Another brilliant man he wanted her to meet.

"To my beautiful Lulu," he toasted, "whose success I have never doubted." He picked up the bill for the next round. His pals—

everyone seated at the bar knew him—cheered him on and toasted Lulu as if she too were on the cusp of something brilliant.

As the evening wore on, Lulu regarded her husband with an increasing sense of concern. Any minute now, his mood might change. She was exhausted and soon realized this party was not for her. Too many of Roy's comments were directed to the men at the bar. He rode the roller coaster of their responses, turning to her only when he wanted to emphasize a point. How much of his erratic behavior was fueled by whatever drug he was taking? Hollywood was his world, so different from hers, and he had dragged her into it. The jarring contrast of the bar scene to Daniels's orderly office and the hushed reverence of the Riverside Library only further disoriented her. This was a place she most certainly did not belong.

The crowded bar was smoky and the evening long. At first, when Lulu noticed a familiar face at the far end of the bar raising a glass in her honor, she thought it was a hallucination. But then Roy shouted out with glee, "Annabelle, my dear, I'm so glad you could join us!"

* * *

Annabelle threw him a kiss.

"Annabelle's here to audition for the role of Calamity Jane," Roy explained as Annabelle made her way across the bar. Every male drinker's eyes pivoted to watch her progress. Her blond curls framed her lovely face, her eyes were smoky, and her lips were painted a bright red. Smoke wafted from her silver cigarette holder.

"Lulu, my dear," she said. "I've been wondering when Roy would let you come out and play. All he ever tells me is that your studies have consumed you."

Lulu was speechless. Her old college friend was gorgeous. Annabelle's hips swayed as she crossed the room. She claimed the bar stool on the opposite side of Roy, her long, tan legs escaping the slit in her red spangled dress. Every move she made was languid, every gesture studied. She accepted the glass of champagne that the bartender carefully tendered. "Roy, my love," Annabelle said. "Did you bring any goodies tonight?"

Goodies. Annabelle's question confirmed Lulu's worst fears.

Roy ignored the request. "Lulu got a promotion today," he said. "We're celebrating."

"How sweet," Annabelle cooed.

He's using drugs again, Lulu thought. *Just as I suspected. And Annabelle had been in town long enough to know it. The two of them were in this together.*

Lulu wrapped her sweater tighter and waited for Roy to explain. The crew at the bar switched their attention to a heavyset man with a waxed mustache who described an encounter with his greedy boss in New York. Each story topped the last and Roy held his own, on top of the pile. Listening to him crow about his successes, one might think he too was a movie mogul. Annabelle's hand rested on his arm, egging him on.

Lulu watched Roy's antics and Annabelle's gestures with growing anger. Her working day had been long and the scene in the bar frazzled her nerves. The smoke irritated her lungs. With each wave of laughter, her stomach clenched. Like a fist ready for a fight. He had dragged her here, humiliated her, and now acted like nothing was wrong. And all under the pretense that he was doing it for her. *Who did he think she was? A member of his fan club, easily swept off her feet?*

When Roy finally turned to face her, she confronted him. "You didn't mail those checks for your mother's mortgage, did you?" She didn't care who heard. He had probably used the money to buy his drugs. She held onto the bar to steady herself, determined not to let him get away with his shenanigans this time around. "Roy, how could you do this to your mother? How could you do this to me? Is there no one you will not hurt? Do you even know how to love? Must it always be all about you?"

The question hung in the air, open to misinterpretation.

Like the heroine of a silent film, Annabelle's eyes opened wide, and her red lips formed a shocked "Oh."

Roy stared at Lulu as if she had gone mad. She knew immediately she had made a mistake going there with him. She should have known better than to expect Roy to admit the truth. Hadn't he avoided every uncomfortable reality since they had arrived in this God-forsaken state, even those he'd brought about himself? Did she really expect an apology? Instead, he excused himself to use the men's room again.

This time, Annabelle followed him. Lulu watched them go and then collected her things.

She headed out into the dark streets, retracing the route to the trolley. She rode home through the darkness, jolting to attention only when the trolley approached the familiar streets of Riverside, whooshing by the solemn shadows of the library. *One more block and I'm home*, she told herself, holding back her tears until she reached the privacy of their spartan room. Once there, she curled up into a ball and pulled the sheets over her head. She thought of her mother, also left behind by a man. What would she say now if she could see Lulu alone in this dreary room? Far from the independent woman she had set out to be, Lulu admitted defeat. Her pursuit of passion had brought her to her knees. The heady sense of adventure she had first discovered in the arms of a Frenchman had been nothing more than a girlish illusion. A pipe dream replaced by disappointment, disillusionment, and a fury she had not known herself capable of feeling. *Damn that man*, she thought. *Damn Roy and his romantic promises. I won't be fooled again.*

Roy arrived home an hour before dawn.

"When did Annabelle arrive in Los Angeles?" Lulu demanded. Keeping her back to him, she did not allow him to see her eyes, swollen and red after a night of crying. She tucked in her white blouse and buttoned her skirt. It was all making sense now, Roy's distraction, his late nights at the bar. *When had they last made love?*

Roy sat down on the side of the bed, still wearing yesterday's clothes.

"A few days ago. You know the girl is dying to be a star. I didn't pull any strings. I told her about the audition. Who knew she would come?"

"And when she did, you didn't think to tell me?" Last night's anger still simmered, not at all extinguished by the night's tears. "Just like you didn't think to tell me that you had decided not to pay your mother's mortgage."

"Dear, you've been running around every night with your lady friends." Roy twirled his bowler until it cast a shadow over his bad eye and wiped his nose with a silk, monogrammed pocket square. He smelled of tobacco smoke with an undertone of something sweet. Lulu, convinced now that he had succumbed to his addictions, wondered if he had visited one of the city's thriving opium dens.

"At least I have not been running around with my former boyfriends," she said. "Annabelle seemed right at home in that stinking hellhole you call a bar."

"She's good, you know. She'll get the role on her own merits."

"That's not my concern."

"Are you jealous?" Roy asked. "Aren't we past that by now?"

Lulu glared at him. "And your mother's mortgage? What's the story there?"

He yawned. "Cash flow, my love. Don't worry about it. I'll take care of everything."

"Don't expect him to take care of you." Lulu heard Roy's mother in her head. *She knew,* Lulu realized. Lulu couldn't depend on Roy any more than Alice had been able to depend on his father. Lulu could only hope that the poor woman had put aside her own reserves. She would be wise to do the same.

Thank God she had a profession now.

"Don't be mad at me, darling. Things are coming together for me at last."

Lulu knew she couldn't believe this, or anything else Roy said.

What hurt most was his defense of Annabelle. All those nights Roy said he was "brainstorming" with the movie men. Had he been with her? Had he fantasized—because Lulu was certain now that his dream of producing a movie was nothing more than a fantasy—that he would cast Annabelle as Calamity Jane all along? How foolish Lulu had been to believe him when he said she was his model for the role.

His glass eye stared straight ahead, the only honest part of him. *How many times could he ask her to believe in him and expect her to fall for his act?*

Did he even believe his own words?

"Get out," she said. "Perhaps you can share a room with Annabelle. The two of you have so much in common." She didn't turn around. She wouldn't face him.

"Lulu, don't be ridiculous."

"Sweetheart, I couldn't be more serious. Besides, I have more important matters to attend to." She picked up her briefcase. "Today is the day women get the vote in California." He looked at her without comprehension. "I don't have time for your misguided melodrama."

"Congratulations," he said, his voice surly. At her words, his spark had disappeared like air escaping from a popped balloon. She headed toward the door. He removed his glass eye, not bothering to cover the socket with the patch.

"You'd better not be here when I come home," she said. "I'm done."

What would his Hollywood moguls say if they could see him now? Stripped of his bravado, a wounded boy who would never be satisfied. She couldn't bear to look at him, refused to be drawn back in by the pain she had caused.

She didn't say goodbye. She felt a hundred years old as she headed down the stairs.

***

When Lulu closed up the library the day after she told Roy to move out, Lillian was there waiting, her shiny Model T purring at the curb. Despite Lillian's refusal to help Lulu locate an abortionist, the two women had continued to collaborate on brochures and marketing. Now Lillian thanked Lulu once again for her contributions to the cause. "So many girls abandon their efforts the minute a young man winks at them," she said. "But not you, Lulu. You're a keeper."

Lulu concentrated on Lillian's nonstop patter, grateful for anything that would take her mind off Roy. "The early news from the polling stations is alarming," Lillian said, goggles pulled down over her eyes to keep out the dust. As she drove, jerking the steering wheel this way and that, she reported that the measure was not doing well in San Francisco. It appeared to be floundering in southern California as well. "Our hope," Lillian honked her horn instead of braking, "is that the rural districts vote our way. Their results are always the last counted." Expecting opposition by saloon and business interests, the suffragettes had concentrated their efforts on the rural districts. Lulu nodded, recalling the many evenings she had stamped hundreds of envelopes addressed to remote corners of the state.

All night, the women in Lillian's living room refused to give up hope. They chewed on their fingernails. "Patience, ladies," Lillian said. "Patience." By eleven, late reports from far-flung counties began to swing in their favor. Seated on couches and kitchen chairs, cross-legged on the Oriental carpet with their skirts covering their ankles, they crowded around the radio, relaying updated news as more women squeezed into the room.

After midnight, their ecstatic lawyer called to inform the gathering that the bill had passed by 3,587 votes, a slim margin reached only after the last of the votes had been counted. In the end, their work in the rural districts had paid off.

Despite the late hour, Lillian let out a euphoric whoop and popped open a bottle of champagne. "By passing the right to vote for women in California," she announced, "the number of women with full suffrage in the United States has doubled. San Francisco is now the most populous city in the world where women can vote."

The women hugged each other, many with tears running down their faces. Clara Foltz never showed up, but Lillian had enough enthusiasm for both of them.

"Today is the day our hard work paid off," Lulu echoed her friend's euphoric toast. "Cheers!" She raised her glass, hoping Lillian would not get too inebriated to drive her home.

"As of today, we determine our own fate," Cassie said, looking to Lulu for approval.

If only, Lulu thought, *if only.*

Lillian opened another bottle of champagne on the drive home, drinking from it with her goggles strapped to her head. The wind blew her curly hair like a lion's mane. She rattled along the highway in ecstatic celebration as Lulu hung on to the door handle for dear life, her head throbbing.

How she arrived home in one piece would forever remain a mystery. She hugged Lillian goodbye and watched her tootle off into the night, honking her horn for good measure. Then she walked up the dark stairs to her room. The lights were still off, and the room was empty.

He wasn't there.

She sat down on the bed. Too tired to change, she kicked off her shoes and fell back on top of the covers.

They had won. At last. But despite their victory, an overwhelming feeling of loss swept over her. If she closed her eyes, she saw Roy stretched out beside her. To keep the illusion at bay, she passed the night watching shadows dance across her ceiling. Amber streetlights back lit the trembling oak leaves as a warm breeze tickled the trees outside her bedroom window.

* * *

Hollywood, 1912

Ever since Annabelle swept into town, she'd made it her business to learn the name of every man at the Hollywood Hotel bar. David Horsley couldn't take his eyes off her. When the mogul offered her a drink, Roy took advantage of the opportunity to slip into the men's room for a hit of cocaine. He hadn't slept since Lulu kicked him out and was relying on the powder to help him get through the night.

"I hope you intend to share," Annabelle said, swinging open the bathroom door.

Horsley might have the money, but Roy had the pick-me-up. It proved a useful commodity.

Annabelle and Roy snorted the white powder together in the bar's back hallway, sharing the glow of the familiar electricity. Their intimacy inspired Roy to confide in Annabelle, as she seemed to have caught Horsley's eye.

"I've been trying to get that man's attention ever since I sold him the lot in Hollywood," he complained as he laid out another line of the magical powder. "But night after night, Horsley changes the subject whenever I mention my project."

Annabelle looked him over, combed his hair with her fingers, and dabbed at a little powder on his scar. "Don't you worry, baby," she said. "There, you go. Just follow my lead." They walked back to the bar. Horsley immediately ordered Annabelle another drink.

"Where have you two been?"

"Why, Roy is just the sweetest thing," Annabelle said to Horsley, whose thick eyebrows overhung his calculating eyes. "He's been telling me about his screenplay." Her green eyes feigned amazement. "It's brilliant!"

"Please call me David," the Canadian said, extending a beefy hand.

"I've got an idea," Annabelle said, as a jolt of cocaine coursed through her veins. "Give me your jacket." Horsley raised his eyebrows skeptically but handed her the tweed jacket. She put it on, buttoning all but the first button. "Now give me your bowler." She winked at Roy and then strutted the length of the bar with him right behind her. When Horsley turned to them, she held a cautionary finger up to her lips and then acted out the screenplay's crucial scene for the mogul. "I'm Calamity Jane and don't you ever forget that," she said, tipping Roy's bowler as she looked Horsley in the eyes. She slowly unbuttoned the jacket to reveal her spectacular curves.

The movie producer applauded, as did his cronies at the bar. She fluttered her lashes and lifted her skirt to pull out an imaginary gun, which she aimed at Horsley without flinching. "Put your money where your mouth is, David."

The bartenders applauded, recognizing a star when they saw one.

Horsley whistled. She introduced herself as Roy's leading lady.

"You got yourself a winner here," he said to Roy, who stood beaming at her side, grinning through clenched teeth.

"And I refuse to play this role or any role," she simpered, "unless you gentlemen immediately sign my dear friend to write the screenplay."

* * *

A beautiful woman on his arm. That had always done the trick. After all Lulu's negativity, her nagging, and her lack of faith in him, Roy relaxed under Annabelle's loving gaze. If only she had arrived a few days earlier.

"You got it, babe." Horsley took another drag on his cigarette and told his lawyer to prepare the contract. "We'll sign up Biograph to write the film with Roy as head screenwriter." If the contract had been in place one day earlier, Lulu could have popped the champagne cork herself. Instead, Roy celebrated with Annabelle, toasting and hyperbolizing until late into the night.

"Lulu didn't look so happy to see me last night." Annabelle sipped the last of the bubbly, licking the side of the glass with the delicate pink tip of her tongue. Their eyes met, hers asking, his searching for an answer.

"Nah, it's me she's pissed at," Roy said. "A screenwriter and a librarian. We're an unlikely duo these days. The woman works all day long, and when she has any leisure time, she spends it writing or convening with women campaigning for the vote."

Annabelle placed a sympathetic hand on his knee. "She looks like such a matron these days, like somebody's mother. What happened to the charming, go-get-'em Lulu of our college days?"

"She's all about security now. Reliability." Roy said the word with scorn. The champagne didn't sit well in his stomach. "Brainwashed by the suffragettes, I fear. Not a lot of fun, I have to admit."

He didn't tell her Lulu had kicked him out. *What business was that of hers?*

"Lulu always did take things too seriously," Annabelle placed a cigarette between her shiny red lips and waited for him to light it. He did, looking into her green eyes as the flame lit her flawless skin. They watched the smoke drift toward the ceiling fan. "But when our film takes the world by storm, she'll see what she's missing."

"You think so?" Roy's elation faded as the buzz of the cocaine faded. He felt a world-class headache coming on and ordered a shot of whiskey to chase it away.

"The girl adores you. Always did." Annabelle ordered two more shots and picked up the tab.

"I'm not so sure that's true anymore."

Annabelle blinked once and blew smoke into his eyes.

By closing time, they were both drunk. Unsteady on his feet, Roy agreed to walk Annabelle to her hotel room. She still wore his hat on her curls and wrapped his jacket tighter to fend off the cool night air. They stumbled down Hollywood Boulevard, discussing their future stardom.

At the revolving door of her hotel, they paused. Roy wondered if she would invite him in. Annabelle kissed him on the cheek. "You sure you're okay to go home?"

"Sweetheart, I'm not sure of anything anymore."

She didn't offer to return his bowler. Without his jacket, he shivered.

"Roy, Roy. Whatever am I going to do with you?" Annabelle led him into the lobby. "Tomorrow is your first day as a bona fide screenwriter. I'm counting on you to make me a star. It's late, why don't you take a nap in my room? I'm sure Lulu wouldn't want you traveling in this state."

Roy didn't argue. Nor did he protest when Annabelle lay down next to him in the narrow hotel bed.

But when he closed his eyes, Lulu scowled at him, grilling him about his finances, questioning his every move. He placed several drops of the dark tincture he had coaxed out of the bartender on his tongue to make her angry visage disappear. It took a few more to slow the beating of his cocaine-fueled heart. How sweet it was to lie next to Annabelle, whose delicate perfume filled the room. Who loved him as he was. Who shared his wild and explosive dreams.

When he woke the next morning, sweating and swearing, Annabelle laid a wet towel across his forehead.

"Okay if I stay with you a few more days?" he asked. "I'm not ready to face the librarian. Maybe I can ride out the storm with you?"

"Whatever you need, sugar. We've got a movie to make."

Like his nugget of gold, Annabelle was there when he needed her.

He would go home when he was ready. He wasn't giving up on Lulu, he told himself, but he needed space and some time to figure things out. In the meantime, he and Annabelle could get this show on the road.

Chapter 15 Roy Comes Home

"This is for you," Mr. Daniels declared, tacking a copy of Bertha Boye's vibrant "Votes for Women" poster to the wall behind the circulation desk. Boye's design featured a draped Western suffragist posed against the Golden Gate, the sun setting in rosy hues behind her. "A momentous day, my dear," he said. "You must be very pleased."

If Lulu's wan smile disappointed him, he didn't show it. His pale face exuded a fatherly pride. Lulu's head throbbed. A searing pain pounded behind her eyes, but she thanked him for his support and settled behind the desk, hoping he would let her be. Of course, the previous night's vote had been a victory, but there were books to catalog and a pile of returns that needed to be logged in and loaded onto carts. After a moment's hesitation, Daniels headed back to the library office, his disappointment conveyed by the reluctance of his steps.

Lulu watched his back, regretting her curt response, and wondered if she should apologize. But he returned a moment later.

"She's on the phone," he said, his excitement renewed.

"Who's on the phone?" Lulu asked.

"Clara Foltz," he said. "She's asking for you."

Lulu followed Daniels into the office and picked up the heavy black phone receiver that lay on a pile of papers.

"We did it!" Even Daniels, hovering behind her, must have heard the exultation in Clara Foltz's voice. "I wanted to thank you personally for all your efforts. I'll be in Riverside tomorrow. Perhaps we can have lunch?"

Under her mentor's watchful eyes, Lulu agreed to meet her. She could use a dose of the woman's inspiration, even if it was doubtful she would get a word in. Mr. Daniels told her to take all the time she needed.

When Foltz stopped by the library to pick Lulu up, Mr. Daniels insisted on showing her the poster he had hung behind the desk. "Congratulations on your victory," he said. "It's a privilege to meet you."

Clara had reserved a table at the Mission Inn. Lulu and Roy had long admired the eclectic hotel, which attracted wealthy tourists and investors from around the globe. The Inn, a hodgepodge of wings, each inspired by diverse historical periods, was a local landmark. A waiter in a crisp white shirt and black vest escorted the two ladies to a table overlooking a medieval-style clock atop the Spanish wing.

"We talk at last," Clara said.

"It's been a whirlwind," Lulu said. "But all our efforts paid off in the end."

"I must say, you look like a woman who needs a good night's sleep."

"Long nights. Lillian is in celebration mode. As a working girl, I struggle to keep up with her."

"That woman is a pistol."

Clara was full of plans. "Now that the campaign is over, I am thinking of publishing a magazine. A women's magazine, of course. While your husband is at work on his screenplays, perhaps you could provide editorial guidance?"

Clara looked at her like a doting grandmother handing her an expensive gift. The clock's hands clicked around its face, counting out the seconds until Lulu gathered her thoughts. Clara tapped her fingers on the table.

"I'm sorry. My brain is mush today. My husband and I have hit a rough patch," Lulu said, abandoning her resolution to keep her troubles to herself.

"Aha," Clara set down her water glass and leaned in toward Lulu. "Do tell."

"There is another woman, an old friend of ours. He asked her to Hollywood to audition for a role in his film."

Clara, a few years older than Lulu's mother, nodded. The contrast to Kitty's tight-lipped disapproval felt like an invitation to examine, at last, her complex attraction to the man who had let her down.

"Roy is a complicated man."

"As are you, my friend, a complicated woman."

"I divorced another man to marry him." Surely, Clara would see her lack of faithfulness as a complication. "A good man who didn't deserve it."

Clara listened attentively, her head tilted as if expecting more. Lulu tried to fill in the silence.

"Roy is as brilliant as he is troubled. He had a terrible accident when we were all in school and lost an eye. Despite chronic pain, he is the most creative person—man or woman—I have ever known..." Lulu stopped, realizing that, on this day of hard-won victory, the renowned woman who had invited her to lunch had many more important things to talk about than her tawdry affair. "I'm sorry," she apologized. "I'm out of line here, but we had a dreadful blow up..."

The waiter arrived with their lunch plates. He filled their water glasses. They sat there in silence, waiting for him to finish, Lulu's face red with embarrassment. When at last he departed, Clara reached for Lulu's hand.

"Dear, the choices we face as women are never easy. What is important is that you do not let your sex influence your decision. Every day, I speak to juries of men. I remind them that, yes, I am a woman, but I am also a lawyer. What about it? We must not let men see us only as caretakers."

"But he is in so much pain."

"As are we all. Never forget that." Clara launched into what sounded like an excerpt from her stump speech. "For almost five decades, whatever I did and wherever I went, I was the first woman. As lonely as it was to be first, it was also a towering advantage. With no standard for comparison, there's little room for failure. Being first was success itself."

"I admire your accomplishments," Lulu said. "I would give everything to follow in your footsteps. But how do you and Lillian fight day after day? Sometimes I feel my husband has sucked me dry. It is all I can do to show up at work and get through the day."

Clara wiped her mouth with a flourish and reapplied her purplish lipstick. "Don't let this man, no matter how brilliant, put out your spark." Finishing her spiel, she placed her napkin on the table, signaling her readiness to move on.

Lulu thanked her, buoyed by the unflagging encouragement of the powerful woman. "I'll think over your generous offer. Give me a few days?"

Back in the library, she quoted Clara's words to Mr. Daniels without providing the context. All afternoon, she mused. The woman's declaration glossed over the emotional realities that must have accompanied the lawyer's arduous journey, no matter how successful she had become. The sacrifices Clara extolled could only have been achieved at significant cost and great loss. It occurred to her that the woman's children and ex-husband might see her choices in a different light.

Lulu returned to her empty room, avoiding the other tenants and skipping dinner rather than face them. The evening was no easier than the one that had preceded it. There was no towering advantage in freeing herself from Roy's dependencies. Her room's silence was louder than his booming voice. His absence created an aching hole in her heart. Lying alone in their bed, apprehension flooded through her.

She supposed Annabelle had taken him in. That woman had always adored him.

***

Three days after Roy left, Lulu read an item on the first page of the Oregon newspaper.

"Professor Thomas Scott, the beloved Oregon geologist, passed away in his sleep on February 11, 1911. Eighty-six years old, he continued to teach at the University of Oregon up until the day of his death. The geologist was a humble man who loved nature and his fellow man, the good, the true, and the beautiful. The university will hold a memorial service for the popular professor this coming weekend."

Lulu pictured Al's grandfather, the inspiring professor of geology who had come to Al's defense. The only member of his family who had welcomed her to their dinner table and charmed her with stories about exploring the Oregon mines. A devout man who always had a twinkle in his eyes.

Lulu had not visited Oregon since starting library school. She had rebuffed repeated invitations from her mother, saying she lacked the time to travel. Between her studies, her work in the library, and the campaign for the vote, she seldom thought of her family. But with Roy gone and the election behind her, she missed her mother and the comforts of home with an intensity that alarmed her.

There were so many people in Oregon she had taken for granted. But Al's grandfather had always been kind to her. He supported her and Al on their journey toward independence.

She held the article in her hand, thinking about the old man, about Al, about the pickle she was in. A change in scenery might be just what the doctor ordered.

I'll go home this weekend, she decided on a whim. This was as good a time as any. She could check in on Lizzie, visit her mother, and attend the memorial service. See old friends. She might even find out from Vesta what the hell Annabelle was doing with her husband.

The long train ride would give her a chance to think. Better that than sitting in an empty apartment, talking to herself.

As Lulu descended from the trolley, she spotted the crowd assembling on the lawn of the university to pay homage to their beloved professor.

Front and center, Judge Bartlett had taken a seat directly behind the speaker, his face solemn but unemotional as he rested his hands on a cane. Beside him, Cornelia wiped her eyes with a series of embroidered white handkerchiefs. Al, seated next to a plain-faced blond woman with glasses, listened to the speaker and did not notice her. Lulu skirted the crowd, an intruder, hoping the family would not see her.

Clarissa Carson, as impressive as ever, stood at the podium, praising Scott's lofty vision. "He followed the creation of Oregon step by step through her long geological history and then entered with enthusiasm into the industrial and educational development of our present life." She spoke with confidence, commanding the audience's attention, with her head held high, her words carefully crafted to capture Scott's contributions to the university community.

Standing on the common, Lulu recalled the girl she had been when she first met Clarissa. Headstrong, bold, and ambitious, determined to change the world. Now she hid in the shadows, afraid of being seen. A disappointment, if not to her friends, then definitely to that early version of herself. A path-treader undistinguished in a distinguished crowd.

Professor Scott believed the earth was God's holy book. Its seas, lakes, rivers, mountains, and valleys were his word. All his life, he had aspired to a higher plane. She, in contrast, had succumbed to her own ambitions, blinded by lust and pride. No wonder her life paled in the light of his. A failed marriage. An empty, dark apartment. A choice of careers more practical than illustrious.

Lost in thought, Lulu nearly walked by Ted and Vesta. She startled when Ted whistled and pointed out the seat they had saved for her, his loopy grin wider than ever, with no trace of animosity. Vesta reached for her hand and refused to let go, even once the ceremony began.

Lulu couldn't take her eyes off the judge. Certainly, at this moment, he would reach out to his eldest son, see the error of his ways, and embrace him. Cornelia would channel her father's compassion. Lulu may never have told Al she was sorry, but his family would grant him the compassion that she, in her self-involvement, lacked. As students and faculty members filed by the grieving family, expressing their sympathy, Lulu watched Al, willing this reconciliation for him.

The judge stood up, leaning on his cane. Cornelia wiped away tears, her eyes red with grief, and then took his arm. Students on the mall moved aside to let the mourning family pass. Al and the blond woman remained behind on the dais, deep in conversation. *Would Al turn away if she offered her condolences? Should she even be here?*

Vesta, as usual, was oblivious. She invited Lulu to join them for supper. "We can all ride together on the new electric railroad to Portland. You can spend all day tomorrow with your mother."

"We want to hear all about Hollywood," Ted said. Dinner was on him. It always was.

"Our kids are in school now," Vesta said. "We never get a night out."

"That would be delightful," Lulu said. "Who's the woman with Al?"

"His fiancée. Daughter of a Norwegian fisherman," Ted said. "Swears a blue streak and can drink me under the table. Al met her at church."

"Church? Al?"

"She plays the pipe organ. They're getting married in the fall."

"She's sweet," Vesta added. "It must drive the judge crazy she doesn't have a university education."

"But she's smart as a whip," Ted said.

"And she adores Al," Vesta said.

At Vesta's insistence, the three of them joined the cluster of students waiting to offer Al their condolences. Vesta hugged the Norwegian woman at Al's side. "Astrid, this is Al's old friend, Lulu."

Astrid extended a sturdy hand. "A pleasure." Al put an arm around his fiancée and smiled, seemingly undisturbed by the surprise of Lulu's presence.

"Sorry, old man," Ted said to him. "It's your turn to grow out your beard now."

"That'll be the day," Astrid chuckled. "I can see it now, Alton walking into his office with a beard down to his belt and a handful of rocks."

Imitating his grandfather's melodic delivery, Al said, "Now that we have provided electricity to our state, divinity pulses through the wires."

"Stop! I'm going to pee in my pants," Astrid shrieked. "My mountain man."

Al laughing? Astrid poked him in the ribs, and he jabbed back, like two children jostling in play.

"Vesta tells me your career is going well," Lulu said. If she couldn't ask for forgiveness, at least she could let him know she was happy his life was going well.

Before Lulu could probe further, Astrid intervened, inserting herself into the conversation. "You betcha," she said, a subtle lilt in her speech revealing her Scandinavian roots. "Western Electric has offered my genius a regional position in Seattle."

"Will you be moving, then?" Lulu asked.

"We're considering it," Al said. "Astrid's family lives in Ballard." He added, "Though the prospect of a weekly dinner with her five brothers is alarming. I can smell the lutefisk just thinking about it!"

"Sweetheart, they'll love your beard." Astrid held her hands up to Al's chin, squinting as if visualizing a beard.

Ted winked at Lulu as if to say, "See? He's okay."

Lulu couldn't imagine Al with a beard. Nor could she remember ever seeing him laugh with such vigor. Their lives together and short-lived marriage had been such a serious undertaking.

Al's happiness should have relieved her. Dispersed the guilt of her infidelity. Instead, she felt only envy. She might as well have been a generation older than her friends, who had not lost the frivolity of their youth.

"Join us for a drink?" Ted asked.

"I'd love to," Al said, "but Mother is expecting us back at the homestead."

Astrid sighed, turning to Lulu. "You can imagine how much I look forward to that." Her good humor did not mask the recognition this time. She knew who Lulu was, but it didn't bother her in the slightest.

"My sympathy," Lulu said.

"Since his stroke, the judge is even more demanding than ever," Astrid said. "But he never misses a chance to remind us that President Taft invited him to the White House."

Al groaned.

Astrid's smile lit up her otherwise unremarkable face. "Cornelia will need my help in the kitchen, poor thing." She had things well in hand.

Al had moved on. The reconciliation with his family was not Lulu's to ordain. Lulu tried her damnedest to look happy for him; for both of them. As she bid the couple goodbye, Vesta's eyes followed her every move. She turned back to her friends, smiling to cover the turmoil the encounter had triggered.

"Annabelle says Roy is taking Tinseltown by storm," Vesta said.

"You know Roy." Lulu searched for the dean, but Clarissa had already disappeared from the stage.

Al laughing. That was the last thing she had expected when she boarded the northbound train, prepared to proffer heartfelt sympathy. As she left the Oregon campus, an inescapable sense of loss overtook her.

"A lovely memorial service," Lulu told her mother. "I'm glad I made the trip."

Kitty asked about her studies. Even before she asked about Roy.

"Library school is good, Mother. I expect multiple job offers when I graduate. Although, if I want, I always have a job in Riverside."

"At least you've chosen an appropriate career for a woman," Kitty said. Lulu could see that her mother was trying. For once, Kitty didn't mention her father. Instead, she spoke of her charity work at the settlement house, reciting the three R's that guided the mission: residence, research, and reform. "We try our best to provide alms, tracts, love, and education to the poor of the city," she said, "but they need so much more."

Her mother's bodice flattered her narrow waist. Her skirt was shorter than normal, with her black pumps visible beneath the ankle-length hem.

"I hope Roy's taking good care of you," she added.

"I take good care of myself, Mother," Lulu said. And then, to placate her well-meaning mother, she continued, "Roy is doing well. He is working on a screenplay. Did you know women can now vote in California?"

They left it at that, soon changing the subject to Lizzie, who had a new beau now and was top of her class at the university. They had sold Diamond in the fall. "Your sister wasn't here to care for the horse, I'm afraid," Kitty said. "Besides, your father bought me an automobile." Glowing with pride, Kitty pointed out the window at a shiny black roadster on the flagstone driveway.

"I'll drive you to the train station later." Kitty's face, lit with excitement, never seemed more beautiful. She showed Lulu the most recent books she had borrowed from the Portland Library. "Have you read Colette?" she asked. "She's French, you know, and an independent woman like you."

Lulu assured her mother she was familiar with the French author but seldom had time these days to read. "My French is frightfully rusty."

After a comforting afternoon sitting in the sunshine of her mother's kitchen, sipping tea, Lulu once more found herself in the passenger seat of a shiny new automobile, this time with her timid mother grinning behind the wheel.

* * *

"Lulu, open the door!" Roy stood on the street, pounding on the front door of the rooming house.

It was ten o'clock at night and Lulu had just pulled down the bedcovers when she heard him shouting in the street below. On the other side of the room's paper-thin walls, she could hear the squeaks of the Japanese men tossing in their beds. "Lulu, let me in!"

Trust Roy to make a grand entrance.

In her stockinged feet, she ran down the stairs and swung open the front door. "What the hell do you think you're doing? The entire neighborhood can hear you yowling."

There he was, a lost puppy angling for a home, sloppy drunk and repentant. "Baby, I've come home," he said. "I'm here to stay." Embarrassed to be standing there where anybody could see, she waved him in, and he followed her up the stairs. Once she locked their room's door behind them, Lulu turned her back on him, eyes fixed on the tree outside their window, invisible in the darkness. "Quite the grand entrance," she said, making it clear her words were not a compliment. She could hear her mother in her voice, adding insult to injury.

"Listen to me, baby. I'm a mess. You know that. I have been for a long time." He put a hand on her shoulder. "But I never meant to hurt you. Lulu, you are the glue that holds me together. Everything else, everybody else, is dispensable."

"Annabelle?"

"Her most of all."

"It's time you take responsibility for your actions," she said. Her mother again. She was one thousand miles away and right behind her, a judgmental hand on her hip.

But he had an excuse for everything. "The pain never goes away. I do what I can to keep it under control, but sometimes it gets the better of me."

Lulu sat down at her desk, still keeping her back to him. She aligned the spines of her textbooks.

"I have every intention of paying the bank. It's all a matter of cash flow. If Litel would only work with me..."

Lulu dusted the windowsill.

"Annabelle means nothing to me, the silly girl. We'll make this film and then she'll be out of my life."

Lulu turned around but still refused to look at him. "When did you start taking the drugs again?" she asked.

"Everybody in Hollywood does a little coke. There's no harm in it. It's the painkillers I have to watch."

She studied the cobwebs in the corner of the ceiling. She'd heard this all before.

"I have it under control. I need an occasional drop of laudanum, but never to excess. You of all people should understand the stress of the creative process."

"And you can live with this, your mother and sister homeless? You, a drunk at the bar like your father, spinning a golden tale and then leaving them behind, penniless?" Her voice shook. As soon as the words left her mouth, she regretted them.

"Leave my father out of this." He grabbed her shoulders and forced her to look at him. She had never been afraid that he might hit her, but she was now. She flinched at his touch. But when she finally met his eyes, she knew better. Roy's most crushing blows always came via his words.

They fought late into the night, knowing Mrs. Shumway and the Japanese tenants heard every angry word through the open windows of the rooming house. Lulu berated Roy for his irresponsibility. Roy belittled Lulu for her conventionality. He kept returning to her comparing him to his father. This, more than anything else, seemed to stick in his craw.

"If I remember correctly, your father absconded to Boston years ago. How is that any different?" Roy said.

"At least he supports us: me, my sister, and my mother."

"Even when he shacked up with another woman?"

"You're one to talk," Lulu said.

When one argument failed, he turned to another.

"My mother can take care of herself," he said. "You don't hear her complaining."

"No thanks to you."

Lulu tried to picture how Clara Foltz would respond to his arguments. The suffragette lawyer had emerged from a bad marriage unscathed. She recalled Clara's words: "Don't let this man, no matter how brilliant, bring you down."

But he wouldn't leave it at that.

"Lulu, you are the only woman in my life."

"You expect me to believe you?"

"I know you believe me."

And although she wouldn't admit it, she did.

"I cannot survive without you." He was on his knees now, pleading.

She knew that was true. She had promised Alice she would care for him. It wasn't as if she hadn't been warned. She had walked into this with her eyes wide open.

Like the acolyte he once was, he knelt before her, waiting for forgiveness.

"You are my wife," he said.

"Then act like my husband," she said, wondering if her mother had said the same to her father with the same effect. This tie would define them and shape the rest of their life together, for better or for worse. Roy reached out for her hand, and she pulled him to his feet. They faced each other, neither speaking now. She traced the scars on his face. He outlined her lips with his finger, his touch alarmingly gentle.

When there was nothing more to say, Roy declared he had a splitting headache and, without hiding it, slugged back three capsules with a glass of water. Lulu watched as the taut muscles in his face and neck relaxed. He folded back the sheets on their bed, climbed in, and soon drifted off. Lulu, who could not so easily escape, stood at the window, letting loose the sobs she had swallowed all night long.

She supposed the neighbors could hear. She breathed in the evening air, struggling to calm herself. Roy called out, lost in a dream now. *How long had she watched over him, believed in him, caught in the web he had spun? How much had she sacrificed?* She thought of Al, his patient accommodations, and her callous disregard for his kindness. Perhaps Roy was God's calculated revenge. A lesson she had yet to learn.

But was it Roy's fault that all eyes turned to him whenever he entered a room? His passion, light and dark, fulfilled her every girlhood desire. At his side, she came alive. His drive inspired her to reach for the stars. His anger fired her fury. Only with him did she feel bold and alive.

She had felt no sympathy for Al, and she regretted it. Now she had a similar decision to make. Was she destined to end up alone, too self-involved to share another person's life? Or was she brave enough, noble enough, to finish what she had started?

Perhaps this time she could work harder, consider her husband's needs as well as her own. Wiser now, she would be kinder. Surely, she could care for Roy's injured soul at the same time that she forged ahead with her plans. They had come too far to turn back now. She could not imagine life without him.

There would never be a parakeet singing in their window in California. Riverside was not a storybook ending. This was life, real life. Not one of her stories.

Unable to sleep, she sat at her desk and turned on the lamp. The short story she had been working on lacked a satisfactory ending, always the hardest part. The comic tale of a love triangle gone wrong, a soldier thought dead returning from the war to the two women he loved, his wife and the woman who carried his baby.

Lulu reread the story now, realizing that the soldier was in a pickle. Both women loved him and there was no simple resolution they could reach.

She had started the story in those heady days after they arrived in Riverside, basing the characters on her college friends. "But no one ever thought Jane and Ted might care, 'specially about each other. Jane was a woman's woman and Ted—well, he was a woman's man."

The window faced west. One minute it was dark outside, and the next the sun had climbed into the sky. She realized that it was morning. She had drifted off, her head pillowed by the pages of her manuscript. Daniels expected her back at the circulation desk by nine.

Roy was still asleep in their narrow bed. She covered him with a blanket, kissing his forehead with a sigh and tracing the socket of his damaged eye with her finger, the void as familiar to her as her reflection.

Even now, the man's electricity burned brighter than any source of energy Al could have discovered in his lab. It always had. Their passion may have ebbed, but what remained was an ache of tenderness. She had chosen him. Now, she would have to decide what to do about it.

She would pay off Alice's mortgage, even if it meant asking her father to provide the funds. Perhaps Mr. Daniels would pay her more if she increased her workload at the library.

* * *

"Konbanwa," Mr. Homma greeted her when she returned home that night. She avoided his gaze, preferring his usual distant gaze to the pity she saw in his face. "Yoi tsuitachi," she answered. When she opened the front door, she felt his eyes on her, as well as those of his compatriots. Inside their room, Roy was still there. He had showered and changed his shirt. Reeking of repentance, he handed her his stash. "I won't be needing this."

"That's your decision, not mine." She closed her hand into a fist. "I am not your keeper."

Roy nodded.

"But I'll help if I can," she said.

"There really IS a script," he said. "And Calamity Jane, she's all you, no matter who portrays her."

Lulu placed her books down on the desk. "I'll be working evenings from now on. I've taken on an extra shift to cover the cost of Alice's mortgage. Don't hurry home if you have some place you'd rather be."

A flash of hurt replaced Roy's pleading expression. "This is where I want to be," he said.

They did not discuss Annabelle, nor his bravado at the bar. But in the weeks that followed, he arrived home each evening sober. By midnight, he set aside whatever he was writing and lay down beside her in the bed. When he did, she breathed a sigh of relief, even when she did not turn over to face him.

He spooned her, his body exuding heat. "There really is a contract," he said. "I didn't lie to you." In fact, the movie company bought Roy's screenplay for a respectable sum. That might have been enough to win back her trust if he hadn't invited Annabelle to audition for the role of Jane.

She let him talk but shook off his hands when they sought out her breasts.

He swore he was off the drugs, but his nightmares woke them both. The shock of the explosion still lodged in his brain. He would startle in alarm, his hands flying to his face, and check for damage. At those moments, Lulu assured him matter-of-factly that he was okay.

Even as she cared for him, she heeded Carla's warning. She refused to be bullied or worn down by his insatiable need. His survival, and their stability, depended on her successful career.

Mr. Daniels, a consummate professional, was teaching her everything he knew. His example carried Lulu through the hard months after Roy returned. From the moment she dressed in the morning, in her white blouse and conservative dark skirt, until she set her alarm clock at night, she emulated the elegant man who had made it his life's work to establish the validity of her profession. Lulu was the first student in the program offered a full-time position in the library and the only one he trusted to assist in the instruction of new students.

Arriving home, under the scrutiny of the Japanese men watching her walk up the stairs of the boardinghouse, she channeled him, careful to hold her head up high, an accomplished professional. She hoped that was who the men saw, not the woman they heard fighting with her husband in the middle of the night. Roy, of course, paid the other tenants no mind. With his Hollywood swagger, he assured her they envied every night of passion they might have overheard. He was certain they longed to be in his shoes.

Chapter 16 The Making of Calamity Jane

The camera kept rolling. Annabelle recited her lines, mouthing the words Roy had written with exaggerated precision. Her deliberate movements were as integral to the plot as the mimed dialogue, which, in this age of silent films, the audience would never hear. Roy shifted in his seat, sighed, flipped through the script.

David Horsley chewed on his cigar, watching every studied gesture Annabelle suggested. "Dance into his arms, darling," he said. "Glide across the room." Annabelle pantomimed the scene in slow motion with languid concentration.

"Like a rodeo clown," Roy mumbled under his breath as he watched the makeup "artist" transform Annabelle's precious face into a theatrical mask.

"Not a clown, my friend," Horsley said. "A blank canvas on which to paint. The girl is a natural." When the scene required emotion, Annabelle raised an eyebrow. When the actor playing Buffalo Bill crossed the set, her lip quivered. The cameraman moved closer, urging her to give him a little more to work with.

At the end of each scene, the camera clicked off. Horsley and Ira Christie—another Canadian, whom he had hired to direct—adjourned to the adjoining projection room. In the flickering light, they reviewed scenes they had printed. Once a scene met with their approval, the technicians changed the backdrop while the director discussed angles with the cameraman. Roy's script remained on the table, discarded.

"We'll pass it on to the musicians once we've got the scenes blocked," Christie said.

Roy, sober as a judge, twitched with restlessness, smoking cigarette after cigarette. His knees jiggled; his foot tapped out his annoyance. This was not how he had imagined filmmaking. When Lulu and he had edited the *Bonville's Western Monthly*, they had reveled in the creative process, working together like a finely tuned instrument. But Horsley seldom consulted him, and when he did, his demands were infuriating.

"Too many fucking words," Horsley said. "Think sound effects. Instead of the actors blubbering on, give us background noises we can ask the musicians to simulate. Heartbeats, cars honking, clocks ticking, horses neighing."

Even Annabelle disappointed him. He had offered her the role of Calamity Jane, a role he had developed. Lulu had been right when she said Annabelle was too soft for the role, but he had imagined coaxing the tough frontierswoman out of his friend. He had looked forward to drilling the actress until he transformed her into the rough and tumble heroine, a role he had modeled on the barmaids he had befriended as a boy at the Crystal Saloon.

"Dig deeper," he said to her now. "Calamity Jane wasn't a beauty queen. She was an expert markswoman and fearless rider. Men feared her." He pulled a photograph of the real Jane from his pocket. The woman, handsome at best, wore men's clothing, a well-worn leather jacket, heavy pants and boots, and hair tucked into a wide-brimmed hat.

"Lordy," the producer said, "this ain't a history class. We're making a movie here."

"But the story—"

"Damn the story. Leave the girl to us."

Annabelle didn't protest. Instead, she preened as the hair and makeup girl "touched her up." Roy seldom spoke to the actress outside the studio these days. When Roy headed home, determined to demonstrate his sobriety to his skeptical wife, Annabelle headed to the Hollywood Hotel bar with the production crew, ready for yet another night of revelry.

Wasn't that always the way? People let you into their lives only as much as they needed you. Lulu had summoned him to Portland when she discovered she couldn't produce a magazine on her own. Annabelle followed him to Hollywood so he could make her a star. The moment somebody more useful extended their arm, they left him behind. Even Reverend Rose had used his oratorical skills to fill his empty pews.

Not one of them had the loyalty of a barmaid in Kennett.

Calamity Jane, to keep her household afloat, worked as a cook, a nurse, a dance-hall girl, a dishwasher, a waitress, an ox-team driver, and, according to some, a prostitute. What did these Hollywood types, with their New York accents and expensive, shiny jackets, know about survival? Not one of them had overcome the hardships that Roy had. How dare they cast him aside? He was an artist, a creative talent. He had sworn off cocaine and could no longer count on the euphoric rush that a toot provided. The businessmen who held his work in their hands didn't have a clue.

His headaches had returned. Big time.

Lost to his musing, he didn't notice the producers reassemble in the room. Annabelle posed on the X, marking her opening position for the next scene. She straddled a sawhorse topped with a leather saddle, framed by two extras playing the role of soldiers. Off-screen, Christie imitated the hollow thumping of hoofs, the whoops of approaching Indians. Horsley pounded his fists, adding a volley of gunfire.

Annabelle, as Calamity Jane, turned in her saddle, golden curls swirling about her shoulders. The soldier recoiled as if hit by a bullet. Annabelle reached out for him with a delicate hand, guiding him onto her lap. Out of the range of the camera, his feet remained on the ground. With an exaggerated sweep of her lovely arm, she spurred the wooden horse onward with a flick of the reins.

"Atta girl," Christie said.

Annabelle rocked as if in motion, the man tucked under one arm.

"Give me more," Christie said. Always more.

Rhythmically rocking, she simulated the soldier's rescue. The actor in her arms, head resting on her breasts, mouthed Roy's words to the camera: "I name you Calamity Jane, heroine of the plains."

Roy exhaled. He mouthed the words along with the actor.

"Brilliant! We got the whole damn thing in one take," Horsley said.

Annabelle shot a victorious "I told you so" his way, her bosom still heaving with simulated exertion and passion. Not a hair out of place. Although she had not ridden the wooden horse sidesaddle, her petticoats covered all but her precious white ankles. She wore dancing shoes instead of boots.

"An angel, an absolute angel," Christie said, kissing her on the lips.

"Calamity Jane was a whore, not an angel," Roy said, slamming his fist on the table.

Annabelle, queen of the dramatic gesture, raised her expressive brow. "Roy, get a hold of yourself. No one wants to hear your sad tale."

"The kindest people I ever knew were whores," he said. "To hell with you. Every one of you." He stormed out the door.

* * *

Lulu, on her way home from the library, stopped at the mailboxes in the rooming house entryway. Sorting through the bills and fliers, she discovered a letter from *Sunset* magazine, a response to the poem she had submitted after their last night in Portland. Expecting the usual form letter rejecting her work, she climbed the stairs and unlocked the door to their room before opening the letter. In the darkened room, she saw Roy stretched out on the bed.

"Congratulations," the letter read. "We are pleased to inform you..."

"Oh, Roy," she said. "You were right." He had encouraged her to submit to a national magazine. Unlike her, he had never lost faith.

She set the letter down on her wooden desk and did a celebratory twirl in the middle of the room. But when she turned toward Roy, expecting applause, she realized something was not right. Roy rested peacefully on the bed, the muscles of his face relaxed. Perhaps he had dozed off at last, momentarily freed from his demons. She approached him, willing him to roll over and hear her good news. Then she saw the syringe. It lay next to him on the rumpled sheet. His face had an unnatural pallor. She shuddered and put her cheek to his, listening for his breath.

Her heart pounded so hard she wasn't sure at first if he was alive. She remained there for what felt like forever, holding her own breath. Finally, he inhaled, a startled intake of air, as if he had remembered something at the very last minute.

He was alive, pale, and faintly breathing. Had he accidentally overdosed? Or had he done this on purpose, intent on performing one last dramatic act to get her attention?

It hardly mattered. Weeks of stoic self-control flew out the window.

"Roy, how could you?" Lulu pounded on his chest with her fists, fierce with fury. He had said he couldn't survive without her. And she had believed him. Had he said the same to Annabelle? He convinced her they couldn't live without each other, but, just as she had feared, his words could not be trusted.

"Roy, I need you," she sobbed, the stark truth he had once elicited and now she could no longer deny.

But he was out like a light. He didn't hear a word she said. *This is where it ends*, she thought. She placed two fingers on his neck again, allowing his faint heartbeat to calm her.

It's over, she thought. This was the final blow. She couldn't do this anymore.

"I've been a bad, bad boy," he wheedled. She removed the wet rag she had placed on his forehead. She had spent the night in the armchair, unable to sleep. Reliving that first time he had collapsed in the collegiate church. That time he had revived in time to sully her reputation with his disgrace. She remembered every promise he had made to her and to his own mother, most of which he had failed to keep. Over and over, she pictured him disappearing down the dark hallway of the Hollywood Hotel bar with Annabelle in hot pursuit.

Earlier that year, Congress had passed the Harrison Act, which said cocaine and heroin could be sold only as prescription medications. But in Hollywood, Lulu knew, you could find anything for a price. Cocaine use was rampant among Roy's cohorts at the bar. Recently, he now told her, laudanum had been harder to come by. He should never have tried the alternative, heroin.

"You nearly died," she said. "You're lucky I didn't call the police."

"I'm sorry, Lulu. You shouldn't have to see me like that."

"I thought you had quit the drugs."

"I did. I tried. You know I tried. But you have no idea how much stress I'm under at the studio. I just needed to take the edge off. Last night, I went to the local pharmacy, but they wouldn't sell me laudanum. I had to buy heroin on the street." Listening to his story, Lulu suspected he enjoyed the drama of purchasing the narcotic from hoodlums and shady characters.

Roy repentant. How many times had she been the audience for this drama? Clara's advice rang in her ears. "Don't let this man bring you down."

"The craving overtakes me," he struggled to explain. "It's like a tightness in my chest. If I don't feed it, I'm certain I will die."

"And if you do?"

"At least I have one moment of peace."

"And the cost? I suppose that's where all your money has been going?"

He didn't answer, only groaned. "I have the worst headache of my life."

No matter the cost, it was more than she was willing to pay.

She had tried kicking him out, but he always came back. Wherever they lived, the cycle repeated itself. She pulled away; he reeled her back in. He couldn't live without her. But could she live with him? Was this destined to be her life? Nursing an addict in a dismal rooming house, never knowing what she would find when she opened the door.

Finally, so many of her dreams were in reach. A woman with a profession, she was a suffragette who had successfully fought for the right to vote. She had loved freely and had experienced her share of passion. There was no reason she could not be the independent, self-sufficient woman she had set out to be. A major magazine was going to publish her poem! Yet, here she was, sitting at the foot of the bed as Roy gazed at the ceiling, lost in his own thoughts. Making his own reckoning.

Was she willing to sacrifice it all for him? The time had come to choose.

She called Annabelle. The actress was the only person who knew Roy, who understood him. Annabelle would not ask questions she could not answer. Not now, if ever.

Annabelle arrived within the hour. A cloud of lavender followed her into the stuffy room.

"He needs your help," Lulu said. "He can't continue on like this."

Annabelle squinted at Roy, taking his measure. "We have a movie we need to finish. That's my priority. If you're washing your hands of the matter, I'll take care of him."

The matter. Annabelle's cold-hearted pragmatism took Lulu aback.

"He's all yours," Lulu said. "I'm tired of picking up the pieces."

* * *

Lulu packed up Roy's belongings. His jaunty fedora. His colorful shirts and pad after pad of notepaper filled with poetry and edited lines for his script. She changed the sheets on the bed, throwing away those that reeked of his sweat, his urine. Before leaving for work, she opened the window wide. The morning breeze rushed in to fill the room with the scent of orange blossoms.

Lulu dropped off the boxes at the studio and then returned to the library. From the circulation desk, she called Mrs. Shumway and apologized. "My husband and I are on the outs."

"Don't I know it," the nosy landlady said. "The Japanese farm workers know it, and they don't speak a word of English.

"He's moved out for good this time," Lulu assured her. "You've heard the last of our quarrels."

Mr. Daniels hovered in the background. Better he heard, she thought. Better he knew. She'd rather he thought of her as a suffragette than a long-suffering wife. She wondered if the dedicated man had a family of his own. If he did, he certainly had never mentioned them to her. Maybe he lived alone.

Maybe that was the key to his tranquility.

She asked Mrs. Shumway to change the lock on the building's front door. The woman, usually gregarious and always on the prowl for gossip, didn't ask why. "Sure thing, sweetheart," she said. "My Japanese men will be glad to hear you've let that man go. If he shows up, I'll call the police myself. No woman should have to put up with that. Especially a classy dame like you."

The embarrassment of being told that her private life was fodder for the building's residents only strengthened Lulu's resolve. She promised Mrs. Shumway she'd pay the month's rent by the end of the week. Three months remained until she graduated. She would pick up extra hours at the library and call Lillian to offer to help register women for the vote. She debated accepting Carla's offer of an editorial job at the fledgling woman's magazine. But Clara expected so much, of herself and everybody else in her orbit. The last thing Lulu wanted now was to fall under the magnetism of another charismatic character. This time, she was going to succeed on her own.

Daniels wandered back to his office without saying a word. That afternoon, while she sat at the information desk, she researched the steps she would need to take to dissolve her marriage.

The evenings were the hardest part. The evenings were when she missed him, the storm of his emotions, the promise in his schemes. To distract herself, she edited her short story, exploring night after night the distinction between being a path-treader and a trailbreaker. Blurring the line she had painted between the two. Neither choice was straightforward. Both required sacrifices, but she resolved to help her characters find a balance between the two.

Bolstered by the reassuring routine of her chosen profession and the discipline of her art, she slowly came to treasure the peaceful evenings in her room. The quiet that accommodated her thoughts and allowed her to adjust to her new circumstances. Time to smell the orange blossoms. She completed her story and submitted it to Scribner's magazine, optimistic that she had done work worthy of the prestigious publication. Even so, from time to time, Roy's voice competed with the cautionary voice in her head. A month after he left, she started a poem, a vehicle for exploring her grief in words she never intended to share.

"Well-Beloved

'Until death do us part,'
Ah, dearest heart,
We scorned the ancient lie
And death defied.
You and I!

Mayhap you'll journey far
From star to star;
On earth, the paths you trod
Lead up to God,
Lord knows, you spurn the sod:

Mayhap you know the rest
What we deemed wasn't always best;
But even apart, you and I are one—
Such love begun
Is never undone.

Until we flame or dust,
Serene I trust
Fate will be kind
To you and me
A taste of eternity!"

The composition brought her as close to Roy as she wanted to be. Roy would have noticed that she included the word "love," the word they swore never to use.

Now she was prepared to set out on another journey, this time on her own.

* * *

"I hope I'm not unwelcome." The woman wore her dark hair in rows of crimped waves. Her lipstick was bright red and her eyes wide with curiosity.

Hidden behind a redolent wreath of lilies, Lulu watched as she approached, unable to place the familiar face. At her side, Annabelle snapped to attention. "Louella," Annabelle said, "how kind of you to come. Lulu, surely I've told you about my good friend Louella Parsons. She's visiting from New York, and the studio has asked me to show her around Hollywood."

Oh her, Lulu thought. *The gossip columnist.*

"Readers will eat up an untimely death," Louella said, casing out the room. She looked Lulu up and down, "especially when there is a hint of an unconventional love affair."

"Darling," Annabelle said, shaking the woman's outstretched hand, "You're more than welcome. I understand. The lives and deaths of movie stars are your stock in trade."

Roy's death became Hollywood fodder the minute Louella Parsons showed up at his funeral.

Lulu didn't recognize anyone else in the dimly lit room. When the last of the guests settled into the cream-colored upholstered chairs, Lulu and Annabelle walked down the aisle together, eyes fixed straight ahead. The usher pointed them to seats only feet away from Roy's open coffin.

The second time Roy overdosed—this time in the studio where they were filming Calamity Jane—Annabelle had discovered his body. She handled everything. She called the authorities even before placing a call to Lulu at the library. The gossip columns caught wind of the whole torrid affair, rallying around the beautiful actress who discovered the promising scriptwriter prostrate on the floor of the production studio where they were filming his work. Annabelle made all the arrangements, called the funeral home to pick up Roy's body, notified his next of kin.

"He was a family friend," she told the reporters. "Mr. Bacon suffered from chronic pain. He must have misjudged his medication dosage accidentally. His wife," Annabelle provided Lulu's name and position, "works at the library in Riverside. I've called her. She'll be here any minute now."

Lulu received the call at the library hours after the incident occurred. For the second time in his life, Annabelle informed her, the man they both loved had been carried off by an ambulance, only this time the hospital turned him away, sending his body on to a mortuary. "I promised you I would take care of him," Annabelle said, with a dramatic and yet convincingly sincere sob, "but in the end, all he wanted was you." Lulu heard the pain in her friend's voice. She thanked Annabelle for handling everything so efficiently, surprised by the wave of gratitude that replaced the animosity she had felt since Annabelle's arrival. Now, they would need to get through this together.

Mr. Daniels extended his sympathies and offered to drive her to the mortuary. He was somewhere in the crowd, invisible in the throng of colorful Hollywood stereotypes craning their necks, hoping to see a celebrity.

Horsley sat on the opposite side of the room, among his colleagues, ignoring the familiar faces from the studio. Even at that distance, she could hear him assuring his backers that the movie would be completed on schedule despite the tragedy that had taken place on his lot.

Any publicity was good publicity, he assured them. *Calamity Jane* *was* the talk of the town. Its success was guaranteed.

In the casket, Roy lay oblivious to the tumult, his eyes closed to the attention he had always craved. Any sign of his disfigurement was hidden behind a patina of pancake makeup.

The service was short. There was no mention of God.

When it was over, Annabelle placed her hand on Lulu's arm. "Please, can you stick around for a while?" The guests filed out of the room, eyeing the two grieving women. Lulu, numb, debated only for a moment. How could she not? Annabelle was all that remained of Roy. She dreaded returning to the rooming house.

Watching the funeral director close the coffin, she thought of that long ago day when Roy, young and full of vigor, had strutted across the stage of the sophomore convocation. She could see him now, urging the audience to set their sights on the lofty atmosphere. Only a poet could deliver such highfalutin lines with a straight face. His magnetism enthralled the audience. No one could resist his charms.

If Annabelle hadn't tugged at her sleeve, Lulu might have continued to sit there all night, staring at the dramatic wreath of red roses from the studio, their scent nauseating her more by the minute.

"Of course," she said. She followed Annabelle down the aisle.

After Lulu signed the paperwork that released the body for cremation, they adjourned to a nearby bar. The waiter, who knew Annabelle by name, escorted them to a booth and offered his sympathy. At first, they nursed their drinks in silence. Then Annabelle spoke, her low voice musical even when laced with regret.

"I sent out two telegrams, one to Alice and one to Jessie in Hawaii." To Lulu's surprise, Annabelle informed her that Jessie had moved out of her mother's home several years ago to wed a college classmate from Hawaii. Lulu knew Roy had meticulously avoided his mother's phone calls, but Annabelle had his sister's new address in her little black book. They had stayed in touch, she said, and exchanged news over the years. "We used to meet regularly for lunch in Portland before I left for California. Jessie knew how hard it was for me to let him go."

Lulu listened, bewildered by Annabelle's familiarity. She spoke of Roy's family as if they were part of her own.

"I did love him, you know." Annabelle reached out for her hand. "As hard as it was for me, I can't imagine what you are going through now."

They held hands, avoiding the lascivious gazes of the men bellied up to the bar.

"Poor Alice," Lulu said. "I'm glad she is not here to see them gawking."

To shield Roy's mother from the attention of the Hollywood press, they decided not to run an obituary in the Oregon papers. "Let's spare Alice the embarrassment," Lulu said. "That woman has suffered enough. The details of Roy's death are nobody's business but our own." Lulu told Annabelle about her monthly payments to Roy's mother.

"I didn't know," Annabelle said. "I'm sure Roy meant well, but... I appreciate your discretion." She didn't mention Louella again. Despite Horsley's desire for publicity, they both agreed Roy's family should be allowed to mourn privately.

It seemed right. Just the two of them in the shady bar, nursing their grief together.

As the evening darkened, the bar became crowded and thick with smoke. Neither Lulu nor Annabelle offered sympathy to the other. Neither assigned blame. Their grief was a bubble that insulated them from the noisy patrons who surrounded them.

"Do you remember our picnic the day we graduated?" Annabelle asked.

"I do," Lulu answered. "We were so damn sure of ourselves."

"Not Roy," Annabelle said. "He was there with us, but he wasn't. Behind that eye patch, I always wondered what he was thinking."

"I remember how beautiful you were that day, preparing for your role in the final class play."

"And I remember Roy drilling me on my lines, never satisfied that I'd get them right. I kept thinking that if I did, he might love me as much as he loved you."

After that, they sat in a comfortable silence, watching the antics of the increasingly inebriated crowd.

When the closing bell rang, Annabelle asked Lulu to come home with her to her luxurious hotel suite. "I don't want to be alone tonight," she said.

Far from an audience, Annabelle wiped her face clean of makeup. Lulu felt the tension leave her shoulders at last as she stretched out on the actress's large bed. Wearing only the scantiest of white slips, they faced each other, wiping away a few errant tears. Watching Annabelle, Lulu wondered if this was the tenderness a new mother felt when she recognized in her infant's eyes a bond that could never be erased. As the early morning hours passed, Annabelle clung to her like a sibling who had lost a parent. Lulu fell asleep, but Annabelle never turned out the light.

When Lulu woke in the morning, Annabelle's arms still encircled her. In the light of the bedside lamp, her blond hair glistened. Lulu inhaled deeply, breathing her friend in. How different it was to wake to a woman's flowery perfume. For so long, she had braced for the morning jolt of Roy's musky sweat.

Unfortunately, Jessie's new husband mentioned Roy's death to a local reporter, a friend they both knew from school. The *Oregon Coos Bay Times* picked up the story and ran an item on page five of the evening edition the night of the funeral.

"Relative Dead. W.G. Chandler today received a telegram announcing the sudden death of his wife's brother, Roy Bacon, of Riverside, California. Mr. Bacon was married, a graduate of the University of Oregon, and had attained quite a reputation as a magazine writer and for moving picture scenarios. Mrs. Chandler (the former Jessie Bacon) resides in Honolulu. Mrs. Bacon, mother of the deceased, lives in Willow Springs, Oregon."

Vesta saw the article and called Annabelle, all in a tizzy. She wanted to hear every grizzly detail. Annabelle handed the phone to Lulu. "She asked about you. She's certain you will never recover from your grief."

Vesta sobbed on the line. "I always knew Roy was bad news." Lulu hung up on her, swallowing an impulse to tell the girl it was none of her damn business.

"You better hope she doesn't show up in town with her two rug rats in tow," Annabelle said. "She'll want to help you shop for widow's weeds before fixing you up with one of Ted's beer-swilling salesmen."

For the first time since the funeral, Lulu laughed.

Two days after the funeral, Annabelle woke up early and informed Lulu it was time she got back to work. "Help yourself to coffee," she said, all business as she carefully painted her face. "The studio is getting impatient." When she was ready to go, she twirled for Lulu's approval. "Do I look presentable?" she asked.

"Every inch a star," Lulu said.

"Oh, I almost forgot something," Annabelle turned to her bureau drawer and pushed aside a pile of white lace panties. "Here, Roy asked me to give this to you if anything ever happened to him." She handed Lulu Roy's gold nugget.

Lulu held the precious metal, its edges smooth and gleaming, in her palm. Closing her fingers around it, she thought of all the times he had clutched it, counting on the gold to allay his fears.

"If you ever need it, just give me a call," she said to Annabelle.

"No, I'll be fine."

Lulu said goodbye to Annabelle, washed her face, and dressed. Soon, she followed her friend out the door. Left behind were all the words they could not say, the love they had shared, the man who had left them. Lulu knew her life would never be the same.

Kitty called Lulu when she read the item in the paper. "Honey, are you all right? Should I come down? Or would you rather come home?"

"I am home," Lulu said. The last thing she wanted to hear was Kitty's take on the accident. "I have a job here," she reassured her well-meaning mother. "Friends and obligations. I'm going to be okay."

Chapter 17 An Unexpected Offer

Riverside, 1913

The phone buzzed at the circulation desk. The clerk, a young girl named Stella with long braids and thick glasses, rooted Lulu out in the reference room, assisting a patron. "Long distance," the clerk said. "From San Francisco." Stella delivered the message, watching her boss's reaction with curiosity.

Lulu suspected her self-possession and insistence on following the rules intimidated the girl. Her status as a spinster set her apart from the other staff members, who treated her as if she were much older than twenty-nine. Lulu excused herself, apologizing to the patron, a flustered accountant wearing a cardigan sweater. "Stella, assist the gentleman in locating the 1910 tax records." Lulu walked to the circulation desk, wondering who waited on the other end of the line.

"I'm sorry to have called you at work, dear, but this was the only number I could find." Clarissa Carson's voice was a pleasant surprise. The former dean said she had read about Lulu's position at the library in the latest alumni update. "I've followed your career with great pride. Your work with Clara Foltz is impressive." And then she offered her condolences.

Lulu stood at the circulation desk, aware of the staff members' scrutiny. Since graduating from the program, she had a senior position in the library. After Roy's funeral, she had asked Daniels never to speak of it. Like him, she felt her private life had no relevance in the workplace. The newer students and employees knew her as the responsible matron whose job it was to keep them in line. Lulu had, with amusement, overheard the students sharing speculation on her background. Stella thought Lulu had been abandoned at birth and raised in an orphanage. The tall, skinny Priscilla posited that Mrs. Bacon was a secret Wiccan who practiced the magical arts. Stephan, the solitary man on the staff, suggested that the upright librarian abandoned the convent for the love of a man who had deserted her.

Unbeknownst to them, and certainly to Daniels, Lulu was considering making a change. The library had been her refuge in the days after Roy and she split, but as the months passed, she no longer found the work satisfying. There was a position available in the English department at the State Teacher's College in Arcata. She carried the clipped classified ad in the pocket of her skirt. She hadn't applied yet, but she knew she would be a perfect fit. These days she made decisions methodically and only acted after due consideration.

"I don't know if you've heard, but a year ago I accepted the position as president of Mills College." Clarissa got right to the point. "I'm putting together an administrative team of bright and ambitious women. The regents are looking for a skilled research professional with experience teaching in an academic environment. I couldn't help thinking of you. They've authorized me to offer you a joint position as instructor of English and head reference librarian of the college library."

Mills College was legendary, the first women's college in the West, committed to offering opportunities to women from all backgrounds. Lulu had indeed read about Carson's prestigious appointment there. She had also read her mentor's textbook on English grammar and style.

Lulu didn't know what to say. She was no longer the woman Clarissa Carson remembered. But she was qualified to do the job.

"I know Mr. Daniels would be loath to let you go, but I would be happy to assure him that your presence at the university would be a credit to his superb program."

"I'm flattered you thought of me." Lulu turned her back on the staff lurking around the desk and lowered her voice. "I am unfamiliar with the Bay Area. I haven't strayed from southern California since joining the program here."

"Oh, it's a glorious area. I'd be happy to offer you a room in my house while you get settled."

The offer intrigued Lulu. The suggestion that she might again fall under Clarissa's protection and inspiration. So much of what she had achieved in her life had blossomed from seeds planted in those long-ago sessions in Carson's office, discussing women's role in modern society. She struggled to maintain her equilibrium, all the while taking care to hide her reaction from the young people who watched her with unveiled curiosity. "I do appreciate the call."

Clarissa encouraged her to give the offer careful consideration and provided her home number for what she hoped would be a positive response.

After hanging up the phone, Lulu returned to the reference room, where Stella had things under control. Daniels had taken a dozen students on a field trip to the elementary school to look at the basics of a school library. The reference room was quiet, her attention not required. She retreated to her office and sat pondering at her desk.

Could she leave this library behind? Ten years ago, she departed Oregon a young, passionate girl. Now she was a woman, an accomplished professional, but weary in ways that young girl could never have imagined.

She thumbed through the manuscript on her desk, an edited copy of the book she was writing for the American Library Association, a small tome titled *Good English, Reading with a Purpose.* The text laid out the basic rules a writer should follow, the fundamentals of grammar, the tools a writer used to produce a cohesive paragraph of prose. She was proud of the book, already included in the syllabus for next year's students. After some debate, she had decided to publish it under her married name, Lulu Cleaver Bacon. She had continued to use Roy's name when submitting stories for publication.

The publisher had asked for a biography of the book's author. Lulu reread what she had written, realizing her words echoed those early lessons she had learned from Carson: "As a reader's advisor, Mrs. Bacon works with the firm faith that education can liberate minds and enrich lives." If she had learned anything at all, it was that her life required a purpose. Clarissa Carson had taught her that. How could she say no?

* * *

After another busy day in the college library, Lulu greeted Clarissa with a peck on the cheek. "Have you given any thought to our summer vacation? Your ambitious students are wearing me out. I've been counting the days until the end of term."

"I have." Clarissa's hair, once a proud Edwardian pompadour, hung loose, almost to her waist, streaked with gray. Her skin was gently wrinkled, her smile welcoming. She dressed less formally now than she had when it had been important to maintain her dignity as the equal of her male colleagues. "Did you read about the march the East Coast suffragettes are planning in New York City?" She handed Lulu a cup of steaming tea.

"I did." The mission of the march intrigued. "They say that the organizers, tired of being portrayed as militants and misguided housewives, have decided to showcase their beauty and diversity instead. They want the march to be a celebration rather than a demonstration. It sounds rather lovely."

"Doesn't it?" Clarissa asked, raising her eyebrows. "Oh, I almost forgot. This arrived in the mail today." She handed Lulu an envelope.

Vesta had written a long, newsy letter. As the women sipped their tea, Lulu read the letter out loud. Vesta reported that Annabelle had been offered the lead in another film. "Who would have ever guessed that our friend would become a movie star?" Vesta wrote, but it did not surprise Lulu at all.

"And then she goes on and on about the success of her own children, both brilliant and accomplished of course, and about to enter the Portland preparatory school," Lulu read. "Al has apparently moved to Seattle, where the Graybar Electronics Company offered him a lucrative management position. He and his Norwegian wife are expecting their first child in the spring."

Clarissa laughed. "I wonder what Judge Bartlett will say to that?"

"I doubt the judge's opinion carries any weight at all," Lulu answered. "Al is a man of admirable integrity."

"That he is."

Over a light supper, the two women chatted about the past, comfortable in each other's presence. The strengthening rays of spring sunshine lit the cheery kitchen. A warm breeze filled the room with the perfume of the lilac bushes in the yard.

"So, about that vacation," Clarissa said as Lulu carried their dirty dishes to the sink. "I am rather in the mood for a celebration. Would you be interested in joining me on a trip to New York?"

"To take part in the International Women's March?"

"Exactly. I picked up a train schedule today. I was thinking of a leisurely trip across the country followed by a week or two in the city."

"Nothing would please me more," Lulu said, forgetting her exhaustion altogether. She clapped her hands in delight and then hugged Clarissa. "It's perfect. Absolutely perfect."

"There's my girl," Clarissa said. "That's the enthusiasm I love." Side by side at the kitchen sink, they cleaned up after their simple meal. The older woman washed the fine china while the younger dried and put it away. Outside, a flock of migrating birds sang, evoking the melodic trills of Sacajawea, the parakeet Lulu had released in Portland such a long, long time ago.

★ ★ ★

1915

Fifteen years ago, at seventeen, Lulu had traveled these same rails, thrilled to be so far from home. Seventy-one hours from Portland to Chicago and twenty-one more from there to New York City. The days had flown by, lost in anticipation of the upcoming Atlantic crossing her father had proposed. She remembered the journey as a blur of high, snow-topped mountains and endless plains, horizons of setting suns and stars blazing brightly in the night sky.

Clarissa and Lulu's trip to New York City to attend the women's march was a more leisurely affair. In 1913, the Overland Limited had become an extra-fare ($10) train, cutting its running time to sixty-four hours and adding amenities such as a barber, manicurist, stenographer, and bath. In its dining cars, white-gloved attendants catered to their every need.

Stopping for a night in Chicago, the two women stayed at the Palmer House. While Lulu admired the breathtaking ceiling fresco by French painter Louis Pierre Rigal, Clarissa read to her from the hotel brochure: "Bertha Palmer was a friend of Claude Monet. He helped her select pieces that reflected her French heritage."

"When I was young," Lulu admitted, "I met a young Frenchman on my first, and only, transatlantic crossing. 'In France,' he told me, 'women are as free as men.' I practically swooned at his words, or perhaps it was the accent, and decided then and there I would surrender my virginity to him."

"You always were a plucky young thing," Clarissa said, amused by the story. "I will never forget the day you cruised into my office, determined to change the world."

"I must have seemed ridiculous," Lulu blushed. "So full of myself."

"You were a breath of fresh air among the proper young women who were your classmates."

"I was in awe of you, determined to prove myself."

"And that you did." Clarissa regarded her fondly. "Look at you now. Accomplished, yet still beautiful. Preparing to march with women from all over the world who have shared our long journey. You have much to celebrate."

"We both do," Lulu tucked in her hand into the crook of Clarissa's arm. The two women strolled through the carpeted lobby, one on the cusp of middle age and the other on its other side. Accomplished, self-confident women at home in the world, admiring the Impressionist works of art from Bertha Palmer's collection.

Two days later, having settled into New York City's new Biltmore Hotel, a part of Grand Central's Terminal City, they rode the subway train to Washington Square. There, they joined the clusters of assembling delegates from labor unions and suffrage groups preparing to march up Fifth Avenue. Women in white dresses carrying placards, holding hands, festooned with garlands and flowers.

"There must be a thousand people here already," Lulu exclaimed. Clarissa positively glowed. Here at last was the "life beautiful" she had promised so many Oregon coeds decades before. Crowds of spectators lined the street, prepared to cheer the marching women on.

In what the *New York Times* later called "more poem than procession," a wall of women walked up the avenue. Lulu and Clarissa took their place in what seemed like endless rows of demure women. Behind them, a breastfeeding mother nursed along the route to a chorus of cheers. Four women wearing white hats and matching high heels wheeled ballot boxes on a stretcher, as if accompanying a sick patient to the operating room.

"What a beautiful gesture." Lulu strained to hear Clarissa above the joyful din of the crowd. "We suffragettes have surely turned a corner here. The right of every woman to vote becomes inevitable today."

"I hear you, lady," an enthusiastic young girl, freckled and in her teens, cheered them on. Although too young to vote, her bright smile declared that this parade was her destiny. Beside her, an elderly woman walked jauntily, tapping her cane on the pavement in time with the women's steps. The afternoon was chilly, but the press of bodies kept them warm. A great army of women whose white costumes glittered in the sunlight. One group of women twirled parasols (a challenge in the wind) and demanded: "March with us."

The parade made its triumphant way up Fifth Avenue in the shadows of towering commerce. When the wind whipped off a woman's hat, a laughing spectator retrieved it and placed it back on her head. Women carrying inscribed banners fought to tame unruly skirts blowing about their ankles.

"We walk with you, we eat with you, we dance with you, we marry you, why can't we vote with you," Lulu's favorite banner said.

Others reflected the international nature of the march: "King Albert of Belgium favors votes for women," "Australian women have the ballot," "Queensland women vote," "Bohemia was the first in the world to pass a law for women's suffrage in 1861," "Oestreichischer Komite fur Frauenstremrecht."

Clarissa was ebullient when they reached 59th Street, pointing out each new row of women. Her deep laugh echoed off the tall buildings. The men's brigade—thousands of supporters this time in place of the ninety-two who jeered the first parade four years previously—strutted along in front of an army of automobiles that ended the procession.

"Marvelous," Clarissa crooned. "Simply marvelous."

The parade ended with a concert of thirty bands and a giant chorus singing patriotic songs at Central Park Plaza.

"If only Annabelle and Vesta could be here now," Lulu said. "They might finally understand my passion for women's rights. I have never felt prouder than I feel today. And to think, because of our efforts, California has been on the forefront of this movement. I, a lowly librarian, have been on the forefront of a movement that will benefit women for years to come."

Clarissa beamed like a proud parent.

Lulu watched as the marchers dispersed, heading off in every direction.

"I only hope their idealism doesn't backfire now," Clarissa said as they walked south toward their hotel. "Our struggle is only beginning."

In the large display windows of the Fifth Avenue department stores, Lulu studied their reflections, two women strolling arm in arm.

"Do you ever wonder," Clarissa asked, "what your friends make of our life together?"

"I couldn't care less," Lulu said, kissing the halo of exuberant white hairs that framed Clarissa's dear, sweet face. They stepped off the curb, barely avoiding a large muddy puddle. Lulu held Clarissa closer, shielding her from the chilly wind.

<<<>>>

Author's note

I first discovered Lulu, this novel's protagonist, in a cardboard box maintained by the University of Oregon's special collections. The librarian retrieved three boxes of my family history from the University's collection and allowed me to peruse them if they remained in the library. One contained material about geologist Thomas Condon, my great-great-grandfather, the first State Geologist in Oregon, and the first professor of geology at the University of Oregon. The second contained material on Justice Robert Sharpe Bean, my great grandfather, the 16th Chief Justice of the Oregon, and a member of the first graduating class at the University. The third box, simply labeled "The Bean Family," contained information on their progeny, including my grandfather.

Although I had been raised on stories about the two illustrious men above, I had not come to learn more about their well-documented lives. Instead, I was pursuing a mystery. According to family lore, my grandfather, Condon Roy Bean, had mysteriously divorced in the early 1900s. At the time of his death, I knew nothing about this marriage, not even his first wife's name.

I skimmed the boxes' contents. Letters from my grandfather's brother who was gassed in world war I. A formal note from President Taft inviting my great grandfather to the White House, The histories of Condon Hall and Bean Hall on the University campus. A researcher at the other end of the table described how the first women students were told not to enter the classroom buildings until the men had fired up the stoves That way, there would be no chance that the men might glimpse a woman's ankle as they climbed the stairs.

A half hour into my search, I discovered the following announcement in a Sigma Nu fraternity newsletter.

Condon Bean, Sigma Nu, and Miss Lulu Cleaver were married at the home of the bride's grandmother in Baker City, Oregon, on Feb. 22nd. This wedding, together with several others of Gamma Zeta Chapter, was the culmination of a romance developed in the shady walks and winding streams of the University of Oregon.

Miss Lulu Cleaver. I was on my way. The University of Oregon's extensive digital collection includes all the yearbooks and literary magazines published since the University opened. I discovered Virginia "Lulu" Cleaver, a classmate of my grandfather and an instructor of English. How thrilled I was when Google uncovered her poems and short stories in literary magazines of the time! I spent so much time on the internet in her company that Wikipedia added an article about her. The Wikipedia entry is for Virginia Cleaver Bacon and does not acknowledge Lulu's earlier marriage to my grandfather. Instead, it says that she married Ralph Bacon, another University of Oregon graduate and classmate. The account of Bacon's injury came from an archived newspaper article. Copies of The Bonville Monthly documented Lulu and Bacon's early careers there, with the dates auspiciously overlapping those of her marriage to my grandfather.

Lulu's voice was loud and clear. I have included short quotations from her work throughout the novel, as well as Bacons. A full list of their work follows with notations where I have included their words in mine.

Between the University publications, family lore, and Cleaver and Bacon's published works, this story wrote itself, leaving me to imagine the emotional journeys that accompanied the characters' vivid and resonant lives. A few peripheral characters inserted themselves. Classmates of the main characters were drawn from the faces in the University yearbooks. A striking photo of the Dean of Woman Clarissa Carson, with its caption recording her plea to the women students to pursue a Life Beautiful, could not be passed up.

This is a work of fiction. Because the novel takes place at a time of intense suffragette activity, it seemed natural that Lulu would want to be involved. Lulu and Clarissa's relationship is strictly a figment of my overactive imagination.

Bacon's premature death preceded Cleaver's illustrious career as Oregon's State Librarian. By the time my father came on the scene, my grandfather had married the spunky daughter of a Norwegian fisherman, my beloved grandmother, and theirs was the story I was told.

But I am delighted my characters insisted on filling in the blanks. What a wild ride it has been.

Publications by Virginia Cleaver (Bacon):

"In an Oregon Orchard," Sunset: The Magazine of the Pacific of All the Far West, 1913.

"Trail Song," Out West, p. 39, 1915.

"The Well-Beloved," The Overland Monthly and Out West Magazine, 1915**

"On Fickle Hill," and "Romany Song," The Overland Monthly, 1916.

"The Path-Treader," Scribner's Magazine- Volume 72, p. 187, 1922. ** (Also included in The Best American Short Stories 1923.)

Six Books in Search of a Library, 192? Short, humorous play about a librarian deciding which books to buy.

Good English, Volume 4. American Library Association, 1928.

Publications by Ralph Bacon:

"Ballad of Love Triumphant," The Overland Monthly, 1913.

"Rest Time," Out West-Volume 7, Issue 3, Page 113, 1914**

"Crater Lake, Oregon," The Overland Monthly, 1914.

"In Retrospect," Munsey Magazine, 1914.

"The Great Panorama," Literary California, 1918.

About the Author

Raised in Seattle and the Santa Clara Valley of California, Kathryn Holzman left the west coast of the US seeking adventure in the Big Apple where she met her husband at a poetry reading. After attending Stanford University and NYU, she chose Health Care Administration as a career, working with public inebriates, dentists, urologists, and cardiologists. When the right side of her brain rebelled against endless databases and balance sheets, she moved to New England with her husband, now a digital artist. Both flourish in the lush beauty of Vermont and the creative communities of New England.